Michael Underwood and The Murder Room

>>> This title is part of The Murder Room, our series dedicated to making available out-of-print or hard-to-find titles by classic crime writers.

Crime fiction has always held up a mirror to society. The Victorians were fascinated by sensational murder and the emerging science of detection; now we are obsessed with the forensic detail of violent death. And no other genre has so captivated and enthralled readers.

Vast troves of classic crime writing have for a long time been unavailable to all but the most dedicated frequenters of second-hand bookshops. The advent of digital publishing means that we are now able to bring you the backlists of a huge range of titles by classic and contemporary crime writers, some of which have been out of print for decades.

From the genteel amateur private eyes of the Golden Age and the femmes fatales of pulp fiction, to the morally ambiguous hard-boiled detectives of mid twentieth-century America and their descendants who walk our twenty-first century streets, The Murder Room has it all. **>>>**

The Murder Room
Where Criminal Minds Meet

themurderroom.com

Michael Underwood (1916–1992)

Michael Underwood (the pseudonym of John Michael Evelyn) was born in Worthing, Sussex and educated at Christ Church College, Oxford. He was called to the Bar in 1939 and served in the British army during World War Two. He returned to work in the Department of Public Prosecutions until his retirement in 1976, and wrote almost 50 crime novels informed by his career in the law. His five series characters include Sergeant Nick Atwell and lawyer Rosa Epton, of whom is was said by the *Washington Post* that she 'outdoes Perry Mason'.

By Michael Underwood

Simon Manton

Murder on Trial (1954)

Murder Made Absolute (1955)

Death on Remand (1956)

False Witness (1957)

Lawful Pursuit (1958)

Arm of the Law (1959)

Cause of Death (1960)

Death by Misadventure (1960)

Adam's Case (1961)

The Case Against Philip
   Quest (1962)

Girl Found Dead (1963)

The Crime of Colin Wise (1964)

The Anxious Conspirator (1956)

Richard Monk

The Man Who Died on
   Friday (1967)

The Man Who Killed Too
   Soon (1968)

Martin Ainsworth

The Shadow Game (1970)

Trout in the Milk (1971)

Reward for a Defector (1973)

The Unprofessional Spy (1975)

Rosa Epton

A Pinch of Snuff (1974)

Crime upon Crime (1980)

Double Jeopardy (1981)

Goddess of Death (1982)

A Party to Murder (1983)

Death in Camera (1984)

The Hidden Man (1985)

Death at Deepwood
   Grange (1986)

The Injudicious Judge (1982)

The Uninvited Corpse (1987)

Dual Enigma (1988)

A Compelling Case (1989)

A Dangerous Business (1990)

Rosa's Dilemma (1990)

The Seeds of Murder (1991)

Guilty Conscience (1992)

Nick Atwell

The Juror (1975)

Menaces, Menaces (1976)

The Fatal Trip (1977)

Murder with Malice (1977)

Crooked Wood (1978)

Standalone titles

A Crime Apart (1966)

Shem's Demise (1970)

The Silent Liars (1970)

Anything but the Truth (1978)

Smooth Justice (1979)

Victim of Circumstance (1979)

A Clear Case of Suicide (1980)

Hand of Fate (1981)

Shem's Demise

Michael Underwood

An Orion book

Copyright © Isobel Mackenzie 1970

The right of Michael Underwood to be identified as the author of this work has
been asserted in accordance with the Copyright, Designs and Patents Act 1988.

This edition published by
The Orion Publishing Group Ltd
Orion House
5 Upper St Martin's Lane
London WC2H 9EA

An Hachette UK company
A CIP catalogue record for this book is available from the British Library

ISBN 978 1 4719 0810 1

www.orionbooks.co.uk

I

Kenny watched with an air of absorption as Shem industriously stuffed pieces of screwed-up newspaper into his left boot. From his expression he might have been trying to detect the sleight of hand required by some particularly baffling conjuring trick. Indeed, a conjurer might surely have had his own professional interest aroused by the quantity of newspaper which disappeared into Shem's footwear without any sign of overflow. They were like two antique receptacles of inexhaustible capacity.

It had been an agreeable surprise to Kenny coming across Shem. He'd found him sitting against a hedge on the farther outskirts of the village. Kenny had been mooching aimlessly along when he had suddenly decided to cut up one side of a wheatfield and make for a thicket of especially luscious blackberries. And there suddenly was the old man, looking, as he always did, like something left behind after a wild storm. A piece of gnarled but lively flotsam.

It never occurred to Kenny to wonder how Shem always managed to look precisely the same. Dirty, though never any dirtier despite an obvious contempt for washing; unshaven, but never more than scruffily bewhiskered; and swathed in numberless layers of baggy garments. He merely accepted him as Shem who turned up in the district each year with the regularity of a migrating swallow – save that autumn was Shem's season for arriving in the village – and who, after two or three weeks, would simply vanish again.

Kenny inhaled slowly but deeply. Yes, Shem even smelled the same. An acrid smell of dog-ends, booze and musty flesh. In a curious way, Kenny found this reassuring. Healthy twelve-year-olds are not normally given to self-analysis, but if Kenny had been so morbidly inclined he'd have realised that reassurance was something which had been missing from his life since the departure of his cousin Brian from the village three years before.

Though eight years his senior, Brian had been his idol. He was the only person for whom the younger boy had ever felt any devotion – and Kenny could still recall the mental – almost physical – numbness he'd experienced when Brian had told him that he was going away. It had been like an injection of some paralysing drug.

Brian had left the village and had never come back, and the only news of him – scant in any event – had been of trouble with the law and a spell of Borstal. By now, Kenny didn't suppose that he'd ever see him again. He'd passed out of his life for good, like nappies and rusks and short trousers and so much else of what one grows up with and discards along the way. Except that he never thought of it as discarding Brian. Brian who, with all the advantage of his eight added years, had taught him so much about growing up.

Kenny's reaction to his cousin's defection had been to avoid all the places which had been their special private haunts as if they'd suddenly acquired a supernatural chill. Like someone leaving untouched the bedroom in which an adored one has died, then locking the door and throwing away the key. Save that Kenny had not been so morbidly motivated. He'd reacted that way because he had. That part of his life which had been shared with Brian had come to an end. You couldn't do Brian things without Brian. It was as simple as that.

'What you staring at, boy?' Shem asked, shooting Kenny a sharp side-glance, as he plugged his boot with another ball of paper.

'All that paper you're poking into your boots!'

Shem grunted. 'Know anyone who's got a pair to give away, boy?' Kenny shook his head. 'Too mean, that's what,' Shem observed sourly. 'World's full of mean people.

No one wants to help his neighbour these days.' Then in case Kenny hadn't caught his meaning, he added, 'I'm a neighbour just as much as the people what lives in the next house, that's what the Bible says!'

'Is that why you're called Shem? Because you spout the Bible?'

'Don't you know who Shem was, then?' the old man crowed. He and Kenny were given to communicating in a bizarre exchange of near non-sequiturs.

Kenny shrugged as if the answer was of no importance to him. 'He was in the Bible,' he replied off-handedly.

'You don't know who he was, do you, boy?'

' 'Course I do, but I'm not telling you.'

'Because you don't know.'

'I do.'

'Who, then?'

'You! You're Shem.'

'Because I'm old enough to be one of Noah's sons, that's why. Know who Noah was, boy?'

'He was the bloke with all those animals in the ark.'

'So they do teach you something after all!'

'Never heard he had any sons, though,' Kenny observed in a moment of confession.

'Who do you think looked after all them creatures, then? Old Noah couldn't have done it all on his own.'

'Hired help.'

'Hired help in an ark, boy!' Shem said derisively, while Kenny shrugged again. 'It was his sons, Shem and the other two.'

'What was their names?'

'What's it matter what their names was?' Shem growled defensively. Then suddenly he began chuckling. 'Shem, Ham and Spam, those was their names.' He repeated them, rolling the names round his tongue with obvious relish while Kenny grinned.

With an abrupt change of mood, he asked, 'What you brought me, boy?'

3

'I haven't brought you nothing. I didn't know you was back until I found you sitting here, did I?'

'Don't you get mean like the rest of 'em. You fetch me something.'

'What?'

'It's been cold sleeping out these last few nights.'

'There's lots of barns you could sleep in.'

'Pah! Who wants to sleep in a barn!'

'You'd be warm there.'

'And have a bloody farmer sticking a pitchfork into my arse.'

'You could probably get a room at the Tall Man.'

'Who'd pay? You, boy?' Shem scoffed.

Kenny edged away slightly. 'They do say you're stuffed with money,' he said, fixing Shem with a weather eye.

Shem swung round on him sharply. 'They! They! Who's they, boy? Who tells bloody lies like that?'

'They say,' Kenny went on boldly, 'that your clothes are stuffed with lots and lots of £5 notes. That you're stiff with money.'

'Who says, boy?' Shem demanded angrily, thrusting his face close to Kenny's, his eyes darting like agitated black buttons.

Kenny wriggled away. 'People. People in the village. But I don't expect they mean it,' he added soothingly. 'It's just sort of a joke.'

'People shouldn't say such wicked things,' Shem said, his sudden spurt of anger subsiding as he leaned forward to pull on the boot which had been claiming his attention. Kenny watched with renewed interest. Wherever all the paper had gone, there still seemed room for Shem's foot.

'How long are you going to stay around?' he asked, after Shem had been twisting his foot about for some time like a duchess trying on a new pair of shoes.

'Depends, doesn't it? Depends on how neighbourly people are. Last year when I came, they were downright mean. No point in hanging around if they just treats you

4

like dirt, instead of like a neighbour.'

Kenny knew well enough what the general reaction in the village was to Shem. Most people viewed his annual visit without enthusiasm. He was a misanthropic old scrounger whose presence they could well do without. There were a few – mostly women – who regarded him with a more tolerant eye and who were ready to give him food. One or two – women again – would even add advice to the proffered food. Advice on how to get closer to the Lord and ensure the salvation of his soul. From these, Shem would back away with dark mutterings, like an affronted monkey. His soul was his concern and, moreover, he'd got thus far through life without accepting anyone's advice and he didn't intend to start now.

It was generally believed that he passed the winter months at a hostel in London and the summer ones on the road in southern England. But all anyone knew for certain was that he invariably turned up in the village in the second half of September, would stay anything from five days to a couple of weeks and then vanish again until the same time the following year. While around he was usually prepared to do a few light jobs in exchange for food or a bit of money, though if he could come by either without he was never averse.

'You run off home, boy, and get me a bite of food,' Shem said, breaking in on Kenny's thoughts. 'A nice bit of cold beef and a bit of bread. Your mum won't miss that.' Observing that Kenny appeared to be giving the suggestion favourable consideration, he reached into the ditch beside him and came up with a battered billy-can. 'And a drop of hot tea, too. With lots of sugar, but not too much milk.'

Kenny stood up slowly. He was a short, sturdy boy with a somewhat wooden expression until he smiled, when his stolid features would become transformed as by a stage effect. The semblance of a dimple (to his intense distaste) appeared in one cheek and his mouth became the focal point of an engaging grin. His hair, which was the colour of ripening corn, grew generally upwards and outwards but to no recognisable plan. This was hardly surprising since it had never been cut by anyone other than his father, who proclaimed it a waste of money to go to the barber when he could do the job himself with the kitchen scissors in half the time it took to smoke a cigarette. His father was a long-distance lorry driver.

Kenny was the youngest of six children. Much the youngest, in fact, his three brothers and two sisters all being in their twenties and married, apart from Susan, his younger sister who was twenty-three. One by one they had left home and now Kenny lived alone with his parents. Not that he saw a great deal of them. His father was frequently away for several nights at a time and his mother had so many part-time jobs in the village that she was seldom home until late evening. Though Kenny had never been actually ill-treated (not counting the fairly regular and usually deserved wallopings he got from his father), the unintended circumstance of his birth had resulted in his being largely left to look after himself. Susan apart, his older brothers and sisters had tended to treat him with haphazard tolerance. Susan had always liked playing the part of little mother. She was genuinely fond of him and remained so despite a scornful rejection of her more pressing attentions. Though he had come to appreciate her rather more this past year since she had left home and moved in with a girl-friend in Arlebury where she had a job in a solicitor's office.

'You be here when I get back?' he asked as he turned to go.

' 'Course I will, boy. And don't forget, lots of sugar in the tea. But not too much milk.'

It took Kenny about twenty minutes to reach home, the end house of a row of small grey-stone Victorian villas on the main street. As he reached the village, he glanced at the large clock in the butcher's shop. It was a few minutes after six. His parents had gone into Arlebury and wouldn't be back until bed-time, which meant the house would be empty. However, he was still unsure to what extent he was going to be able to execute Shem's requirements. He'd certainly make him the tea and he could sneak out a few slices of bread without being questioned later, but when it came to meat ... His mother had cooked a joint that morning, but it would be more than his skin was worth to start hacking that about. Two of his brothers and their families were coming over the next day and the joint was intended for them.

He had just gone into the kitchen and was surveying the larder when he was startled by a voice.

'Hello, Kenny, I thought everyone must be out.'

He turned guiltily to find Susan standing in the doorway.

'Oh, hello,' he said uneasily.

'Are you hungry? Do you want me to get you something? Where are Mum and Dad?'

'They've gone into Arlebury. Anyway, what are you doing here?'

'I had some curtain material for Mum, so I thought I'd bring it over. But it seems I've had a wasted journey.'

'How long are you staying?'

'I'm not in any hurry. I'll get you something to eat if you want.'

A sly look crossed his face. 'Thanks. I'd like a couple of sandwiches. This beef'll do. Shall I cut some off?'

'Don't you dare! Fetch me a knife and I'll do it.'

Kenny turned away and, with a smug expression, got a knife out of the table drawer.

'Where are you going to eat it? Here in the kitchen?'

'No, I'm meeting Ray up by the quarries. We're having a feast together. Can you make some tea, too?'

'Tea? Wouldn't you prefer Coke? I'll give you money for Coke if you like.'

'No, thanks, I'd prefer tea.'

'What are you going to carry it in?'

'I've got an old can.'

He picked Shem's billy-can up from the floor and Susan

looked at it with distaste.

'You're not going to drink out of that dirty old thing?'

'Why not! It's all right.'

'As you please. It's like that thing that terrible old tramp used to carry around. Where'd you get it?'

'Found it.'

While she made the sandwiches and tea under Kenny's watchful eye, Susan plied him with questions, most of which he answered briefly and without interest. Sometimes her prattling got him down.

'Go on, give us another bit of meat in that one,' he urged at one point.

'What'll Mum say? Has she cooked this joint special for something?'

'She won't mind. Anyway, I'm hungry.'

'How's old Mrs Parkin?'

'I dunno. Where's the sugar?'

'Usual place I imagine. Mum said she was pretty ill.'

'Well, she ain't dead yet. I can't find it.'

'Here, let me look! *There*, at the end of your snub little nose. She's not all that old as a matter of fact. Well ... I suppose she must be nearer eighty than seventy ...'

Kenny's lips moved as he counted out six large spoonfuls. Susan who'd been bent over the table as she cut the sandwiches suddenly looked up. She seized the packet out of Kenny's hand.

'That's quite enough. It'll be like syrup.'

'I like lots of sugar.'

'You've got lots. How's school?'

'How's what?'

'School! the place you go to learn things.'

Kenny wrenched his mind from contemplation of Shem's forthcoming meal.

'All right, I suppose. At least, it isn't all right. I don't like it.'

'Did you ever?'

'Some of it's all right, but most's not.'

Susan shook her head in a resigned sort of way. Kenny seemed happy enough in one sense and yet she worried about him, which, admittedly, was more than any other member of the family did. He'd become curiously distant in some ways since Brian had departed from the village. She found it hard to particularise, but he seemed far too wrapped up in his own thoughts. Perhaps it was because he was more like an only child. Though an only child with a difference, most only children being doted on by their parents. This had certainly never been Kenny's lot. Indeed, his conception and birth had caused first dismay and then recrimination in the Bostock household. Susan who had been ten years old at the time could remember it clearly. She'd been thrilled to have a baby brother, but all the others had viewed the new arrival with dubiety if not actual hostility.

'What are you looking for now?' she asked as Kenny began rummaging in a cupboard.

'A bit of newspaper to wrap the sandwiches in.'

'O.K., let me do it. Anything else you want?'

He thought for a moment. Shem hadn't mentioned anything else, but Kenny didn't imagine he'd reject a few extras.

'What about a bit of cake?'

'If there is any.'

There was, and Susan cut a wedge to Kenny's specification.

'That should do you. If you get through all that, you'll be too bloated to walk home.'

Kenny grinned. 'Thanks, Susan.'

'Tell Mum I came. On second thoughts, don't bother. I'll leave her a note.'

'O.K. See you soon.'

'I'll be over again next Saturday.'

Kenny slammed the door behind him and hurried back to where he'd left Shem. It didn't occur to him that if Susan was watching his departure she might wonder why he was setting off in the opposite direction from the quarries which he'd said were his objective.

It was while on his way back to Shem that a thought suddenly struck him. He almost stumbled over as he dug one hand energetically into a trouser pocket which was stuffed with a collection of items such as to excite a magpie's envy. His fingers closed on what they sought and a small secret smile sped across his face.

He found Shem reclining languorously on one elbow like a bored courtesan.

'What you got there, boy?' he asked, beadily eyeing the package which Kenny was clutching under one arm.

'Beef sandwiches.'

'Let's see.'

'My sister made them.'

Shem held out a predatory hand. He wasn't interested in who'd made them. He unwrapped the sandwiches and held them up to his nose.

'They smells all right,' he observed cautiously, 'though a bit of onion pickle would've given 'em a nice bit of flavour.' He looked up sharply at Kenny. 'Didn't think of that, did you, boy?'

' 'Fraid not.'

'Anyway, they'll do for going along with. But put a bit of pickle in next time.'

'Here's your tea. I put in lots of sugar like you said.'

Shem accepted the billy-can, removed the lid and sniffed. Then he held it to his lips and drank half the contents before putting it down beside him.

'All right, but too much milk.'

Having made the remark, he settled back on one elbow and gazed out across the field, ignoring Kenny's presence. A slight mist was rising and the air was rich with the agreeably dank smells of autumn.

Kenny remained standing. He was always intrigued by Shem's seasonal visit and it required more than the old tramp's quirky moods to deter his interest. Indeed, in one sense they excited it. He was the only tramp Kenny had ever met, and his little-known way of life was enough to seize a boy's imagination.

He wondered whether it was really true that Shem's clothes were stuffed with £5 notes ... that he was even a millionaire ...

'Did you ever have to go to school?' he asked suddenly, giving expression to a thought which had been occupying his mind for the past few seconds.

' 'Course I went to school. Everyone has to go to school. I'm not ignorant.'

'Where'd you go to school?'

Shem's eyes darted maliciously.

'A place called Bollockstown.'

Kenny grinned uncertainly. 'I don't believe there is such a place.'

'Just because they don't teach you nothing at school these days, I'm not a liar.'

'Where is it, then?'

'Where? You ask your teacher.'

'How old are you really?'

'Old enough to skin your arse if you go on with your plaguing questions.'

Kenny moved a prudent step back out of Shem's reach.

'Have you got any brothers or sisters?'

'None what I know.'

'Who'll look after you when you're too old to get around?'

'Who looks after animals when they get too old?'

'Do you mean like dogs and cats?'

'Dogs and cats!' Shem snorted. 'I mean proper animals. Foxes and badgers and them sort.'

'They just die in their holes. Nobody looks after them.' Shem nodded fiercely and gave Kenny a hostile look. 'But you're not an animal.'

'Some people thinks so the way they treat a man these days. No neighbourliness.'

'What about me? I've brought you something.'

'Didn't put any onion pickle in them sandwiches, did you, boy?'

'I will next time. And, anyway, I've thought of something else.'

But Shem appeared to have sunk into a morose contemplation of his hat, a piece of apparel which resembled a misshapen steamed pudding of predominantly grey ingredients. He had removed it and was holding it out in front of him.

'I've thought of somewhere you can spend the night,' Kenny went on.

'I don't want any of your dirty old coal-sheds,' Shem retorted.

'It's not a coal-shed. It's somewhere very special.' He paused as he observed the old man's flicker of greedy interest. 'Do you want to hear about it?'

For several seconds they stared at each other in silence. Then Shem said testily, 'Well, go on, boy.'

II

It was four days later, on the Wednesday to be exact, that Kenny hurtled downstairs and through the kitchen towards the back door. He had got the door open and was about to disappear when his mother who was peeling potatoes called after him.

'Where are you going?'

'Out.'

'Don't forget Mr Gladwell's expecting you.'

Kenny looked round, his expression a mixture of resignation and exasperation.

'Oh, Mum, do I have to?'

'Yes.'

'Why?'

'Because I said you would.'

'But I'm in a hurry.'

'Where are you going?'

'Out . . . out to meet Ray.'

'Ray won't mind waiting. It'll only take you five minutes to make the two deliveries he wants.'

'It won't, Mum. It always takes much longer than you think.'

'Anyway, it's what he pays you to do.'

'A mouldy three bob a week.'

Three evenings a week, Kenny would make late deliveries for Mr Gladwell the grocer. There were seldom more than a couple of houses to go to and normally he was quite happy to perform the duty and collect the meagre payment. But tonight he had intended to slip out and pretend he'd forgotten.

'How do you know it's two deliveries?' he asked with sudden curiosity.

'Because I saw him on my way home just now and he told me. I said I'd send you along straight away. One of the things is a bottle of tonic wine for Mrs Parkin. She's been ill.'

Not ill enough, Kenny thought savagely.

'The other's a packet of biscuits for Mr Shelley.'

Kenny groaned. Getting away from Mr Shelley was like trying to free yourself from a fly-paper. He was always wanting Kenny to go in and see the rotten old model ship he'd built about a hundred years ago, or get him to move some stupid old piece of furniture from one side of the room to another. At best, he'd simply keep him standing at the door while he went drearily on and on with some anecdote. And Mrs Parkin wasn't much better, though, with luck, her illness may have helped to curb her natural flow of words.

'Well, don't just stand there glaring,' Mrs Bostock said

as she reached for another potato. 'That won't get the job done.'

Kenny departed, giving the door an extra vigorous slam to help relieve his feelings. His mother sighed. She couldn't wait for him to be grown up like the others. She just hoped that she'd still have the will and energy to enjoy herself. She didn't really blame Kenny, nor even herself or her husband. It was just a rotten bit of luck that she'd fallen for another baby at that late stage. Nature could play mean tricks on the unsuspecting.

Meanwhile Kenny stood silently fuming as Mr Gladwell carefully wrapped Mrs Parkin's bottle of tonic wine.

'A nice bit of paper round it will help to cheer her up,' he remarked, groping for the piece of green ribbon he'd dropped on the floor.

'Just knock on the door and go in,' he went on. 'She can't move around much yet.'

'Can't I just leave it on the step?'

'No, certainly not! Seeing you will cheer her up as much as the wine will. Now, here are Mr Shelley's biscuits. Off you go, Kenny. By the way, tell Mr Shelley they're not his usual but I think he'll find they have a nice flavour. The ones he likes best should be in next week.'

When he reached Mrs Parkin's cottage, Kenny tiptoed up the path and knocked lightly on the door. He hoped there'd be no response and he'd have an excuse for leaving the bottle of tonic wine on the step and departing with the same stealth which marked his arrival. But whatever had been wrong with the old girl, it clearly had nothing to do with her hearing for there was an immediate, almost eager, summons to enter.

'Hello, Kenny dear, have you brought my tonic?'

'It's wine.'

'Yes, tonic wine, dear. Now, just sit down for a minute and tell me how you are.'

'I'm afraid I mustn't stop. I've got to take something urgently to Mr Shelley.'

'I'm sure he can wait a few minutes longer. What is it, anyway?'

'His biscuits.'

Old Mrs Parkin let out a cackle. 'Who ever heard of biscuits being wanted urgently! Someone's been teasing you.'

Kenny flushed crossly. 'I've also got to get back to help Mum,' he added.

'How is your mum?'

'She's fine.'

'And your Susan?'

'Fine, too. I really must . . .'

'I remember Susan when she was just a little girl. Sweet little thing she was. And then you come along and . . .'

'I hope you'll feel better soon, Mrs Parkin,' Kenny broke in and turned tail.

If he had hoped to avoid seeing Mrs Parkin, there was certainly never any question of his being able to do so with Mr Shelley who was standing at the window like a sentinel awaiting his arrival.

He had opened the door before Kenny reached it, his face creased in an oleaginous smile.

'Come in, I've got something to show you.'

'I'm afraid I can't stop. My Mum wants me.'

'It won't take a minute.'

'Here are the biscuits. Mr Gladwell says he'll have the right ones in next week.'

Mr Shelley accepted the packet, at the same time giving Kenny's cheek an affectionate pat. If it wasn't your cheek, it was your bottom or a gentle squeeze of a biceps, while his eyes bored into you and his creepy smile remained a fixture on his face.

'I've been repainting my ship. Would you like to come and see?'

'Not now, I've got to go.'

'My, you are in a hurry, young man!' Mr Shelley remarked with a certain amount of asperity. He didn't like being quite so obviously rebuffed by a twelve-year-old. 'What is it your mother wants you to do?'

'Eh?'

'You said just now that your mother wanted you back.'

A light dawned in Kenny's eyes and he nodded vigorously. 'Yes, that's right. I've got to help her with something.'

'May one ask what?' Mr Shelley had been a schoolmaster before retiring to the village and the precision of his speech was matched only by the prissy neatness of his appearance.

Kenny was a slow-thinking boy and simulation didn't come to him easily.

'I've got to help her move furniture around,' he said after an uncomfortable pause.

'Then you must certainly hurry back,' Mr Shelley replied coldly. 'Far be it from me to detain you when you have promised to help your mother.'

To give effect to his reproof he closed the door firmly in Kenny's face, not that it took Kenny more than a couple of seconds to turn on his heel and run.

He ran with a sense of excitement and exhilarating release which grew with every yard of ground covered by his short, powerful legs.

He felt somehow certain that this time his hopes were going to be fulfilled. As he pounded along, lips parted and eyes bright with eager expectation, his mind had but one thought...

And to think that it was all because of Shem.

III

Shem's body was found about six o'clock the next evening. Found by Kenny's friend, Ray – or rather by Ray's dog, Leo.

Ray had called round at Kenny's place about half past five to suggest they went up to the quarries together. It was one of their regular haunts, providing, as it did, an almost unlimited range of pleasures. One could scramble over the tussocky mounds, which surrounded the quarries, until one dropped in delicious exhaustion. It was ideal ground, too, for stalking and fighting and springing out on unsuspecting enemies. And finally there were the quarries themselves, one large and two smaller ones, with waters almost as deep as the ocean itself, it was said. Round their precipitous edges were hefty stones and lumps of wood and, best of all, one or two ancient rusty pieces of machinery, left behind when the quarries had ceased to be actively worked, which could be put to a dozen fascinating uses.

Just recently he and Kenny had begun to build a raft from some of the larger lengths of wood and four old oil drums which they had collected and brought to the scene.

On the particular evening, Ray found Kenny sitting at the kitchen table with a magazine in front of him whose pages he was mechanically turning.

'Coming up to the quarries?' he asked.

Kenny shook his head firmly.

'Not tonight.'

'Why not?'

'Don't feel like it.'

Ray gazed at his friend with a puzzled expression, while Leo made a round of inquisitive sniffs in the Bostock kitchen.

'Anything wrong?'

'Nothing. I just don't feel like it, that's all.'

'I thought we could get on with the raft.'

Kenny glanced up. His face had a blank, forbidding look. 'You go if you want.' And then he lowered his head again and began turning the pages of the magazine more rapidly than before.

Ray stood there nonplussed for a while, then, making a grab at Leo as he started on another circuit of smells, said with a tinge of sadness, 'Come on, Leo, you and I'll go.'

In fact, though he'd have preferred to have had Kenny's company, he was always perfectly happy provided Leo was around.

Leo had a soft black and white coat, appealing eyes, an impudent tail, which had seen as many fights as a boxer's nose, and a store of restless energy surpassing that of the two boys. Though he reciprocated his small owner's affection, and regarded him as the liberal dispenser of treats, obedience was not among his qualities. Hence no amount of whistling or shouting had the slightest effect on him. If Ray whistled or called out his name and Leo came running up, it was no more than coincidence. On the rare occasions when his young master fastened a length of washing-rope to his collar and kept him on a lead, irksome though he found it, it was Ray whose spirit broke first.

On the evening in question, Ray had made his way rather disconsolately to the quarry where the raft was under construction. He wished Kenny had come. Apart from anything else, there was awfully little he could do on his own. It needed the two of them to manhandle the great lumps of wood and to hold steady the oil drums to which the wood was being lashed with anything that came to hand for the purpose; odd bits of string, short lengths of twisted wire and some rather fibrous grass which they had found near by.

After about ten minutes of largely fruitless effort, Ray decided to give up. All he had succeeded in doing was to gash one of his thumbs on the sharp edge of an oil drum and turn his ankle when trying to prevent the same drum from rolling away into the water.

He clambered up the sharp sandy slope from the water's edge and cast an eye around for Leo.

There was no sign of him; and still none after Ray had whistled and shouted out his name for a full half-minute. The only thing to do was to make his way across to the small knoll which commanded an all-round view of the area. From there one could see all three quarries and their surrounding hillocks.

He and Kenny would frequently race each other to the top of the knoll, with Leo joining in vociferously if he had nothing better to do at that moment. On this occasion, how-ever, Ray arrived breathless on the summit without having caught so much as a glimpse of Leo on the way.

He stood up and looked all around him. Vapour was beginning to rise off the water in one of the quarries and the sky was streaked with red and grey in the softly blurred light of an autumn evening.

Suddenly about fifty yards away in a declivity between two ridges of hillocks, Ray thought he saw the unmistakable waggle of Leo's tail. He called out to him but nothing hap-pened, save that the tail continued to waggle in a manner which indicated that Leo's other end was busily occupied.

Ray clambered down from the knoll and ran over to where he had spotted his dog.

At first he thought Leo was burrowing away at a bundle of old clothes, but then he saw him lick at something lighter in shade and realised with a sickening feeling that it was a man's head. Shem's head.

Although he had never seen a dead person before, he knew in an instant that there was no life left in the prone figure under his gaze. There was something almost carefree in the scattered arrangement of Shem's limbs.

Seizing Leo by the tail, he tugged him away. He was forced to pause while he then removed his own belt and fastened it to the dog's collar, for Leo showed no inclination to quit the scene voluntarily, but, after that, he ran and didn't stop running until he arrived home.

Ten minutes later a police patrol car had been directed to the village and was speeding on its way with the brutish disregard for anything in its path of a hunger-crazed rhinoceros scenting food.

IV

Detective Superintendent Daniel Page was looking forward to retirement. Only six weeks to go before he moved out of his small bachelor flat in Arlebury and settled into the cottage in Somerset which he had bought several years ago with a legacy left him by an affectionate aunt.

He had let it in the meantime, but now the tenants had departed and it awaited his occupancy.

For years he had been looking forward to the day; not impatiently or with any sense of frustration, but calmly and hopefully. He was used to living on his own and perfectly capable of looking after himself. Being the person he was, he knew exactly how he was going to spend his retirement. He would garden and keep bees (a subject on which he had read a great deal recently) and he would read history. After thirty-five years in the police, he was determined to catch up on an education which had ended when he was only fifteen years old. He was a reflective man and he wanted to spend his remaining years, of which he hoped a score might be left, to understanding something of the world into which he had been born and he had long realised that only a knowledge of history could fill this deeply felt need within him.

Though he had on the whole enjoyed his time in the force, he had frequently wondered how he came to be there. And, to be fair, the same thought was not unknown to his fellow-officers, superior and lower in rank.

It wasn't that he was a misfit, for if he had been he wouldn't have survived thirty-five years and risen to his present appointment. On the other hand, he lacked the sense of dedication and of *esprit de corps* possessed of most of his generation of police officer. He worked hard and never did less than his duty, but a sense of detachment had led him to be regarded as 'a bit of a funny one'. He was liked without being popular and was respected without commanding any great loyalty.

About a year ago his force had been amalgamated with those of two neighbouring counties, and Arlebury, which had previously been the constabulary headquarters, was now no more than a divisional headquarters of the combined force. Page, who had been head of the C.I.D. of his force, had been left to mind his old manor, but was now answerable to a Detective Chief Superintendent who hung out at constabulary headquarters forty miles away from Arlebury.

Though he recognised the changes as being in the greater interest of all-round police efficiency, which was more than most of his contemporaries found themselves able to admit, they had served only to increase the quiet satisfaction with which he viewed his approaching retirement.

On this particular evening he had been home about half an hour and was in the midst of grilling himself a steak when the phone rang.

'Sergeant Machin here, sir. Someone's found a body out at Long Gaisford. Looks like murder. Shall I come round straight away and pick you up?'

'I'll be ready, Sergeant,' Page said equably, even though the steak had reached a tantalising stage and its succulent aromas were assailing his nostrils as he stood at the phone. 'Do we know who the victim is?'

'Some old tramp, I gather. Found near a quarry on the

outskirts of the village.'

'Oh well, we shall doubtless discover more when we get there.'

Page replaced the receiver and went and took the steak from beneath the grill. With a faintly sad air, he put it on the larder shelf.

Long Gaisford was fairly free of crime, if only for lack of opportunity, Page reflected while he waited for Detective Sergeant Machin to come and pick him up. It had bred a few criminals over the years, but they had gone farther afield to more fruitful areas to commit their offences. There'd certainly never been a murder there in all the years he'd know the village. It was a pleasant village, without any particularly memorable features, and was far enough off the main road to have remained unspoilt. Page hadn't set foot there for over a year and then only to have a pint of beer in the local on a summer evening's drive out into the country.

It was three years since the local constable had been withdrawn and the small police station closed; this in the interests of conserving manpower. Now, its police needs were met from a larger village about five miles away and by irregular visits of a patrol car.

Page put on his ancient raincoat and the brown felt hat which he wore meticulously straight with the brim turned down in front and went downstairs to wait for Machin at the street door.

He was glad that it was Machin who'd been on duty and who'd be going out to the scene with him. He was a promising young officer, still only in his mid-twenties, whom Page had recommended for early promotion on his general record in the C.I.D. One day he should be a Detective Chief Superintendent or even a Chief Constable, if they hadn't by then been replaced by computers – or one of the other pieces of electronic apparatus with which the police were being increasingly equipped.

An Austin A40 swung round the corner and pulled up where Page was waiting.

'I tried to get a patrol car, sir, but they were all out.'

Page nodded briefly. 'They always are except in TV serials, but I've no doubt this'll get us there.'

C.I.D. officers were often forced to use their own cars on duty, claiming an allowance for such usage, and at Arlebury they had only two cars officially allocated to them. The A40 was at least the better of the two.

'I'd better tell you what I've done, sir,' Sergeant Machin said, as he engaged first gear and let in the clutch with a Jehu's sense of urgency. 'I've let headquarters know and I've asked one of the photographic boys to get out there as quickly as possible. I've also passed a message to the Coroner, seeing that he's a bit touchy about these things, not that there's anything for him to do at the moment.'

'No, but you were quite right, Sergeant. He always likes to be consulted about which pathologist should do the P.M.' Page braced his legs against the floor of the car as it sped round a wide bend, leaving the town behind. 'We'll have to see when we get out there whether we want the pathologist and one of the lab people to attend the scene.'

'I should think it would be a good thing to have the pathologist.'

'Probably.'

'The lab never seem too keen unless one pulls out all the stops.'

'I don't blame 'em. They're often called out unnecessarily. And if you have a good scene-of-crime officer, he should be able to cope in nine cases out of ten.'

'I've got Detective Constable Stevens for that. He's pretty keen since he went on that course.'

'Let's hope his practical application matches his enthusiasm.'

'Don't you think it will then, sir?' Machin asked in a faintly worried tone.

'Oh, I'm sure it will,' Page replied blandly. 'He's a competent officer.'

For good reasons, Machin held his Detective Superintendent in higher esteem than most, but he still found him-self nonplussed from time to time by his superior's uncom-mitted air.

'Do we know who discovered the body?' Page went on.

'I gather a boy found it when he was playing near the quarry.'

'And the cause of death? Any information about that?'

'The message I got just before I left, sir, said that it was believed to be a blow on the head.'

Page received the information with a grunt and relapsed into silence. This was not the moment he would have chosen to become involved in a murder enquiry. He could only hope that it would be cut and dried and not a pro-tracted investigation in which a hundred false leads pre-sented themselves. He'd scarcely be able to retire in the middle of the enquiry unless it had come to a complete full-stop.

As they approached the village, they found a police car parked at the end of a track leading off to the right. A small knot of people stood staring and whispering at the side of the road. Sergeant Machin pulled up and a constable in uniform came over to the car.

'Up this track, is it?' Machin asked.

'That's right, sir. You can drive about a quarter of a mile, but you have to get out and walk the last bit.'

Neither of them spoke as the car bucked and lurched its way up the rutted track. At the end they found a number of cars parked and a further group of hovering villagers.

Page got out and looked across to where the reflected light of some torches was coming from behind one of the hillocks.

'Got a torch, Sergeant?' he asked as Machin came up beside him.

'Yes, sir.'

'Better get it, then. It may save us breaking our necks.'

He frowned as a sudden thought occurred to him. If the victim hadn't been killed at the scene, he must have been brought there. And if he'd been brought there, it must have been by means of a vehicle using the same track they'd just traversed and parking where four cars and a dozen-odd people were now industriously obliterating possible vital traces of evidence. He swore under his breath as the full force of the implication flooded through his mind.

'Is there a police officer here?' he called out.

A figure detached itself from the chattering group fifteen yards away.

'P.C. Carver here. Who's that?'

'Detective Superintendent Page. Get those people back on to the road, but don't let them use the track, and tell the officer on duty at the other end that no one else is to be allowed into this area until I say so.'

'Yes, sir.'

'Now, let's go and discover the worst,' he said morosely, as he and Sergeant Machin set off in the direction of the torches.

Twice he tripped and once he half fell over when one foot caught in a tussock of coarse grass. He was aware of feeling faintly irked that Machin didn't appear to be similarly troubled.

There were three officers at the scene, two patrol car officers and Detective Constable Stevens, who seemed to have justified Sergeant Machin's confidence in his keenness by arriving ahead of anyone else from the C.I.D.

'Nothing's been touched pending your arrival, sir,' Stevens said.

'Let's have a bit of light,' Page remarked as he bent down to stare at the corpse.

At once, four torch beams wove together and settled on Shem's last remains. Page observed the hair matted with blood at the base of the skull. It certainly looked like the result of a blow which could have caused death. A brief further examination failed to reveal any other injuries to the head.

'Anyone know who he is?' he asked, as he straightened

up again.

'An old tramp, known to everybody in the village as Shem, sir,' Stevens replied.

'Anything else known?'

'He was discovered by a young lad who was playing out here.'

'So I've heard. Any rumours as to who might be responsible?'

'None, sir.'

'Why should anyone want to murder an old tramp?' Page said aloud, though without expectation of an answer. The question merely reflected a dawning realisation that this was unlikely to be a quickly solved case. And yet he knew that this was a premature judgement. Indeed it wasn't so much a judgement as a *cri de coeur*. The two uniform officers stared at him stonily from the shadows. There'd been little love lost between Page and the car and motorcycle patrol section since he had been heard, in an unguarded moment, to liken its officers to Hitler's stormtroopers. Cold-eyed, square-jawed and thriving on the harassment of others, he had gone on to say somewhat bitterly after a brush with a speed cop who had failed to recognise him when he was out driving one Sunday afternoon. It wasn't the failure to be recognised which had irritated him, but the wholly unjustified action of the officer in waving him down in the first place.

'I'd better get to the village and arrange for a pathologist to come out,' he now went on. 'As soon as he's been, we can move the body to the mortuary. Meanwhile, you stay here, Stevens, and get on with what you can. You'll need to be here anyway when the doctor comes, though there's probably not a great deal you can do until it's light. We'll see what the night brings, but it'll be necessary, I suspect, to examine the whole area for clues. It looks like that sort of case, unless there's already someone waiting to confess. You'd better come with me, Sergeant,' he added, turning to Machin. 'After I've made some phone calls we'll go and see the boy who found the body, not that I imagine he'll be able to tell us very much more than we already know.'

'It must have been a nasty shock for the kid,' Sergeant Machin remarked.

'I would think so,' Page replied, 'though with twelve-year-olds these days you never know. Anyway, let's go and find out.'

V

When Page and Machin arrived about half an hour later at Ray's home, the door was opened by his father, a small, anxious-looking man whose eyes flickered behind glasses as restlessly as a home movie. The two officers introduced themselves.

'It's given him a nasty turn,' Mr Nutter said accusingly.

'I can quite understand that,' Page replied, 'and we certainly don't want to make it any worse for him, but we should like to put a few questions to him.'

'I'd sooner he wasn't mixed up in it.' Mr Nutter's tone was belligerent as his gaze darted from one face to the other.

'I quite understand that, too, but he *was* the person who found the body and we'd just like to have a bit of a talk with him. In your presence, of course.'

'I don't hold in getting mixed up in things which don't concern you,' Mr Nutter observed.

'A very good principle,' Page agreed.

'Particularly with the police,' Mr Nutter added.

'What's wrong with the police? They only do a job like everyone else.'

'Well, I still don't like it and I assure you I know my rights so don't you try anything on with the boy.'

'That's the last thing I'd dream of doing and I'm sorry to hear you even suggest it.'

At this moment, a woman appeared in the doorway behind the man.

'Are these the police?' she enquired.

'Yes. I'm just telling them I don't want Ray upset.'

'You'd better come in,' she said, ignoring her husband. 'Ray's more likely to be upset if he's *not* interviewed by the police,' she added with a wink. 'You don't want to take too much notice of Mr Nutter. He fusses a lot. I'm always telling him so. Come on in, Ray's in the kitchen.'

Mr Nutter added a few baleful mutterings, but otherwise appeared to retire from the exchange.

One glance at Ray was sufficient to confirm to the police that his mother's assessment of the situation was considerably shrewder than his father's. He was sitting composedly watching television with Leo stretched out asleep at his side.

'Here are two policemen come to ask you some questions,' Mrs Nutter announced as they entered. She went across and switched off the sound, but left the picture showing.

'I'm Detective Superintendent Page, Ray, and this is Detective Sergeant Machin.'

'I'm sure I've seen you in Arlebury,' Mrs Nutter said chattily to Sergeant Machin.

'Very likely. That's where I'm stationed.'

'We were really sorry when Constable Holmes left the village,' she went on.

'I wasn't,' her husband put in. 'I don't hold with the police.'

'Oh, we all know you and your ways,' his wife retorted, though with perfect good humour. 'Anyway, it's Ray they've come to talk to, not you.'

Page seized the cue and in an easy conversational manner began eliciting Ray's recollection of events while Sergeant Machin jotted down notes.

Having established the approximate time of his discovery of the body and exactly how he had come across it (Page's heart sank a little further when he realised what Leo's intervention might mean by way of destroyed clues), Page went on:

'Do you often go and play near the quarries, Ray?'

'Yes, with Kenny.'

'Who's Kenny?'

'Kenny Bostock.'

'Does he live in the village?'

'Yes.'

'But this evening, you were on your own?'

'Yes, Kenny wouldn't come.'

'Oh, why not?'

'He said he didn't want to.'

'Did he give any reason?'

'No. He seemed sort of funny.'

Page and Machin exchanged a swift look, before Page went on.

'In what way, funny?'

Ray shrugged. 'Just funny.'

'You mean, he wasn't his usual self?'

'That's right.'

'What've all these questions about Kenny Bostock got to do with my boy?' Mr Nutter demanded to know.

'I was just interested in trying to find out why Kenny hadn't accompanied Ray this evening, that's all,' Page replied soothingly.

'Well, you can ask young Bostock himself, can't you?'

'Certainly.'

'Would you like a cup of tea if I put the kettle on?' Mrs Nutter now chimed in.

'That would be very kind. I'm sure we could both do with one.'

Page marvelled at the way Mrs Nutter, who had twice her husband's bulk, appeared completely unruffled by – almost unnoticing of – his querulous interventions. Perhaps it was because she realised that it was she who had command of their married situation. Page suspected they'd find that Nutter had a criminal record when they came to check. His likes usually did. He turned his attention back to the boy.

'Did you immediately recognise the dead person as Shem?'

' 'Soon as I saw his face.'

'How long have you known him?'

'I dunno. Kenny knows him better 'n I.'

'When was the last time you saw him alive?'

'Yesterday, I saw him and Kenny together.'

'What time was that?'

'Dinner-time.'

'What time is dinner-time?'

'One o'clock, I suppose.'

'Where were Shem and Kenny when you saw them?'

'Top end of village, by Garstang's field.'

'What were they doing?'

'Talking, I suppose.'

'Did Kenny say anything to you about Shem afterwards?'

'Yes.'

'What?'

'He said Shem kept on about people being mean and not helping him.'

Warning mutterings came from Mr Nutter. 'What's all this got to do with my boy?'

'It's just a question of finding out everything he can tell us. What's important or not important, we'll know later.' He paused. 'Perhaps, at this stage, I could ask you something, Mr Nutter. Did you know Shem?'

'What are you accusing me of! I didn't have anything to do with his death. I didn't even know he was back here.'

'There's no need to get so excited,' Sergeant Machin said. 'Mr Page hasn't accused you of anything. He's merely asked you a simple question.'

'Of course I knew him, sort of. Everyone did,' Mr Nutter

replied in a grudging tone. 'He's been turning up regular for years.'

'Do you happen to know what his real name is?'

'No. He's always just been Shem.'

At this moment, Mrs Nutter returned to the room from the adjoining scullery in which she had been making the tea. She was carrying a tray with four cups and saucers, milk jug, sugar bowl and tea-pot covered by a home-knitted cosy with a pom-pom on top.

'Everyone take milk and sugar?' she asked, as she began to pour.

'I don't want any,' her husband said sulkily.

'You'd better have a cup, it'll make you feel yourself.'

'I'm not thirsty.'

'You don't have to be. Have a cup.'

'No.'

She shrugged. 'Please yourself.'

'Can I have something to drink, Mum?' Ray chipped in.

'You don't drink tea.'

'I know. Is there any fizzy?'

'You'll go up in the air like one of them balloons with all the fizzy you drink.'

Ray grinned and went to a cupboard on the far side of the kitchen, returning with a glass and a large bottle of faintly yellow liquid.

As he sipped his tea and listened with one ear to Mrs Nutter's flow of conversation, Page decided that they had probably exhausted their present line of enquiry and could profitably move on. He had never ceased to be surprised – though by now in a rather mild sort of way – at the vagaries of human behaviour and the curious relationships which existed. Mr and Mrs Nutter were a case in point. It was difficult to see what had brought them together, let alone what had kept them together. Luckily, their son seemed to take after his mother, rather than his father, which, Page reflected, provided a better prospect for society.

'How long had he been dead before Ray found the poor old chap?' Mrs Nutter asked suddenly.

'We shan't know that until the doctor has examined him,' Sergeant Machin replied.

Page watched her as she appeared to be digesting his answer. Then she said, 'If you want to know what I think, it was one of them tip-and-run drivers.' Observing the mystified expressions on the faces of her audience, she went on, 'These lanes round here are death-traps. Cars come flying along like they were scalded cats and never mind what's in the way. I reckon one of them knocked the poor old boy over and then they dumped his body by the quarries.'

Page nodded gravely. 'But supposing it didn't happen that way, Mrs Nutter, and that Shem really was murdered by someone. Have you any idea who might have done it?'

'Well, that's the whole point. Why should anyone want to murder a poor old tramp?'

It was a question which Page had already asked himself and was destined to hear echoed from all quarters in the course of the days ahead.

It was a question, however, which remained resolutely unanswered even though, before that night was out, he became certain he had found the person to whom the answer was known.

VI

The lane outside was quiet when Page and Machin emerged from the Nutters' house.

Mr Nutter had made a final declaration that he knew his rights, coupled with a denunciation of what he called an attempt by the police to involve his son in other people's trouble, and Mrs Nutter had invited them to drop by again.

Ray had begun to look heavy-eyed with sleep and Leo hadn't stirred once all the time they'd been there.

'What's the time?' Page asked as they got back into the car.

'Just after nine, sir.'

'Think Dr Leary'll be there yet?'

'It'll take him at least an hour, sir, even if they find him straight away. I doubt whether he'll get here before ten at the earliest. And you know what a man he is to run to ground! If he's not cutting up another body, he's speaking at some dinner. He's never without a knife of some sort in his hand.'

'We'll let the officer at the end of the track know where we'll be, so that he can send us a message as soon as Leary arrives.'

'We'll probably hear him. That fish-tail exhaust on his car almost bounces sound waves off the moon.'

'I've not seen his latest car.'

'It's the sort of thing James Bond might care to buy, second-hand at that.'

Page had considerable respect for the pathologist's professional ability, though rather less for his schoolboyish enthusiasms. Nevertheless he was glad that the Coroner had expressed the wish for Dr Leary's services.

'Let's be on our way.'

'Where to, sir?'

'Where do you think?'

'To see this Kenny Bostock.'

'Correct.'

'What do you make of him?'

'Ask me after we've talked to him.'

Page pulled out his pipe and Sergeant Machin grimaced in the dark. It seemed that the Superintendent was slipping into one of his Maigret moods.

To do Page justice, his thoughts were in fact running on the line that it might be better if he left the questioning of the Bostock boy to his sergeant. Though he had interviewed hundreds of children over the years, he never felt entirely at ease when doing so. He was aware that his efforts at establishing rapport were sometimes stilted and unsuccessful. Some bachelors can get along famously with children – too famously – but Page was not among these. It wasn't that he disliked them as a breed, just that he found it difficult to get on easy terms with them. And something told him that the way Kenny Bostock was handled might prove all important.

He cast a surreptitious glance at Sergeant Machin who looked little more than a boy himself – heaven knew what it denoted when police officers began to look so young to their own species – and was, Page knew, the eldest of a large family, with brothers little older than Nutter and Bostock.

They pulled up outside the short terrace of Victorian villas where the Bostocks lived.

Machin was about to get out of the car when Page said:

'I'll leave you to conduct the interview with young Bostock, Sergeant. I'll just chip in when I want.' His tone was awkward and Machin felt momentarily nonplussed.

'Very well, sir,' he said, masking his curiosity.

'I think it'll be better that way,' Page added, opening the door on his side of the car and getting out.

A light shining through the glass panel over the front door appeared to indicate that someone was at home, but it took three hefty knockings on the door before it was opened.

Kenny stood there, staring at them as if they were straight from Mars. His mouth was clamped shut as though he felt that he was going to be sick at any moment.

'Kenny Bostock?' Machin asked in a friendly tone.

Kenny nodded, without relaxing his facial muscles.

'We're police officers. This is Detective Superintendent Page and I'm Sergeant Machin. Can we come in for a few minutes, Kenny, we have some questions we'd like to ask you? I suppose you've heard about Shem?'

Again the tense nod.

'Is either your mum or dad at home?'

This time he shook his head.

'Oh! Well, we don't want to ask you questions without one of them being present. And I expect you'd sooner have it that way, too. Will they be back soon?'

'Mum will.' His voice came out as a nervous croak.

'Where is she?'

'Mrs Parkin's.'

'And your father?'

'Driving his lorry.'

'Do you think it would be all right if we came in and waited, Kenny? Your mum wouldn't mind that, would she?'

'No.'

He turned and led the way into the kitchen.

'Cosy place you've got,' Machin remarked, looking about him. 'Do you have a dog, too?'

Kenny shook his head.

'We've just been to see Ray and I took rather a fancy to his dog. I've forgotten his name now . . .'

'Leo.'

'Yes, Leo, that's it.'

There was a sound of footsteps along the path at the side of the house and a few seconds later, the back door opened and a woman entered.

'Mrs Bostock?' It was Page who spoke.

'Yes.'

'We're police officers. Your son very kindly said we might wait inside. Actually, it's him we wish to talk to, but we didn't want to begin until you were here. It's your right as a parent to be present.'

'What's he done, then?'

'He hasn't done anything. Sergeant Machin here just wants to ask him a few questions about Shem.'

'You'd better go ahead, and you'd better tell them anything you can, Kenny.'

She laid the bulging plastic carrier-bag she had in her hand on the table and took off her coat, hanging it on a peg behind the door. Then she flopped into a chair and let out a heavy sigh.

'Don't take any notice of me. I've been on the move all day and must get the load off my feet. Putting old Mrs Parkin to bed is more than I should have taken on.'

'Will your husband be back tonight?' Machin asked.

'Not till the day after tomorrow. He's on the lorries – long distance. He's on the Glasgow run at the moment.'

Turning his attention to Kenny who was sitting at one end of the plain deal table, on two other sides of which he and Page were seated, Machin said:

'When did you first hear about Shem's death, Kenny?'

'This evening some time.' As soon as the words were out, he shut his mouth tight again, as though still fearful that he was going to vomit.

'Who told you about it?'

'I think I told him,' Mrs Bostock chimed in. 'I heard it in the village and when I got home I naturally mentioned it to Kenny. It was after that I went round to Mrs Parkin's to get her some supper and see her to bed.'

'Have you seen Ray this evening since he found Shem?'

Kenny shook his head.

'Did you know Shem quite well?'

'No.'

'But you talked to him when you met him?'

'Yes.'

'When did you last talk to him?'

'Yesterday.'

'What time yesterday?'

'Dinner-time.'

'Did you see him today?'

'No.'

'Sure?'

'Yes.'

'How many times have you seen him over the past week?'

'A few.'

'Three? four? five?'

'About four.'

'Where used you to see him?'

'All over.'

'By the quarries?'

Kenny shook his head vigorously. 'No.'

'Never there?'

'No.'

'Where?'

'In fields mostly.'

'What used you and Shem to talk about?'

'Nothing special.'

'But what sort of things?'

'I can't remember.'

'Did Shem ever tell you he was afraid of anything?'

'No.'

'Or anyone?'

'No.'

'Do you know where he's been sleeping these past few nights?'

'Different places, I suppose.'

'But you don't know where?'

'No.'

Sergeant Machin had maintained a friendly expression throughout the questioning and his tone had been as quiet as it had been unhectoring. He now said:

'Are you worried about anything, Kenny?'

The boy stared at him and for a moment even stopped fiddling with his hands as he'd been doing ever since the inteview began. Then he shook his head vigorously.

'No.'

'Are you sure?'

'What've I got to be worried about?' His tone had a hoarse urgency about it.

Machin smiled disarmingly. 'I don't know. Probably nothing. It's just that you seem worried ... very worried.'

'I'm not.'

Mrs Bostock was watching her son with a puzzled frown.

'You sure there's nothing the matter, Kenny?' she broke in.

'Nothing's wrong, Mum. Don't keep on.'

'O.K.,' Machin said quickly, 'there's nothing worrying you, so that's fine. Tell me, Kenny, why didn't you go with Ray when he went to the quarries this evening?'

'Didn't feel like it.'

'Why not?'

'Just didn't.'

'There must have been a reason.'

'I had a pain.'

'Where?'

'In my tummy.'

'Has it gone now?'

'I think it's coming back.'

'What's that you're playing with in your hands?'

As Machin spoke, Kenny whipped his hands beneath the table and thrust one into his trouser pocket.

'Just a bit of stone.'

'Why were you fiddling with it?'

'No particular reason.'

'People usually do things like that when they're worried about something.'

Once more Kenny clamped his mouth tight shut and glared straight ahead of him.

'But you still say you're not worried; that nothing's the matter?'

This time Kenny didn't make any answer and Sergeant Machin turned to Page.

'I don't think we can take this any further at the moment, sir.'

Page pursed his lips in thought, then looking at Kenny he said, 'Listen to me, Kenny. It's pretty obvious that you do have something on your mind and that you haven't told us all you could. We have a lot of other enquiries to make but we shall certainly want to talk to you again. Probably tomorrow. I hope that between now and then you'll think very carefully about what I've said, and that when we see you again you'll be much franker than you have been this evening. Hiding things is only going to make you feel much worse. I'm sure you've always been taught to tell the truth, so make up your mind to do that when we come back and see you. You've certainly got nothing to be afraid of if you're truthful.'

On this exemplary moral, but dubiously practical, note, Page concluded what, even to his own ears, had begun to sound like a not very good sermon.

'Perhaps you'll have a word with him,' he murmured to Mrs Bostock as he turned to leave the room. 'Stress how important it is that he tells us all he knows. I'm sure he's holding something back. It mayn't even be anything relevant, but only the police can judge that.'

Mrs Bostock met Page's gaze but her expression remained non-committal. Whatever she intended doing or not doing after the officers had gone was not going to be disclosed.

Kenny remained seated at the table, staring white-faced ahead of him, as the officers left the room.

Mrs Bostock bade them a formal good night at the front door which she closed as soon as they'd stepped outside. They heard her shoot the top and bottom bolts before they were off the step.

'What did you make of him, sir?' Machin asked when they were back in the car.

'We'll have to search around for a lever or two to prise him open.'

'Do you think he could have done it?'

'Murdered Shem, you mean?'

'Yes.'

' "Could have", yes. "Did", too soon to say.'

'What motive would a twelve-year-old boy have for murdering an old tramp?' Machin asked in a tone of self-bewilderment.

Page gave an abstracted shrug. Experience had taught him that the most unlikely people could commit the most improbable crimes, for the most trivial of reasons. He hoped that the post-mortem examination would provide them with a lead. It might even provide an answer to the question as to whether Kenny Bostock could have committed the crime.

'Back to the scene,' he said as Sergeant Machin turned the car. 'If Dr Leary's not already there, we'll wait for him. And it looks as if tomorrow we'll have to start knocking on every door in the village.'

VII

A police car was still parked at the end of the track which led to the quarries, but the villagers had melted away and a young police constable kept a lonely vigil. One day if he ever got round to writing his memoirs he would doubtless claim Shem's murder as one of the earlier cases on which he worked. He informed Page that Dr Leary had arrived about five minutes earlier.

As Page and Machin reached the end of the bumpy track they recognised the pathologist's scarlet coupé parked a little way off from the police vehicles as though it didn't wish to be seen in their company. Its chrome dazzled the eyes as the headlights of Page's car swept over it.

Dr Leary jumped up from his examination of the body as Page and Machin joined the small group which was there. He was wearing a dinner jacket with an ancient mackintosh over the top. Page knew that he always kept this in the boot of his car for such occasions and had noticed a vicuna coat flung over the driver's seat when they parked. He was a small, compact man with reddish brown hair, of which there was only a soft fuzz left on top of his head, bright blue eyes with tufts of hair on the cheekbones beneath them and a small button of a mouth which was his weakest feature.

'Good evening, Superintendent,' he said briskly. 'Nothing further to be done here. You can remove the body.'

'You've been very quick, Doctor,' Page remarked with some surprise.

'I don't know what more I'm expected to do by the light of a torch in these miniature Himalayas. I'll certainly come back and look at the scene by daylight, but meanwhile let's get the body to the mortuary. Incidentally, where'll you be taking it?'

'Arlebury public mortuary if that suits you.'

'It has fewer amenities than a Victorian kitchen, but couldn't otherwise be better.'

Page turned to Detective Constable Stevens. 'We must preserve the scene until we've been able to examine it properly. You'd better arrange that and then come along to the mortuary as soon as you can. You'll be needed there to take possession of the deceased's clothing and all the samples Dr Leary produces.' He turned back to the pathologist. 'Have you been able to form any preliminary view, Doctor, as to cause of death and when it took place?'

'Looks as if it was caused by a blow to the back of the head. As to when, I can't tell you yet. But it was certainly a fair number of hours ago. Possibly over twelve.'

'Possibly longer still?'

'Could be. When was he last seen alive?'

'Lunch-time yesterday is all we have at the moment.'

Dr Leary pulled at his small fleshy lower lip. 'Lunch-time yesterday,' he mused. 'That's approximately thirty-four hours ago. Could be that he met his death in the course of last night.' He stared thoughtfully down at Shem's outflung limbs. 'If he has been dead as long as that, you'll want to know whether he was killed here or brought here after death.'

'Yes.'

'I'll return as soon as I've done the P.M. It won't be far off light by then. Have you got something with which to cover over the area?' He bent down and touched the ground.

'We'll arrange that.'

'Good.' He stood up and gave his black bow-tie a small adjustment as though about to launch into an after-dinner speech.

'I'm afraid we've wrecked your evening,' Page said, as they prepared to move off in the direction of the cars.

'With the murder rate going up, I reckon I soon shan't get farther than the soup before being called out. This evening, I was actually about to tackle a peach melba when I received your message. Luckily I wasn't due to speak at this dinner.'

Page realised that the reference to luck applied to himself and not to the pathologist's fellow-diners.

As Dr Leary strode briskly back to his car, an acolyte's torch lighting the way for him, he turned towards Page and said, 'Why should anyone want to murder an old tramp? Any ideas?'

'None,' Page replied gloomily. 'I'm hoping you'll provide some.'

'Hmm! It's quite possible.' They had reached the cars and he had flung off his raincoat and put back on his vicuna. He got agilely into his car and pressed the starter. The engine sprang to life with a powerful, full-throated roar. 'See you at the mortuary,' he called out, as he engaged first gear and shot away while a volley of small stones thrown up by his rear wheels spattered Page and Machin round the legs.

'Glad I didn't put on my white tie and tails,' Sergeant Machin remarked as he bent down to brush his trousers.

Arlebury public mortuary was no better than Dr Leary had described, and so long as it remained as low as it did on the council's list of priorities it was likely to go on resembling a Victorian kitchen minus its amenities. It had flaking white-washed walls, a floor of undulating red tiles and, in one corner, an ancient sink fed by a cold-water tap and a small temperamental gas geyser, which had been installed just after the war and was one of the more recent fixtures. For the rest there were two long trestle tables, and, in the middle of the room, something akin to a marble tomb on top of which the bodies were laid to await the pathologist's attention. The whole was bleakly illuminated by strip lighting which did nothing to mitigate its starkly morbid ambience. Never to be seen at its best, it could scarcely look worse at one o'clock in the morning.

In the absense of its normal attendant (a retired police constable who sensibly declined to get out of bed once there until his alarm clock went off at half past seven the next morning), it fell to Sergeant Machin and Detective Constable Stevens to undress Shem and prepare him for Dr Leary who hadn't yet arrived. Page watched them with an expression of mild distaste as they peeled off one filthy layer after another and popped the items into polythene bags, which Detective Constable Stevens carefully labelled.

Eventually, Shem's begrimed and skinny body lay before their gaze.

'Looks much the same as anyone else now, doesn't he?' Machin remarked. 'Apart from the bit of extra dirt. No wonder the poor old boy needed all those clothes, he's hardly got any flesh on him.'

'No wonder the boy's dog sniffed him out. He's as fruity as a ripe old bit of cheese,' Detective Constable Stevens said, exhaling vigorously through his nostrils.

Page said nothing, but went across to the table on which Shem's belongings had been placed. Before, however, he had time to start examining them, the outside door opened and Dr Leary came in carrying a canvas bag.

Looking about him as he walked briskly over to one of the tables he said, 'Place is a disgrace. An absolute disgrace! Millions spent on building schools which look like some eskimo's dream of paradise and they can't find a few thousand to put up a proper mortuary. Serve them right if an epidemic started. That'd shake them and send them dipping into their pockets.'

As he talked, he unpacked his instruments and put on the green nylon gown he always wore. Finally he pulled on a pair of rubber gloves.

'Well, let's to work.' He glanced at Detective Constable Stevens. 'This your first murder case as a scene of crime officer?' Stevens nodded. 'Come and stand on the other side of the body, then, and get ready to catch the bits.'

For the next hour and a half, Dr Leary worked away industriously, maintaining a running commentary all the while, watched by the three officers.

Page spoke when spoken to, but otherwise remained silent. His predominant thought was that he was becoming too old for this sort of thing. It required a resilience, he now felt himself lacking, to be up all night directing enquiries without any certainty that one was using the time profitably. He thought of all the hours, running into days, which he had spent standing in mortuaries waiting for the pathologist's verdict; of all the weeks, running into months and years, which had been occupied investigating crimes with varying degrees of success. One thing he knew for sure was that most crimes were solved, if at all, by a combination of slogging work and luck. Often it was an element of pure luck which put one eventually on to the right track. He brought his mind back to Shem as he idly watched the doctor peel off the back of his scalp. He hoped that luck would come to the rescue, and quickly at that. At the moment, the prospect of reading history and of minding bees seemed depressingly remote.

'He must have received quite a blow,' Dr Leary observed. 'This isn't just a linear fracture of the skull, it's comminuted. Looks like somebody cracked him one with a hammer.'

'Could it have been a stone or something of that sort?' Page asked.

'Could have been, though it has more the appearance of a hammer blow. You can almost see where the head of the hammer fits.'

Page peered where the pathologist pointed and nodded.

'Is his skull normal thickness?'

'Near enough.'

'And there are no other signs of injury to the body?'

'None. A few old scars, but nothing associated with death. A bit of hardening of the arteries, but probably a good deal less than yours will show at his age.'

Or yours at a rather earlier age, Page thought to himself.

'How old is he, by the way?'

'No idea. We don't even know his proper name yet. How old would you guess?'

'Late sixties. Early seventies at the most. Though they live good healthy lives in one sense, these old tramps don't take much care of themselves. And the body does need care, though, perhaps, not as much as we're liable to smother it with these days.' He turned away and said casually, 'One of your lads can sew him up.'

Detective Constable Stevens promptly went across to the table where the exhibits had all been assembled and appeared to become very busy, leaving Sergeant Machin to give Page an appealing look.

'Nobody's going to see your handiwork, so you needn't go all modest,' Page remarked heartlessly.

'I daresay not, but I don't reckon it part of my job to tidy up after pathologists,' Machin protested.

'It's one of his little jokes. He likes to observe the re-action.'

'Well, he's welcome to mine. It's one of revolt.'

'Get on with it and don't make such a fuss. Imagine it's a pretty girl.'

'If your imagination's that good, sir, why don't you do it!'

'Because it's your turn,' Page replied with a wisp of a smile, 'and Detective Superintendents are always gentlemen in such matters.'

Ten minutes later the disagreeable task was complete and Dr Leary, who had been making notes over at one of the tables, came across.

'Very good, Sergeant,' he said. 'Very neat indeed! I wouldn't mind having you darn my socks on that showing.'

Sergeant Machin grinned. In a curious way it satisfied him to think he'd been able to do something for Shem, even if it'd only been to cobble him up after death. And it was true that he had overcome his revulsion to make as good a job of it as he could.

Dr Leary glanced at his watch.

'I'm going to get two or three hours kip,' he announced, 'and I'll meet you out at the scene about eight o'clock. Does that suit you, Superintendent?'

'Yes, that'll be fine, Doctor,' Page replied stoutly, clenching his jaw against a yawn. 'Any other conclusions you've reached? How long do you think he'd been dead?'

'I'll have a better idea when I've examined the scene and studied a temperature chart, but I'd say between twenty and thirty hours.'

There was a silence while each stood immobile in his own thoughts. Then Page spoke:

'Would a boy of twelve have been able to inflict the injuries?'

'A normal, healthy boy? Armed with a hammer? Quite easily!'

'I thought that would be your answer.'

'If you're thinking along the line that some lad may have been defending himself against a sexual assault, I'd point out that the blow was almost certainly struck from behind.'

'I wasn't thinking along any particular line,' Page replied slowly.

'It looks like a case of find your motive, find your criminal.'

'I know.'

The trouble was that vagrants such as Shem rarely had any known associates and that meant an absence of suggested motives.

Since he'd been in the mortuary, Page had mentally listed all the possible motives he could conjure up in his weary mind. They ran something like this:

1. Peeping Tom bonked by angry victim – possible.
2. Sexual pass resisted by victim – improbable.
3. Robbery – could be, investigate.
4. Witnessed something and killed by frightened victim – possible, but what?
5. Killed by madman – possible, check on psychopaths in Long Gaisford. Anyone in village with record of violence?

As he now reviewed the list in his mind's eye, it seemed to him that No. 5 presented the most fruitful line of enquiry. It was also a fairly easy one, assuming that the madman was a local person.

He walked across to the table on which Shem's belongings had been laid out. There was a small pile of objects grouped together as in one of those party games in which you are given five seconds to memorise as many of the items as you can. The largest was a flat and much dented tobacco tin in which Shem hoarded the cigarette ends his eyes were ever seeking. There was a crumpled and partially torn ten-shilling note, a two-shilling piece and four pennies. These appeared to comprise his total wealth. On the face of it, robbery was ruled out, not that it had ever seemed a likely motive. There was a matchbox containing two buttons, five spent matches and a single unused one. A small piece of blunt pencil lay beside the matchbox and next to that was another, though smaller, tobacco tin. Page removed the lid and gingerly stirred the contents with the tip of his finger. Gingerly, since he could see a couple of needles among an untidy ball of tangled thread.

Something white beneath the thread caught his eye and he tipped the contents out. Picking the object up, he murmured softly, 'Now, that's interesting!' He walked across to where Sergeant Machin was helping Dectective Constable Stevens lable the exhibits. 'Know what this is?' he asked, holding it out on the palm of his hand.

'A tooth, sir,' Machin replied.

'Yes, but whose?'

'Looks like an animal's.'

'I know, but what animal's?'

'No idea, sir. What animal is it?'

'I don't know either. But I'm going to find out. Doesn't it remind...'

'Of course,' Machin broke in eagerly, 'it's like the one Kenny Bostock was fiddling with all the time we were talking to him.'

'Exactly. Interesting, isn't it!'

For the first time that evening, there was a quietly optimistic note in Page's voice.

VIII

When his alarm went off at seven o'clock Page knew the worst. He was definitely too old for this sort of life. Three hours fitful sleep in his clothes in a chair left him stiff, sore-eyed and feeling as if he existed in a terrible grey limbo.

He shuffled into the kitchen and recoiled at the sight of his half-cooked steak. A couple of minutes later, with a mug of black coffee in his hand he stagged into the bathroom. He drank the coffee while he shaved and felt a degree more human when he had finished, not that that was much of an improvement.

He had known he'd feel like this. It would have been better not to have gone to sleep or, at least, to have undressed and got into bed. Sleeping in his clothes always made him feel tacky in both mind and body.

Just before half past seven, Sergeant Machin called for him, looking as rested as a baby, and they drove out to Long Gaisford in an overpowering silence.

When they reached the end of the track leading to the quarries, Page spoke for the first time.

'Drop me here. It'll do me good to walk. You go on into the village and start organising house-to-house visits. You know the sort of things we want to find out. Last time they saw Shem; who he was with; anything which might shed light on his death.'

'Right, sir. Then I'll see you later.'

Page got out and stumped off along the track, his eyes fixed on the ground. Terrible as he felt, he still had a job to do and who knew but some clue might not suddenly be yielded up.

He had neared the end when a surging whine from behind heralded the approach of Dr Leary's car. He stepped to the side of the track and the car pulled up beside him.

'Found anything useful?' the pathologist called out of the window.

'No. Nor likely to, this track has been like a motorway since last night.'

'And several days fine weather won't have helped either.'

'No, it couldn't be worse for detecting tyre marks or footprints,' Page agreed.

Dr Leary made a helpless grimace and drove on towards the track's end. Page reached there just as he was getting out of the car and together they set off for where Shem's body had been found.

Detective Constable Stevens and another young officer were already there and on Dr Leary's instructions removed the huge polythene sheet which had been pegged down over the site.

Page watched while the pathologist stooped to study the ground with an expression of intense concentration.

It was a cold, grey morning which gave the whole area a desolate appearance. From time to time, Dr Leary pointed at the ground and Detective Constable Stevens scooped up a sample of earth or vegetation.

But it was the area where Shem's head had lain that he examined most closely, even pulling out a large magnifying glass to assist his scrutiny.

When he straightened up, he said, 'I'm pretty sure he was killed elsewhere and that his body was dumped here later. That's a preliminary view subject to lab confirmation when they've examined all the samples. But if he'd been murdered here, there'd have been blood on the ground and so far as my eye tells me there isn't any.'

'That would mean he was probably brought here after all bleeding had ceased?'

'Yes.'

'Possibly several hours after death?'

'Quite possibly.'

Page stared thoughtfully at a tussock of coarse grass which stood apart from others on the slope just above Shem's final resting place. He could see a small black beetle laboriously ascending one of the stalks. If only it realised what a wasted journey it was having. Suddenly it fell, probably to start its climb all over again. The whole episode reminded him of a criminal investigation. Laborious moves which all too often were matched only by their futility.

He reclaimed his thoughts from the tangents along which they had flowed. If Shem had been murdered in some other place and his body had been brought to the quarry area later, it could only mean one thing: that the murderer must have had a very good reason for not wanting the actual scene of the murder discovered. What could that reason be? Surely only that the scene and the murderer were so associated that the discovery of the one must lead to the revelation of the other. So, find the scene and know the murderer.

He even began to feel warmer as his reasoning gathered pace. It was like a game of patience in which the cards all come right. He could take it yet a stage further.

Shem was known to have been in the vicinity for the past few days, so the actual scene of his murder must be relatively near by. There was no question of his having been killed in a completely different part of the country and then, almost irresponsibly, dumped on Page's manor. That possibility could be excluded and the search was correspondingly narrowed.

The answers to all the questions should be found here in the village.

It was with a lighter step that he accompanied Dr Leary back to the car and accepted a lift. He was even able to enjoy the sensation of being a pea adrift in a pneumatic pod as they pitched and tossed their way back to the road. Thereafter the sensation became that associated with the take-off of a jet plane as they completed the journey into the village.

Mr Shelley had just begun his breakfast when Sergeant Machin knocked on his front door.

He peered round the edge of the window to see who his visitor was before going to the door. He saw a young man of medium build, with clean-cut features and thick fair hair which had a parting as straight as a roman road.

Mr Shelley liked his looks. He was also reasonably sure that he was a police officer. For either reason alone, he would have been prepared to admit his visitor.

'Good morning,' he said, with what was almost an overwhelming smile, as he opened the door.

'Good morning, sir. I am Detective Sergeant Machin, I wonder . . .'

'Do come in, Sergeant. I was just about to have my breakfast. Won't you join me in a cup of tea?'

'Thank you, sir. Perhaps you wouldn't mind answering a

few questions while you eat.'

'Not at all. I shall be delighted to help in any way I can. After all, it's every citizen's duty, isn't it, to assist the police?' He cocked his head on one side and smiled as though in anticipation of an accolade for such a public-spirited attitude.

'That's a fairly unfashionable point of view these days,' Machin remarked.

'Not among my generation, I hope.'

They had entered the small front parlour where the table was set for breakfast. A boiled egg in a silver cup, two pieces of brown toast, a pot of Cooper's Oxford marmalade and a large comfortable-looking tea-pot rested on the blue and white check cloth.

'I'll just fetch another cup and I expect we may need a drop more milk.' He was half out of the door when he turned back. 'And do you take sugar? I don't, but there's some in the kitchen.'

'Please.'

'I shan't be a moment. Sit down and make yourself comfortable.'

Sergeant Machin sat down on the arm of the chair and waited. There was a still-folded *Times* on the table and he glanced at the main headlines. It concerned the bank rate which could hardly have been of less interest to him. Clearly, however, Mr Shelley made something of a performance of having breakfast. Machin was making him his first port of call as an officer with local knowledge had described him as running the best one-man intelligence service in Long Gaisford.

'"Everyone's business is my business" is his motto,' the officer had observed.

At this moment, Mr Shelley returned to the room, bearing a tray. 'I thought I'd being a little more hot water, too,' he remarked, with his already familiar smile. 'Now, let me just pour you out a cup and I'll be ready to answer your questions. I assume you've come in connection with the murder?'

'That's so, sir.'

'Yes; a sad affair! Poor old Joshua! After all, homeless old tramps count for as much in the eyes of the Almighty as presidents and prime ministers . . .'

'Poor old who?' Machin broke in.

'Joshua. Oh, of course, you've probably heard him referred to as Shem, but his baptised name was Joshua.'

'Joshua what?'

'Joshua Clapp, with two p's. Not a very pretty name, I'm afraid, though that wasn't his fault.'

'How do you come to know his name, sir?'

'A couple of years ago, I think it was, I helped him with a form in connection with a claim he wanted to make. He'd been slightly injured by a motor-cyclist and thought he could get some money out of someone, but I never heard if he ever did.'

'You knew him quite well, then?'

'I don't think I could go quite as far as that. I doubt whether anyone knew him "quite well", but he knew me as one of the people ready to offer him a helping hand if asked. Not that I ever gave him money, because I don't believe in begging; but my advice was always at his disposal.'

Sergeant Machin nodded gravely. He couldn't imagine that Shem had ever had much use for Mr Shelley's advice.

'Once I tried to get him to accompany me to church,' Mr Shelley went on with a reflective smile, 'but I'm afraid I wasn't successful. However, I always made a point of remembering him in my prayers when he was in this area.'

This struck Machin as being curiously selective, and he presumed that Mr Shelley felt Shem became someone else's spiritual responsibility once he'd left the district.

'Had you seen him around in the past few days?'

'No. I'd heard he was back, but I'd not seen him myself. I'd sent him a message via a lad called Kenny Bostock that, if he wanted any help, he should come and see me. But he didn't do so.'

Machin wasn't surprised having regard to the restricted nature of the help on offer.

'I take it, then, you know Kenny Bostock?' he said.

Mr Shelley slowly spread a finger of unbuttered toast with marmalade before answering.

'I think I can claim to know Kenny Bostock quite well,' he said with a small indulgent smile. 'He frequently calls here on errands and I've always tried to make friends with all the boys in the village. As a retired schoolmaster, I understand their problems and sometimes I've been able to help them in the difficult business of growing up.'

'What sort of a boy is Kenny?'

Mr Shelley popped the last morsel of toast into his mouth and wiped his fingers with fastidious care on his napkin, while Sergeant Machin blew on his tea.

'You obviously ask that question advisedly, Sergeant, so it behoves me to be circumspect in my answer.' He paused, gave a final chew and leant back in his chair. 'In many ways Kenny Bostock is a typical twelve-year-old; in others he isn't,' he said with judicial gravity. 'For example, although he enjoys most of the pursuits of the average lad of his age, he has about him an air of detachment. He's friendly and polite – well, most times he is – and yet I've always felt that he's probably given to fantasy, to retreating into a small world of his own creation. Do I make myself plain?'

Sergeant Machin gave a doubtful nod. He thought he knew what Mr Shelley meant, but it didn't seem to matter too much either way.

'I've known him for about six years,' Mr Shelley went on, 'and when I first came to live here, he was never out of the company of his cousin Brian. Then Brian left the village around three years ago and it seemed that a light went out of Kenny's life, if you will excuse the cliché.' He threw Machin a little conspiratorial smile, which evoked no response, since Machin's mind was occupied in wondering whether to find out who Brian was, apart from being

Kenny's cousin, and what had happened to him. The trouble was that Mr Shelley was one of those people who liked to tell a story in his own way, which was an expansive way, and once embarked upon it there was little his audience could do to affect its course. However, as Sergeant Machin reflected ruefully, it was a police officer's lot to listen in the hope of learning something useful, even though he was more often disappointed than not.

'Curiously enough,' Mr Shelley continued taking the matter out of Machin's hands, 'I was only thinking about Brian Farmer just before you arrived. His parents left the village and moved to London about a year ago. Mrs Farmer was Mrs Bostock's sister, though they were never particularly close, I understand. But as far as I know, Brian never returned here after he left. I did hear that he had fallen into bad company and got into trouble with the police and that he finally ended up in Borstal.' He paused and gave Machin another of his oleaginous smiles. 'You're probably wondering why I am telling you all this?'

'Please go on,' Machin said cautiously. There was something mildly hypnotic about Mr Shelley's flow of words and the bright, piercing gaze which accompanied them. But perhaps this lulled feeling was due more to the warm cosiness of the room and the very welcome cup of sweet tea which he had just drunk.

'Let me give you another cup of tea, Sergeant,' Mr Shelley said, taking the cup from Machin's hand and contriving as he did so to make their fingers touch lightly. At that moment, however, there was a loud knock on the door and Mr Shelley frowned. He rose and went across to the window to peer out.

'It's Miss Jackson,' he said crossly, as though this explained everything. 'What can the silly woman want?'

He went out into the hall and Machin heard him open the front door. There followed a brief murmur of voices, before Mr Shelley said impatiently, 'I'm engaged at the moment, so I'm afraid I can't ask you in or stop talking on the doorstep. Come back later.'

The door was firmly shut and Mr Shelley reappeared, shaking his head as one sorely tried.

'Now, where was I?' he asked, resuming his seat. 'Yes, I remember; I was about to tell you something about Kenny Bostock and Brian Farmer. But first let me give you that cup of tea. And I'm ready for another one myself.' It seemed to Machin that the pouring of two cups of tea was invested with as much ceremony as if they were in Japan. However, eventually, the simple task was completed. 'You'll probably think that this sounds rather far-fetched and that my imagination has got the better of me,' he now went on, giving Machin a tentative smile, 'but you must remember that I've been a schoolmaster all my life and that I've had some experience in observing boys' thoughts and reactions. Anyway, what I'm telling you is this. The day before yesterday, Kenny Bostock came round in the evening on an errand. Mr Gladwell in the grocers had promised to send me a packet of biscuits. The fact that they weren't the ones I wanted has nothing to do with the story,' he added with a small chuckle. 'Kenny arrived here with my biscuits about six o'clock. Usually, he's not averse to stopping and having a little talk with me – I think it encourages boys of his age to know that one is interested in their activities – but that evening he could scarcely wait to get away. He said he had promised to hurry home and help his mother with something, though I subsequently learnt that this wasn't so.'

'How did you learn that?' Machin asked, showing a quickening interest.

'I happened to see Mrs Bostock pass here about half an hour later and I went and called to her from the front door. Without disclosing my motive to her, I ascertained that Kenny had not gone home and, moreover, that she had not been expecting him back at that time.' He threw Machin a triumphant look. 'I might have made quite a good detective myself, don't you think?'

Machin gave a perfunctory smile.

'Go on. I'm afraid I interrupted you.'

'Well, it wasn't just that he was in a great hurry to get away, but he gave the impression of being full of pent-up excitement. So much so, that I didn't really believe him when he told me that his mother wanted him back home. It was obviously something much more than that.' He paused and gave Machin a placating look. 'Now this is where you'll think my imagination has run away with me. Don't ask me to explain what I'm about to tell you, since there is no explanation. It's pure intuition. I know women are supposed to have a monopoly of intuition, but it's not so. I've always regarded myself as having a share of that most useful commodity. Certainly useful to a schoolmaster! After he'd gone, I thought to myself, he's as excited as if he'd heard his cousin Brian was back. Sounds ridiculous, I know, but that was exactly what went through my mind at the time. And then last night when I heard of the murder and I knew Kenny had seen Shem and I thought of Brian who'd been in trouble with the police and I recalled Kenny's ill-suppressed excitement when he brought round my biscuits, well . . . it did strike me that they might all be pieces of the same puzzle.'

Mr Shelley paused slightly out of breath with his own sense of excitement generated by these revelations. He took a sip of tea.

'Anyway, I deemed it my duty to tell you what had passed through my mind. The more so when I learnt that you interviewed Kenny last night. Clearly, you must regard him as an important witness and, therefore, equally clearly it seemed to me that I should give you my own thoughts. What you make of them is, of course, entirely a matter for yourselves. And now, Sergeant, what about one more cup of tea?'

Machin shook his head. 'No thank you, sir. I must be on my way. You've been most helpful.'

'But oughtn't I to sign a written statement of all I've told you?'

'We can do that later, sir.'

The corners of Mr Shelley's mouth turned down in obvious disappointment.

'I thought it was usual to do it now, while the witness' recollection is fresh.'

'I'm sure your recollection will remain fresh for a bit longer. And quite frankly, sir, although what you've told me is most valuable, very little of it has any strict evidential value.'

'Won't that be for lawyers to say?'

'Certainly, and when I come to write down your statement we'll put in everything you've told me.'

'You'll be taking down my statement yourself, then?' Mr Shelley said, brightening.

'Yes, I'll be back to see you. Probably later today.'

Sergeant Machin made good his escape with a combined feeling of relief and burgeoning hope.

At least, there were now some leads to be followed up – and that always afforded grounds for hope.

IX

Machin made for the temporary headquarters, which had been set up in the former police station, to find Page there giving instructions to a number of detectives who'd recently arrived on assignment to the investigation from other divisions.

Police officers, like Boy Scouts, excel at improvisation and although the station had been disused for over a year and had been denuded of its furnishings, it was already, after only one hour, a scene of considerable activity, with a couple of tables in what had been the local constable's office, some chairs and a tray of assorted cups without saucers which somebody had found for coffee. In fact, an elderly detective sergeant who was noted for his insistence on the simple comforts came into the room carrying a huge steaming kettle at the moment of Machin's arrival.

As soon as Page saw Machin, he raised one quizzical eyebrow in his direction and Machin stepped across to tell him of his visit to Mr Shelley.

When he had finished, Page said, 'You'd better go and see the boy again. I'll join you as soon as I can, but the Assistant Chief is on his way over from headquarters and I'd better wait here for him.'

'O.K., sir, I'll see you later.'

Machin arrived outside the Bostock cottage at exactly the same moment as a girl who had come up from the other direction. She gave him a friendly smile.

'Are you police by any chance?' she asked.

'Yes. I'm Detective Sergeant Machin from Arlebury.'

'I thought you must be. Police, that is. I'm Susan Bostock, also from Arlebury.'

'Would you be a sister of Kenny Bostock?'

She nodded. 'Yes. Mum phoned me last night to say you'd called to see Kenny and . . . well, I told her I'd come over on the first bus this morning as she sounded a bit worried.'

'Did she tell you why she was worried?'

The girl hesitated. 'Is it all right to talk to you?'

Machin grinned ruefully. 'I ought to say "yes", and, in fact, I do say "yes", though I wouldn't want you to feel later that I'd tried to trap you into incriminating your brother in any way.'

'Incriminating him!' she exclaimed. 'Surely no one's suggesting that he had anything to do with Shem's death?'

'I'm certainly not suggesting it, but your brother does appear to have something on his mind and to be unwilling to tell us what it is.' He gave her a small hopeful smile. 'Perhaps you'll be able to persuade him to talk?'

She appeared thoughtful for a few seconds. Then turning

abruptly, she said, 'Shall we go inside?'

As she opened the front door, her brother's voice called out from the kitchen, 'Is that you, Susan?'

'Yes. Is Mum in?'

'No, she's . . .' At this point Kenny appeared and stopped in mid-sentence as he caught sight of Machin. 'She's just gone shopping, she'll be back soon.' Immediately, he went back into the kitchen, followed by his sister and Machin.

'Aren't you going to school today?' Susan asked.

Kenny, who had sat down at the table and affected to be poring over a magazine, shook his head. 'I've got a sore throat.'

'You know Sergeant Machin from last night, don't you?'

'Yes.'

'I've come to ask you some more questions, Kenny,' Machin said.

The boy looked up slowly and Machin couldn't help noticing the lustreless appearance of his eyes, also the dark smudges beneath them. At his age, a bad night's sleep left its immediate marks.

His sister gazed at him with a worried expression.

'I haven't got anything to say,' Kenny replied stolidly.

'I'd still like to ask you the questions, but I'll wait till your mother gets back.'

It was five minutes before Mrs Bostock returned. Five minutes during which Kenny stared mindlessly at the rapidly turned pages of his magazine and Susan and Mackin nibbled conversationally at everything save what was occupying each of their minds.

'I wish my husband was here,' Mrs Bostock said worriedly when Machin explained the reason for his visit.

'Have you been able to get in touch with him?' he asked sympathetically.

'I've phoned his firm and they're going to get a message to him.' She stared at her son with an uncomprehending expression as though he had just sprouted a third ear or announced his intention of entering a monastery. 'How are you feeling now?' she enquired in a tone which seemed to imply that her bewilderment at events couldn't be eased, whatever the answer.

'My throat hurts.'

'Badly?'

'It just hurts.'

'I don't know whether he's really up to answering questions,' she said doubtfully. 'You couldn't leave it till later?'

'It's very important that I should talk to him now,' Machin said. 'I'll try and ask him questions which can be answered "yes" or "no", so as to save his throat. Perhaps, he'll even be able to answer some of them by nodding or shaking his head.'

Mrs Bostock shrugged helplessly. 'I suppose if it's that important, you must.'

'I'm sure Sergeant Machin won't deliberately upset him,' Susan broke in.

'No, I most certainly won't. All I'm after is information and I believe that, despite what he says, Kenny *can* help us a bit further.' He sat down at the table and, resting his arms along the edge, leant forward so that he faced Kenny like a chess opponent. 'Do you remember calling at Mr Shelley's house the evening before last, Kenny?'

'Yes.'

'You took him a packet of biscuits from Mr Gladwell's?'

'S'right.' His tone was wary.

'Mr Shelley says you appeared to be in a great hurry to get away, were you?'

'Not more than usual.'

'You mean you're always in a hurry to get away from Mr Shelley?'

'He gives me the creeps.'

Machin nodded. This was something he could well understand.

'Did you tell him you had to hurry back home to help your mother with something or other?'

'Don't remember.'

'Did you in fact come straight home?'

'No.'

'You just said that as an excuse to get away from Mr Shelley?'

'Yes. I didn't want to go in.'

'Where did you, in fact, go when you left his place?'

'Don't remember.'

'Try and remember, Kenny, it could be important.'

'I just went and played.'

'But where?'

'Can't remember.'

'Near the quarries?'

Kenny shook his head strenuously.

'Where, then?'

Kenny made no reply and Machin tried again.

'If you can remember that it wasn't near the quarries, surely you can remember where it was you did go and play?'

Machin's tone held no note of hostility or impatience, even so he could see Kenny closing up before him like a sea anemone. With every question, his expression became more of a blank mask – a mask whose eyes alone reflected any emotion, and that only animal suspicion.

'Did you meet anyone or were you alone?'

'Alone.'

'You didn't see anyone even?'

'No.'

'Sure you didn't see Shem that evening?'

The boy looked up quickly and, as quickly, lowered his glance.

'Didn't see anyone,' he muttered.

Machin gazed at him thoughtfully for a few seconds while his mother and sister stood together anxiously observing the tableau. So far all he was proving to himself was what he already knew, namely that Kenny was holding something back. It seemed that the moment had come for shock tactics, even if only a shot in the dark.

'When did you last see your cousin Brian Farmer?' he asked, leaning forward to add emphasis to his question.

Kenny's head went back as though it had received an under-cut and the colour drained from his face so that the dark patches beneath his eyes stood out as angry bruises. His mouth opened, but no words came and it closed again. He stared at Machin stupidly like a half pole-axed calf.

'You've seen him recently, Kenny, haven't you? Don't deny it because the answer's written all over your face.'

For several seconds, Kenny continued to stare at his interrogator as though hypnotised. Then slowly some colour returned to his cheeks and he took a very deep breath, expelling it like somebody on a bicycle free-wheeling down a long incline, which he'd never expected to reach. When he did reach the bottom of the incline he said:

'Course I haven't seen him. Where'd I have seen him?'

'In this area recently.'

'How could I have! He doesn't live here any more.'

'I know, but you have seen him, haven't you, Kenny?'

'No.' It came out as flat and definite as the slamming of a heavy door.

Machin looked at Mrs Bostock, and then at Susan. It was Mrs Bostock who eventually spoke.

'As far as I know, Brian hasn't been back since he left three years ago. His parents don't even live here any more.'

'Do you happen to know their address?'

'It's somewhere in London. They moved there last year.'

'But the actual address?'

Mrs Bostock shook her head vaguely.

'It was Shepherd's Bush way. We were never that close and I didn't bother about addresses.'

Machin glanced at Susan, who shook her head. 'I've no idea, I'm afraid,' she said. 'Like Mum says, we weren't that close and after they left the village, that was that. I know my uncle was going to a job at the television studios – he's a carpenter – and they found a place to live near there. You might be able to trace him through the studios.'

Machin nodded. At least, that was better than nothing. He turned back to Kenny.

'Now listen to me, Kenny, it's a very serious matter if you don't tell the police all you know, and I'm more than ever certain that you're holding back information.'

But Kenny met the plea with a heavily shuttered expression.

'You liked Shem, didn't you?' Machin enquired. The boy nodded hesitantly. 'You don't want the person who murdered him to go free, do you?' But once more the boy's face froze.

Machin turned again to Mrs Bostock. 'Supposing Brian Farmer has been somewhere in the district just recently, have you any idea who might have seen him?'

'No, I can't think of anyone. If he'd been in the village I'd have been sure to have heard.' She paused, then said with a faint note of defiance, 'I don't believe he has been here.'

Machin made a non-committal face. Looking at Susan, he said, 'Can *you* suggest anyone who might have seen him if he has been in the area?'

'I don't know if he ever kept in touch with any of the boys at the factory where he worked for a short time. I don't expect he did, he was only there a few months.'

'What factory was that?'

'Keenan's Electrics over at Flatchet.'

'When did he work there?'

'Immediately before he packed up and went off to London. It wasn't much of a job. He used to work in the stores, but he wasn't going to stay because he didn't like the cycle ride to and fro in the winter.'

Flatchet was a small town about seven miles from Long Gaisford and Keenan's Electrics was one of those new factory developments which have sprung up like sore thumbs in the unlikeliest parts of rural England over the past two decades.

Machin gave Kenny a last thoughtful look before getting

up and moving towards the door. He had failed to find the key which unlocked the boy's heart and, with it, his tongue – and so all he could do was leave him sitting there mute and unhappy – and uncrackably obstinate.

Susan accompanied him to the front door.

'I think you're right,' she said in a soft tone, when they were out of earshot of the kitchen, 'I believe he has seen Brian recently. His expression gave him away.'

Machin looked at her hopefully. 'Can you work on him?'

She grinned. 'I can try, but you've seen what sort of mood he's in. However, he does occasionally open up to me, which is more than he does to Mum or Dad.'

'I'd certainly be very grateful if you would try. Apart from anything else, if we're right, he's carrying an intolerable burden for a lad of his age. Another couple of days of bottling up whatever it is inside him and he'll be ready for a psychiatrist's couch.'

'I know. He looks terrible. I'll see what I can do, but I don't promise any results.' She gave him the same shy smile he'd been attracted by when they'd met at the gate. 'Do you have any theories, or oughtn't I to ask?'

'Theories?'

'About the murder.'

'I think that Brian Farmer has been in the area and that your brother believes he is somehow connected with Shem's death. But that's the helluva long way from solving the crime. In fact, it poses more questions than it answers.'

'I suppose you'll try and find Brian?'

'That's for sure, if only to eliminate him from the enquiry. But it's going to help a lot if you can get Kenny to talk. Possibly save us a great deal of time.'

Machin turned at the sound of the front gate opening and saw Page.

'I was just coming back to headquarters, sir.'

'Any luck?'

'Yes and no, but more no than yes.'

'Is Kenny inside?'

'Yes. By the way, sir, this is Susan Bostock, his sister. This is Detective Superintendent Page.'

Page held out his hand and Susan, obviously surprised, took it. She didn't appear to expect detectives of that rank to waste time on hand-shakes.

'Come back in a moment,' Page said, entering the cottage.

Kenny was still sitting at the kitchen table, but Mrs Bostock was over at the sink.

'Have you still got that thing you were playing with when we talked to you last night, Kenny?' The boy looked uncomprehending and Page said, 'Turn out your pockets.'

Kenny did so. 'Yes, that's the thing I meant, that tooth.' Page now fished inside his own pocket and brought out the similar one which had been found among Shem's belongings. He now moved closer to the table and picked up the tooth which Kenny had produced. Holding one in his right hand and the other in his left, he said, 'Can anyone tell me what this is?' He raised his left hand as he spoke.

'I can't see properly,' Mrs Bostock complained, trained by countless hours of watching TV panel games.

'It's a badger tooth,' Page observed. 'And this' – he raised his right hand for all to see – 'is also a badger tooth.' He looked around his small audience with an expression of mild triumph. 'And I think there's a rather curious coincidence connected with these two teeth, which calls for an explanation. So what about it, Kenny?'

X

If Page had wanted to create an atmosphere of drama, he couldn't have succeeded better. But, in fact, it had not been his intention to do so. He had been genuinely intrigued by the identification of the two badgers' teeth (it had been made by the elderly tea-brewing constable whose knowledge of country lore had always outstripped his acquaintanceship with police rules and regulations) and felt an immediate explanation was called for. He hadn't wished to give the impression of a conjurer performing his most difficult trick, though that was the effect on his audience. As soon as he finished speaking, they all automatically switched their attention to Kenny. And Kenny reacted in precisely the same way as the bashful boy whom the conjurer tries to cajole into coming up on to the stage. He hunched his shoulders and glowered.

There was half a minute's silence. Then, looking almost crestfallen, Page said, 'Who gave you that badger's tooth, Kenny? Surely you can tell us that?'

There was a further silence and then Susan spoke. 'He's had it ages, hasn't he, Mum?' She sounded anxious and looked from her mother to Kenny and on to Machin as her words hung on the air.

'So it's not something Shem can have given him the last few days?' Page said quickly.

Susan looked more uncomfortable than a moment earlier. 'Let him tell you. It's his thing. I just thought . . .' She gave a helpless shrug.

'You think it's something he's had a long time?' Page said for her.

She nodded unhappily. 'But I could be wrong.'

'How long have you had it, Kenny?'

'Ages,' he said in a gruffly off-hand tone.

'Where'd you get it from?'

'Don't remember.'

'Did Shem give it to you?'

'Don't remem . . .' His expression changed abruptly. 'Yes . . . yes, he gave it to me.'

'When?'

'Ages ago.'

'How many did he give you?'

'Just one.'

Machin noticed that Susan frowned at this answer as though doubting its truth. He would tax her with it later.

'Is that the truth?'

'Yes.' He looked across at his mother. 'My throat's hurting, Mum.'

'I don't think you should ask him any more questions,' Mrs Bostock said. 'He's not well today.'

'O.K., Mrs Bostock, we'll leave now but we shall almost certainly want to see Kenny again.'

As they walked the few hundred yards back to their temporary headquarters, Page said with a heavy sigh, 'How do you make a twelve-year-old boy talk? Or, more to the point, how do you make him tell the truth?'

Machin made a grab at an insect which was patrolling in the area of his head. 'Persuade him that the loyalty which is inducing his silence is misplaced.'

'And how do you do that?'

'I don't know.'

'A fine lot of help that is, then!'

'We've got to find Brian Farmer, sir! I don't know whether he murdered Shem or not, but I'm absolutely certain that he's the key to Kenny's silence.'

'Well, we'd better get through to the Met and see if they can trace him for us. If the family still live in the Shepherd's Bush area, it shouldn't be too difficult to locate them, particularly as Master Brian has form.'

It was about an hour later, after Machin had been out and had returned again to the headquarters which had been set up in the old police station, that he was told someone was asking for him. He went out into the passage to find Susan Bostock standing there.

She gave him a quick, nervous smile. 'I don't know whether I'm doing the right thing or not, but I'm so worried I decided that I must come and talk to you.'

'Fine, let's try and find a couple of chairs and then you tell me what's worrying you. There's a small room at the back where we can talk alone. It smells a bit like a disused tallow store, but at least it's quiet.' He led the way down the narrow passage – 'Mind a couple of steps here' – and flung open a door at the end. 'Hang on a tick while I get another chair, there's only one.'

When he returned, Susan was standing at the begrimed window, gazing out on the now overgrown patch which had been the pride of the last incumbent of the station. He closed the door behind him.

'If we're lucky, somebody may bring us a couple of cups of tea in a minute,' he said, giving her a friendly smile.

For a few seconds, Susan continued standing by the window. Then she came and sat down and said a trifle breathlessly, 'I still don't know whether I'm doing the right thing. I feel somehow disloyal and yet . . .'

'It's about Kenny, is it?'

'Yes. I'm so worried about him. I've never seen him like this before. Something's on his mind and yet he won't say a word. Obviously he didn't have anything to do with Shem's death, but at the same time he knows something . . .'

'That's what I think, too. And I'm sure that Brian Farmer also comes into the picture somewhere.'

'Yes, Brian . . . that's what I've really come to tell you. That badger tooth Kenny has, he has had it for ages as I said.'

'And as he admitted.'

'Yes, he did admit it after a fashion, didn't he, though I couldn't help feeling it was only because I blurted out what I did.' She looked up and met Machin's gaze. 'But the thing is, I'm quite certain it wasn't Shem who gave him the badger tooth. In fact, I know quite well it wasn't. It was Brian.'

Machin frowned as his mind absorbed the implications of this.

'Then it looks as if it was Kenny who gave Shem the tooth.'

'But why?'

'Not so much why did he give it to him? But why has he felt obliged to lie about it? To lie doubly about it!'

XI

All too often a murder enquiry resembles a great jamboree. For a few days there is an impression of immense activity with constant comings and goings, then, as quickly as they have gathered, the hordes depart and those who are left settle down to the laborious business of clearing up.

So it was at Long Gaisford. After the doctors, the photographers and all the other specialists, not to mention the senior visitors from constabulary headquarters who descended like inspecting generals, had departed, Page and Machin and a small team of detectives found themselves left to get on with solving the mystery of Shem's murder. From time to time they would still be nudged from on high, as with diminishing frequency the newspapers would remind their readers that no arrest had yet been made. But no one is particularly interested in the death of an unknown old tramp, even where the circumstances are somewhat mysterious, and so even the initial publicity had been fairly meagre.

Any violent death usually rates a headline in the evening papers, but thereafter newspaper interest in Shem dropped rapidly away.

It was four days later that Sergeant Machin ran into Susan in Arlebury. The temporary headquarters set up in the village had been disbanded, having served their purpose and the enquiry was now being run from Arlebury itself.

In the course of those four days, every single person in the village had been interviewed, though without any hopeful result. No one had been able to throw any light on Shem's death, and this despite an obvious determination by some to remain in the limelight of the investigation if they possibly could. A number of theories were advanced, of which the most popular was that concerning his alleged wealth with the consequent robbery motive. But the upshot was that though several people had seen Shem around no one could advance any helpful suggestions as to who might have killed him. One thing, however, over which the village was united was its view that the murderer must be an outsider. Not even its most virulent gossip-mongers suggested that he might be found within their own community.

And the one person who *could* tell them something remained stubbornly mute.

It was just after five o'clock and Machin had slipped out to buy an evening paper when he ran into Susan on the pavement.

'Hello,' he said cheerfully. 'Where are you off to?'

'I'm going back to my flat.'

'Is this your normal way?'

She blushed. 'I don't have a normal way. I ring the changes.'

'Have you got time for a cup of tea?'

'Yes.'

'Good, well, let's go to that place on the next corner, the one that's changed hands.'

'Do you mean The Muffin Parlor?'

'That's it. Used to be the Merry Clown. Except that we always knew it as Weasel's Place because the chap who ran it looked just like a weasel.'

Susan laughed. 'He did rather.'

They reached the café and Machin fetched two cups of tea from the counter and brought them across to the table where Susan was sitting. 'Would you like something to eat as well? Their doughnuts are pretty good. Home-made and with a decent amount of jam inside.'

'I oughtn't to,' she said doubtfully.

'Why not?'

She looked at him in surprise. 'Because they're about a million calories, that's why!'

'Oh! But surely you don't have to worry about your figure?'

'I certainly do – but I'd love one! Are you going to have one, too?'

'Certainly.'

When he returned with the doughnuts and had eased himself into the narrow space between table and bench, she said, 'I gather you're not married?'

'That's right, but what gave me away?'

'Nothing. I just somehow guessed.'

'You ought to join the police. Good guesswork is our mainstay.' He bit into his doughnut and a squelch of jam went on to his chin. He removed this with one finger which he then licked.

'How's the case going?'

'I'm afraid we're no further forward than we were. We're still looking for your cousin, Brian Farmer, though what joy finding him will bring us remains to be seen. I suppose you've not been able to get anything out of Kenny?'

She shook her head. 'I've not been home again, though I'll be going over this weekend. I spoke to my mother on the telephone last night and I know she's worried about him.' She gave a small wry laugh. 'It's funny in a way because she never has worried about him before. I've always been the one who was apt to fuss over him.'

'Why do you think she should be worried this time?'

'I imagine it's because she's never seen him like this before. Silent and moping and refusing to say what's on his mind.'

'What about your father? What's his reaction?'

'I gather he had a go at Kenny, but achieved nothing except lose his own temper. You certainly won't get Kenny to talk by shouting at him and bullying him,' she added scornfully.

'Do he and your father not get on?'

'Dad doesn't give him much attention normally. It's only when Kenny's annoyed him that he gives him any notice.' She paused a second. 'I don't mean that he's a bad father, at least not in the sense that he's unkind to him. He's just not a particularly good one. Kenny wasn't exactly a planned child, you see.'

Machin nodded. 'Tell me about your cousin Brian, what sort of person was he?'

'Although we were much the same age, we never took a great deal of notice of one another. It was Kenny who used to follow him around slavishly – and Brian was certainly very good to him.'

'Did he have any girl-friends in the village?'

'Not real girl-friends, no. There were one or two girls he used to go out with, but they were the sort who were public property anyway. He used to take them out just for one thing.'

Machin glanced at her keenly. He couldn't imagine Susan Bostock ever falling into that category. She was pretty in an unstartling way, and combined an attractive shyness with an apparent firmness of character. Not the sort of girl, Machin imagined, who would conform merely for the sake of doing so. As he watched her now run her tongue across her lips to remove some of the doughnut sugar, he experienced a sudden quiver of interest. He realised, too, that she had gone on speaking and that he hadn't been listening. He smiled at her vacantly for a few seconds.

'Do you go out much in the evenings?' he asked, breaking the silence which had fallen.

She looked up with an expression of mild surprise. 'No, not very much. Bridget, that's the girl I share a flat with, and I sometimes go to the cinema. And friends of hers drop in quite a bit. I don't know many people in Arlebury myself and anyway it's not exactly a social mecca, is it, even if you happen to have money to fling around, which I don't.'

'Would you like to go out to dinner with me one evening?'

She nodded slowly. 'Very much.'

'I don't have to ask Bridget, too, do I?'

'Good heavens, no!'

'Well, that's fine. What about the day after tomorrow, provided I can get away?'

'I'd like that.'

'But you won't be angry if I have to cancel at the last minute.'

'Because of the case you mean?'

'Certainly not for any other reason.'

She laughed. 'No, of course I wouldn't be angry. Where shall I meet you?'

'I'll call for you at your flat at eight o'clock.'

'Where do you live, incidentally?' she asked.

'In digs. Thirteen Barton Road.'

'Who cooks for you?'

'I only have breakfast there. I have all my other meals out. In the canteen or at cafés. Actually, Mrs Prebble – she's the old girl who owns the house – will always cook something for me in the evening if I happen to be in and it's not one of her Bingo nights.'

'Where's your home?'

'My parents live in Cornwall. My father's a Customs officer.'

'What made you come to Arlebury?'

'I'd always wanted to join the police. I felt I'd like to get away from the district I'd grown up in; on the other hand I didn't want to work in a large city. And that's more or less how I came to end up here.' He paused. 'Except, I hope it's not "end up".'

'You don't like it in Arlebury?'

'Oh, Arlebury's all right, and the job's fine, but I don't want to spend my whole life on the rungs of this particular ladder.'

'That means you're ambitious.'

'You could say that. But I also want to enjoy life.' He glanced at his watch. 'I'm afraid I shall have to be getting back. I'm so glad I ran into you and I look forward to Thursday evening. Keep your fingers crossed.'

She held up her hand.

'See! They are already.'

It occurred to her only after they had parted company, that she still didn't know his first name. She hoped it would turn out to be one she liked.

XII

The next morning Kenny got up early and caught the first bus into Arlebury. He told his mother that he wanted to visit the agricultural show which was being staged there and she, for her part, was thankful for the suggestion. It was the first positive thing he'd done since Shem's death. It had got on her nerves having him sit about the house all day turning the pages of one magazine after another. He had even refused to go out when Ray had called round for him. And in answer to every question as to what was the matter, he just went on saying that nothing was the matter.

Mrs Bostock didn't for one moment think that her son had had anything to do with the murder, though she believed he'd had some fright in connection with Shem's death. However, nothing had persuaded him to talk and each day seemed to find him further withdrawn behind the barricades which his mind had erected.

It was shortly before eight o'clock when he stepped off the bus in the market square and stood for a moment gazing about him. It was a grey day and the forecast of 'showers, prolonged at times' seemed likely to be fulfilled. Kenny, however, was not concerned about the weather. In any event, he was wearing his windcheater, which, at the moment, was zipped up to his chin.

He felt in his pocket to make sure his money was still there and set off in the direction of the railway station where he bought a ticket to London.

While he stood on the platform waiting for the train to come in he became aware that he was the object of a good many curious stares. His mind was too preoccupied with his own thoughts to be seriously embarrassed by this and it was only after he was on the train, seated in a carriage full of businessmen, that it dawned on him that his fellow-passengers weren't used to seeing other than their own sort on their daily ride to work.

The men on either side of him were both smoking pipes and reading the sort of newspapers which Kenny regarded as being as dull as school. He had been undaunted by their lack of welcome when he entered the compartment and had squeezed himself between them and wriggled back until he formed a small, pneumatic wedge in their midst. Thereafter he sat staring at the advertisement above the head of the man opposite. It proclaimed the virtues of life insurance about which Kenny knew nothing and cared less, though by the time the train arrived in London he knew every trite word of the text by heart.

He hung back on the platform and waited until all the passengers had cleared the ticket gate before approaching the collector, a large, moon-faced West Indian.

'Ain't you got no ticket, son?' the man enquired as Kenny sidled up to him, hands in pockets. Kenny pulled out his ticket and handed it over and was rewarded by a surprised grin. 'I thought you was hanging back because you didn't have no ticket.' He gave Kenny a mock salute. 'My apologies to you, sir.'

'Can you tell me the way to Shepherd's Bush?' Kenny asked, ignoring the banter.

'Shepherd's Bush! Why, that's quite a way from here. I don't rightly know ... You see I'm not a London man myself ... But I'll find out.' He glanced about him and then gave a shout at a passing porter. 'Hey there, Joe, does you know the way to Shepherd's Bush? This young gentleman here has to get to Shepherd's Bush.'

Joe paused, jutted out his lower lip and rolled his eyes heavenwards.

'Shepherd's Bush, you say! Now, which way's that?'

'I'm asking you, Joe.'

'It's not my way. I live Brixton way. But I sure heard of this Shepherd's Bush. I tell you what,' he went on, addressing Kenny himself, 'You go ask the lady behind the tea counter. She knows where every place is.'

'Yeah, you go ask her,' the ticket collector chimed in, 'she really knows every place. Why she even heard of Parson's Green!' At this, both he and the porter rumbled with laughter as at some secret joke and Kenny went off in the direction of the refreshment room. One look through the glass-panelled door was, however, sufficient to deter him from entering. The place was packed and, at the tea counter itself, there was a sizeable queue.

Leaving the station, he walked out into the forecourt. A couple of policemen were walking slowly on the far side. They'd certainly be able to direct him to Shepherd's Bush, but he thought it better not to bring himself to their notice. Policemen remembered people and were liable to be inquisitive about twelve-year-olds alone in the capital, who were obviously not sure of themselves.

He joined a stream of people who were making for the main road fifty yards away where buses were passing to and fro.

Now that he'd actually arrived in London, he felt quite composed and though he had only visited the place half a dozen times or so and had no notion of its geography, he didn't feel in the slightest degree overawed.

When he reached the main road, he saw a small confectioner's shop and went in. There was a middle-aged woman behind the counter.

'Yes, duck?'

'Can you tell me the way to Shepherd's Bush?'

'What bit of Shepherd's Bush?'

'The centre of it.'

'Yes, duck, but what's the name of the street you want?'

'I can't remember, but I'll recognise it when I get there.'

'Well, if you take my advice you'll go by bus. You don't want to go by Underground, do you?'

'I don't mind.'

'You go by bus, then. Take one from the stop just outside and ask for Notting Hill Gate. You'll have to change there and ask again. O.K., duck? You got that?'

'Yes, thanks. How far is it?'

'It'll take you best part of half an hour at this time of the morning. Don't forget to tell the conductor to put you off at Notting Hill Gate.'

'No. Thanks.'

'Hey, duck, the advice is free, but what about buying something to show there's no ill will.'

'What?'

'How much do you want to spend?'

'Not much.'

'A packet of gum, then?'

'O.K.'

The transaction completed, Kenny left the shop and joined a queue at the bus-stop. It was almost half an hour later to the minute that he got off at Shepherd's Bush Green. He looked about him in bemusement. Half the road seemed to be up and here was a tangle of traffic which stretched round all three sides of the green.

So this was Shepherd's Bush! In a vague sort of way, Kenny had expected to find something closer to the romantic sound of its name. If not actually sheep and a devoted shepherd, at least an acreage of cool, green bushes. A line of dusty trees and, beyond them, some well-worn grass were scarcely a substitute.

He became aware of a policeman who was eyeing him

and so set off with a purposeful expression. He had gone only a short distance when he noticed a newspaper shop. That would be the place to begin his quest! Newspaper shops always knew where everyone lived because of delivering the papers. He went in. It was small and poky and had the same smell as Mr Peckover's shop at home, which was in itself reassuring.

An old man with a tummy the shape of an over-inflated football emerged from the shadows at the back.

'Can you tell me where Mr and Mrs Farmer live, please?' Kenny asked.

'Who are they?'

'My uncle and aunt.'

'Never 'eard of 'em.'

'Don't you deliver papers?'

'Not to nobody called Farmer.'

'How can I find out where they live?'

'Try the Council Offices, they might know.' He gave Kenny a speculative look. 'Lost, are you?'

'No. Who said I was lost!'

'Nobody did. I asked you if you was lost.'

'Well, I'm not.'

'You'd better hop it, then.'

'Why?'

' 'Cos I don't like your tone, that's why.'

'And I don't like your great fat belly.'

As he spoke, Kenny beat his retreat. There'd been something faintly menacing about the man, something which had provoked a parting shot of abuse.

The Council Offices gave the impression of being run entirely for the benefit of those working in them. A number of people stood or sat listlessly about waiting for attention, but without apparent expectation of receiving it. Kenny marched up to a counter behind which a vinegary-looking female was making entries in a book of forms. After standing there for a time without her looking up, he spoke.

'Can you help me, please?'

She went on writing and he thought that maybe she hadn't heard him. But then she stopped and, raising her head, looked at him with an impatient expression. She didn't say anything, however.

'Can you tell me where someone lives?' Kenny said, when it was clear to him that she was waiting for him to go on. 'Where Mr and Mrs Farmer live?'

'Who are you?' she asked coldly.

'Kenny Bostock. They're my uncle and aunt.'

'These are the Council Offices.'

'I know. I was told you could help me.'

'It is not our practice to supply addresses to third parties,' she remarked with a sniff.

'But I'm not a what-you-just-said. I'm their nephew.'

'How do I know that?'

'Because I say so.'

She gave another sniff. 'I'm afraid you've come to the wrong place, young man. It's not part of our duty to provide that sort of information. We have enough to do without helping every member of the public who wanders in.'

'Where can I find out?'

'You could try the police station.'

'Where else?'

The woman's eyes narrowed, which made her expression even more disagreeable.

'Why don't you want to go to the police station?'

'I didn't say that . . .'

'I noticed your expression,' she broke in. 'Are you in trouble?'

'Are you a nosy old hen?'

Once more Kenny made a rapid exit, though this time he had the satisfaction of hearing an outraged intake of breath as he turned on his heel.

It was while he was putting as much distance as possible between himself and the Council Offices that he suddenly remembered having heard his mother mention that his Uncle Jack had a job at the television studios. He stopped someone to ask the way and a quarter of an hour later arrived at a vast complex of new buildings.

An imposing commissionaire listened gravely while Kenny explained his business and, then telling him to wait there, went off to a nearby phone. When he returned it was to say that nobody was quite sure whether a Mr Farmer still worked there or not, but in any event he certainly wasn't on the premises at that moment.

Kenny received the information with a baffled expression.

'This is a big place,' the commissionaire explained. 'Hundreds work here. But you can always write in,' he added. 'That might be the best way.'

Kenny nodded and turned away.

Two hours later he was feeling lonely and dispirited. His legs were aching from all the walking he had done and he was still nowhere nearer discovering where the Farmers lived. After leaving the television centre, he had hung around outside a couple of pubs, hoping to see his uncle.

As he sat in a cheap café with a plate of greasy chips and one withered sausage in front of him he wondered what he should do.

It hadn't occurred to him that he wouldn't be able to find out where his uncle and aunt lived. Having spent all his years in a small community where everyone knew everyone else's name at the very least, he'd thought it would be the same in London – or certainly in that part of it which enjoyed the rustic description of Shepherd's Bush.

But after a morning of meeting indifference, if not rebuffs, his morale had dipped. Moreover, his disappointment was the sharper since, after several days of inward mental turmoil, he had seen his trip to London as a positive breakout. He would find Brian and Brian would tell him what to do ... after he had told Brian what he knew.

He had been buoyed up with excitement at the prospect of seeing his cousin again and of assuring him of his loyal support whatever happened. After all, nobody had been able to get a word out of him yet, nor would they, but with every day that passed the strain became greater until it had reached the point when he had to share it, which meant with one person and one person only, namely Brian. Brian alone in all the world could help him, could tell him what he must do.

He ate the last of the chips and drained his glass of Coca-Cola. The meal had gone some way to restoring his spirits but had not provided him with any new ideas as to his next move.

Even though his determination had been undermined by dawning realisation of the hopelessness of his mission, in no way did he feel overcome by despair.

In fact it was at this moment as he finished his meal and counted his money to see how much he had left, that he decided he wasn't going back home.

XIII

The next morning, Detective Superintendent Page cut himself shaving. There was a particular angle of his chin where this invariably happened, and had gone on happening despite his changing use of a variety of different razors. He had long come to accept the sudden sharp nick and the ensuing messy escape of blood as one of the trials of his life, and one which he must, as far as possible, ignore. A quick dab with an old-fashioned styptic pencil, a blob of cotton-wool and he forgot the mild unsightliness.

As he got dressed he realised that he felt more cheerful than he usually did first thing in the morning. There were certainly no substantial grounds for this; none, that is, connected with the enquiry into Shem's murder, which had flattened out into one of plugging routine.

But Page, who had always been intrigued by what were often regarded as the fringe quirks of an investigation, had had his interest distinctly aroused by the odd intrusion of the two badger teeth in the case.

In the first place, badger teeth were unusual items of personal possession and, secondly, Kenny Bostock's evasive behaviour invested the two teeth with a mystery which needed to be solved.

Accordingly, Page had arranged to call on a naturalist acquaintance who lived a few miles outside Arlebury. He was an old bachelor of eccentric habits who lived in a small cottage which he shared with a large black alsatian, a goat, several rabbits and guinea-pigs and an assortment of smaller animals, all kept in their respective places by a matriarchal cat.

When Page arrived at the old man's home, he found him eating something out of a bowl which looked like gruel. The goat stood hopefully at his side.

'Ah, Daniel,' the old man cried out, 'enter the cage, though I'm sorry I still lack a lion to make you feel really at home.'

Page smiled. The old boy made the same remark every time he called on him.

Stepping carefully to avoid some of the smaller creatures which occupied the floor, he held out the two teeth in the palm of his hand for the old man to see.

'Badger teeth,' the old man said immediately.

'So I already gathered. What I want to know is whether there are any badger lairs near Long Gaisford?'

'Badger *sets,* not lairs. There used to be one in a wood about half a mile away.'

'Have you seen it?'

'Of course I have, Daniel. I don't give second-hand information.'

'Could you show me where it is?'

'I could. But why?'

'It may have some connection with a murder case I'm on.'

'Who's been murdered?'

'An old tramp.'

'How do badgers come to get caught up in a murder? They're good creatures.'

'The murdered man had this tooth in his pocket and a young boy also had one in his possession. Where would you find a badger's tooth?'

'In a badger's mouth.'

'Yes, even I know that. But do badgers shed their teeth?'

'No, but they die – that is if man doesn't kill them first – and then they're often found buried near the set, so you could also find teeth and bones after a time. I've got a badger's skull somewhere which I found when I was messing around near a set several years ago.'

Page glanced uncertainly at the roomful of livestock. He wondered if the old man would be willing to leave his charges for an hour or so. He knew that the dog and the goat usually accompanied him in his incredibly ancient van whenever he went out, but he would prefer that they should be left behind on this occasion: the goat, at any rate.

'Can you show me now where this set is?'

'I'll get the van out.'

'We could go in my car.'

'Jake doesn't like strange cars.' He gave the goat's beard a friendly tug as he spoke. 'And Bruce feels lost without Jake.' At the mention of his name, the alsatian who had been stretched out by the door, flapped his tail a couple of times. 'Give me half an hour and I'll come.'

'Where shall I meet you?'

'The wood is on the far side of the village from Arlebury, on the slope of Harrier's Hill.'

'I know it.'

'There's a track leads off the lane in the direction of the wood. I'll meet you at the end of the track.' He paused. 'I don't know what you're expecting to see, but all it'll be is a few holes in the ground. Sure you still want to go?'

Page nodded, though he was anything but sure of the

usefulness of the visit. Indeed, he was unable to see what it could achieve, but having pursued his interest thus far, he felt compelled to follow it up until it, too, petered out. Then of a sudden it became freshly stimulated as the old man said:

'There's a very well-concealed cave near this particular set, from which I used to do my observing. Splendid place it was, overgrown entrance and big enough to hold a banquet. I once slept in it for a couple of nights.'

'That sounds even more interesting than the set,' Page said.

'Depends what your interest is, doesn't it! Anyway, that's your business.' He pushed a large white rabbit gently out of the way with his foot. 'Should like to have kept a badger,' he said wistfully as he got up. 'Fascinating creatures and almost as persecuted as the Children of Israel.'

Page had been waiting at the rendezvous for about twenty minutes before the noise of plaintive machinery, which heralded the arrival of the old naturalist's van, greeted his ears. The vehicle juddered to a halt on the grass verge and the old man got out, followed by dog and goat.

'Do they really have to come too?' Page asked. 'We've already had one dog running wild over the scene of the crime. Couldn't they wait in your van?'

'All right, Daniel, you're in charge, but let them just run around for a few minutes.' He flicked his fingers and pointed at a gate into the field and Bruce immediately went bounding away. Jake set off at a more stately pace behind him.

The lane in which they were standing ran round the base of Harrier's Hill and the wood which had their attention covered the middle third of the side they were looking at, and ran like an irregular band round the edge and out of sight.

'That's the place,' the old man said musingly. 'The set's just about in the very centre.'

'Tell me about the cave.'

'Nothing to tell. It's just a cave.'

'Good place to hide?'

'Most caves are.'

'I wonder if old Shem knew about it?' Page murmured to himself.

'Shem! Shem! He's been dead awhile.'

'Not this one. He was found murdered only five days ago.'

The old man let out a soft whistle and almost immediately Bruce appeared. A short while later the hedge shook violently as Jake forced his way through, leaving a jagged hole.

'Suppose we'd better do something about that or the farmer'll be angry. You're younger than I, Daniel . . .'

Page went through the motions of restoring the damage, silently cursing Jake and his forefathers as he did so. By the time he had finished, both animals were back in the van and they were ready to start for the wood.

Half-way along the track, which led into the wood, Page stopped and bent down.

'What's that you've picked up?' the old man asked.

'Looks like something off a car.' He held it out for the other to see. 'If you ask me, it's part of an exhaust pipe.'

'What are you going to do with it?'

'Keep it, for the time being.'

The old man grunted. Five minutes later they reached the lower edge of the wood. Just before they entered its leafy dankness, Page turned and looked back over the ground they had covered. It confirmed the conclusion he'd already come to, namely that the track provided a well-secluded approach to the wood, with a hedge on one side and a high bank on the other. He examined the small bit of exhaust pipe thoughtfully, before hurrying after the old man who was striding out of sight.

The track continued for about twenty-five yards into the wood before abruptly terminating. Page studied the ground carefully, but it told him nothing. There was certainly no sign of wheel marks, but then the nature of the ground was against this. Moreover, there'd been no rain for over two weeks which meant that everything was hard and unyielding. But if a vehicle had come up the track and entered the wood, it would either have had to turn somewhere or to have backed all the way out again which would have been difficult though not impossible. There was certainly nowhere it could have turned inside the wood, the trees being spaced too closely together for such a manoeuvre. On the other hand there would have been room for this just where the track reached the wood. The hedge veered away leaving an elongated triangle of flat ground and a vehicle could certainly have been turned there with a bit of care. He must examine the area more closely on the way out.

'There you are! There's your badger set!'

The old man had stopped and was leaning against a beech tree.

'Where's the cave?'

'Confound the cave! I thought we'd come to look at a badger set.'

Page dutifully stared at a gaping hole in a bank just ahead of where they were standing.

'Any badgers at home?' he asked.

The old man went closer and stared at the ground.

'Could be. Some of the marks look reasonably fresh.' He swung round and gave Page a glinting look. 'Not that you're really interested, are you? All you want to look at is the cave. Well, I bet you can't even see it!'

Page stared about him while the old man watched him with an expression of amused triumph.

Just beyond the badger set, the wood became much denser with a profusion of bushes between the trees and wild creeper festooned between the branches.

The old man suddenly burst out laughing.

'All right, Daniel, don't look so forlorn. I'll help you. See that sycamore tree?' – he pointed in the direction – 'Make your way there and I'll show you the next signpost.' Page picked his way over to the tree in question, then turned and looked back at his friend. 'Now push your way between those two bushes and look to your right.'

But even before he followed the further direction, Page could see that someone else had recently been thrusting their way between the bushes. Bits hung loose and he could see small pieces of material adhering to the thorn bush. Case-hardened though he was, he couldn't help experiencing a jab of excitement. But it was also a moment for a quick decision. If he now forced his way through, he might destroy vital clues. It was better to get someone else along and take possession of these potentially precious items. He turned away.

'What's wrong? Not afraid of a few thorns are you, Daniel?' the old man called out.

'No, but I'm not going any farther until I've got another officer out here.' He wondered whether to ask the old man to go back into the village with a message, but decided it would be better if he went himself. 'Do you mind staying here till I get back?'

'How long are you going to be?'

'Twenty minutes to half an hour.'

'I'll go and wait with Bruce and Jake.'

'O.K., but make sure nobody goes up the track while I'm away.'

'What d'you want me to do? Set Bruce on them?'

'Jake, too, if necessary. He's just the boy to defend the entrance to the track.'

Page had no idea which, if any, officer he might find in the village and so felt that luck was really on his side when almost the first person he saw as he drove down the main street was Detective Constable Stevens, who, it turned out, had come over to collect a further control sample of earth from that area where Shem's body had been found.

'Forget that for the moment and come with me,' he said.

Together they drove back to where the old man was

squatting at the edge of the lane with Jake and Bruce sitting on their haunches either side of him like supporting emblems in a family crest.

A few minutes later, Page was pointing out to Stevens the way to the cave entrance.

'Got some of your little bags with you?' he asked.

For answer Detective Constable Stevens pulled a roll of polythene bags from his pocket.

'Good! Let's begin!' When they had finished, Page gazed at their collection of samples and said, 'Certainly somebody's been pushing their way in and out of here. I just hope that it's someone of interest to us.'

'If you look at this bush, sir, it appears that whoever it was has tried to conceal the fact. The bush has taken quite a bashing, but somebody's gone to quite a lot of trouble to try and straighten it out again.'

'Hmm! It's time we took a look inside the cave. You lead the way!'

'Can't yet see the cave,' Stevens muttered.

'No, but you should do as soon as you've passed that lot. Unless someone's made off with it.'

Stevens grinned. The Super had a funny old sense of humour, so that you were never quite sure when he was making a joke. But that last remark was surely meant to be one, even though it had not been accompanied by so much as a flicker of a smile. Cautiously, and moving sideways, he began to edge his way between the two bushes. Page watched him attentively.

'You're leaving a few samples of your own clothing behind,' he remarked.

When at length Stevens was through he turned and parted the foliage as well as he could to facilitate his Detective Superintendent's passage.

'Now where?' Page asked a trifle testily when he had joined Stevens and they had the impression of standing inside a holly bush.

Stevens pointed between the trees to where the slope of

the hill became suddenly much steeper and a screen of creeper hung down from a small promontory which jutted out about four feet above the ground.

'That must be it there, sir!' Though there was no defined path to the mouth of the cave, the way was much easier than it had been and there were further signs of others having been there before them.

'Got a torch?' Page enquired.

'Yes, sir. A small pocket one.'

Page grunted. 'That's a bit of luck, then. I'd forgotten about caves being dark.'

Stevens stooped and parted the fall of creeper and let out an excited exclamation.

'This is the cave all right, sir. What's more it's been in recent use.'

'How do you tell that?'

'Smell.'

Page bent down beside him and peered in.

'Tobacco smoke,' he remarked. 'Is that what you smell?'

'Yes, sir.'

'Shine your torch on the ground.' Stevens did so and the light showed up several cigarette ends in the beaten earth.

They entered and found that once they were inside it was possible to stand upright. Page took a deep breath and appeared to analyse its content before slowly expelling it.

'Somebody's had a fire in here, too.'

'Yes, over there, sir. You can see the floor's blackened.'

'Give me your torch a minute.'

Page directed the narrow beam methodically over the floor of the cave up to about twelve feet in and then up and down the walls. He then moved forward several paces and repeated the procedure while Stevens collected the cigarette ends and placed each in a separate bag with as much care as if they were precious stones.

'Look!' Page suddenly called out, holding the beam of the torch focused on one spot at his feet.

'It's a button, sir.'

'I happened to unearth it with the toe of my shoe, otherwise I wouldn't have seen it.'

The torch beam darted forward again and a few seconds later Page let out an excited mutter.

'Blood! Dried blood! I'm darned certain that's what it is.' He stooped down to examine the ground more closely. Stevens knelt down beside him. With infinite care they scraped up a top layer of floor and deposited it in a polythene bag.

But this seemed to be the sum of their finds for the present. As the old naturalist had said, the cave was large enough to hold a banquet and it widened out into a larger chamber about twenty yards from its entrance. All signs of recent use, however, were confined to what might be termed the vestibule area.

By the time they emerged into daylight, Page was satisfied that they had discovered all that there was to find. Nevertheless, it would be necessary to give it an even more thorough search with the aid of something stronger than Detective Constable Stevens' pocket torch. It was time to return to the village and organise this.

When they did get there, it was to learn that Kenny had not returned home the previous night.

XIV

Brian Farmer and three other men sat in the front room of a terraced house in a South London side street. He was the youngest of the four and, from appearances, the most nervous. Indeed, the other three were not exhibiting any signs of nervousness at all. Two of them looked faintly bored and the eldest, whose name was Mick Edmunds, was doing the talking.

'For Chrissake snap out of it, Brian! You 'aven't got nothing to worry about. It's a bloody nuisance it 'ad to 'appen, but that's all. Nothing's altered, we just 'ave to 'old off awhile and then we're all set again. Ain't that so?' He looked at the other two who nodded briefly.

'It's right what Mick says,' one of them said. 'All we need is a bit of patience.'

'That's right,' the other chimed in.

But Brian Farmer's expression remained unchanged.

'Anyway,' Edmunds went on, 'if I'm not worried why the bloody hell should you be?'

'Supposing the police . . .'

'Bugger the police! The police can't know a thing.'

'They're looking for who did for that old man.'

'So what! Why should they connect you with it!'

'Me! I didn't . . .'

'O.K., Brian, calm yourself, boy! I know you didn't do it. None of us did, so what you got to worry about?'

'I'm the one who used to live in the rotten village. Not any of you lot.'

'So you used to live in the rotten village,' Edmunds said in a pacifying tone, 'what's that prove? 'Undreds of people lived there once and have moved away.'

'Not hundreds, a couple of dozen at the most.'

Edmunds let out an exaggerated sigh. 'O.K., a couple of dozen then. Why should the police be interested in any of them? They're going to be concentrating on the ones who live there *now*, not on absent friends.' He grinned at the other two. One of them responded with a wink, the other with an exasperated glance in Farmer's direction.

'I've got form,' Farmer said, 'that's why they could be looking for me. Also there's something else!'

'What?'

'Somebody in the village may have spotted me.'

'Who?'

'I don't know. I only said may.'

'You never spoke to no one, did you?' Edmunds asked

suspiciously.

'No.'

'If somebody saw you, you'd have seen them. Did you?'

'No.'

'Sure about that?'

'Certain.'

'Then what the bloody hell are you worried about?'

'I don't like what's happened. I'm nervous.'

'Nobody likes what's 'appened, but it doesn't 'ave to make you nervous.'

'So what are we going to do now?' Farmer asked, looking from one face to the other.

'Same as what we've been doing for the past few days. Lie low and wait for the 'eat to go off. Give it another week and you won't find the law within five miles of the place.' Edmunds got up and walked slowly across to the window, then swung round to face his small audience. He was surprisingly agile for one of his physical bulk. 'Let's 'ave this straight,' he said, 'there's no reason why the police should connect any of us with what's 'appened in that village than they should the train robbers who are under lock and key. And that goes for you, too, Brian, even if you did once 'ave it off with all the local birds.'

Farmer grinned. It was flattering, if not wholly accurate, to be regarded that way by Mick Edmunds, who'd had more women, not to mention more criminal convictions, than the rest of them put together.

'Anyone got anything else to say?' he enquired. Three heads were shaken. 'Good, then that's that!' He glanced at his watch. 'Just about time to down a few pints before the boozer shuts. But we don't want to be seen all together in one. Brian and I'll go to the Essex Arms and you two piss off to another.'

At the pub, Edmunds saw a couple he knew and went over to speak to them, leaving Brian alone with his beer. He sat slouched back on the padded bench staring at a trickle of beer winding its way across the round marble-topped table. It had come from his own mug when Edmunds had put it down roughly and some had slopped over the rim. He wondered idly whether the trickle had sufficient momentum to reach the edge of the table. He felt that his own fate was somehow bound up in the answer. Ever since he was a small boy, he'd had this thing about omens and had often gone out of his way to create his own.

For example, when he had done something naughty, he would go through a lengthy rigmarole of touching certain objects, changing step, scratching an ear and whistling a specific number of times in the belief that he would thereby ward off trouble. The fact that he didn't only persuaded him that he had cast the wrong spells.

The habit, which had turned into an obsession, had died hard and he still found himself looking for portents when he was up against life.

Two inches from the edge of the table, the small probing trickle of beer seemed to have come to a final halt and Brian viewed this with relief. It was a good sign. But then suddenly it started oozing forward again, though on a slightly different course, no longer directly towards the table's edge, but at an oblique angle. He stared at it with fascinated gaze. His eyes were still fixed hypnotically on the top of the table when a hand with a cloth briskly wiped it over. He looked up to find Vera, the licensee's wife, collecting empties and mopping the tables as she went.

'Anything the matter, dear?' she asked.

'No, nothing.'

'That's all right, then. It was just that you looked a bit peaky of a sudden.'

'No, I'm fine.'

She moved on and Brian took a large gulp of beer and lit a cigarette. The truth was that he was still worried and nothing which Mick Edmunds was likely to say could change that. He judged it improbable that the police *did* have any interest in him, but that wasn't sufficient to restore his confidence. What had happened was a bad omen, rather like a flat tyre before you even get out of the garage.

It was six months since he'd been released from Borstal and he was still on licence. He'd been sent there for housebreaking – two offences and three others taken into consideration – and had hated it, every minute of it. The brisk, healthy, turn-you-into-a-useful-citizen attitude had soured him from the start. He resented such obvious, if well-meaning attempts to reshape him in a mould acceptable to law-abiding society.

As he now looked back on his Borstal days and even earlier ones he realised that, perhaps, the happiest had been the last couple of years he'd spent at Long Gaisford. There'd been lots of fumbling fun with various village girls and the companionship of Kenny his cousin. He wondered what had become of Kenny. He must be about twelve by now. A nice kid and it had been flattering the way he always looked up to him. Kenny had been in his mind a good deal these last few days.

He took another deep swallow of beer, holding back some in his mouth as a sudden thought came to him. Then slowly he released it down his throat.

'Christ!' he muttered. 'Surely it couldn't ... and yet ... why have I thought of it only now?'

He glanced across at where Edmunds was engrossed in conversation with a thick-set man and a middle-aged blonde who had a face the shape of a door wedge.

He must get out into the fresh air and think.

Kenny! He was the only one who'd know. How could he possibly get in touch with him without arousing suspicion? Somehow he must think of a way.

With every step that led him away from the pub, the need to see Kenny seemed to become more imperative.

XV

Sharp at eight o'clock that evening, Sergeant Machin rang Susan Bostock's doorbell.

'No, I'm afraid no news yet,' he said immediately, in answer to her look. 'But don't worry, it's a safe bet that he hasn't come to any harm. We know he caught a train to London yesterday morning and I've no doubt that he's alive and kicking somewhere in that jungle. With everyone on the look-out for him, it won't be long before he's found.'

'You really believe that?'

'Yes. You know him better than I do, but he seems a fairly tough twelve-year-old. Not the type to lose his head and do something silly.'

'But isn't the fact of his running away like this a sign of that?'

'Yes and no.' Machin had realised that in his endeavour to set Susan's mind at rest he had been led into illogicality. 'I agree that he has run away because he presumably saw it as the only answer to his problems, but, having run off, I don't see him behaving like a hen without a head.'

'I hope not, but there are so many awful people about and one's always reading of children who get picked up and . . .' She let the sentence trail away.

'Don't think along those lines. We're going to find your brother – and soon. Incidentally, we've already traced the Farmers. They still live in Shepherd's Bush.'

'What did you find out from them?' she asked, with a slight catch in her voice.

'They've not seen Brian for about three months – or heard of him for that matter. He told them he was helping a friend in the decorating business somewhere in South London.'

'Are you still trying to find Brian?'

'Very much so.'

'Do you think that's why Kenny ran away?'

'I certainly think Brian is in some way tied up in things, at least in Kenny's mind.'

'But what on earth can it be that's made Kenny behave like this?'

'I reckon we'll stand a better chance of discovering that when we find him. And now,' he added with a hopeful smile, 'what about dinner?'

'Yes, I'm ready. I'll just fetch my coat.'

As they walked across to his car, Machin said, 'By the way, I never told you my first name.'

'I know you didn't.' She gave a small giggle. 'I've been trying to guess what it is.'

'That's risky. Anyway, let's hear, but don't you dare say Godfrey!'

'Don't you like that name?'

'I do not.'

'No, you don't look like a Godfrey.'

'Thanks.'

'David?'

'Not quite.'

'Derek?'

'No!'

'Darrell?'

'Good heavens, no!'

'Daniel?'

'That's Superintendent Page's name.'

'What other name begins with D?'

'Mine doesn't anyway.'

'But you said "not quite" when I said David.'

'What I meant was that I had a name about as common as David. Same number of letters, too.'

'George?'

'No. Do you like "George"?'

'Not very much.'

'That's lucky then. Also it has one letter too many.'

'Oh, I know, it must be Peter.'

'Peter it is. A prize for the lady!'

'Peter Machin,' she murmured, as though savouring the combination. 'They go well together.'

'I suppose they're all right. Certainly better than some. We've got an Inspector called Percy Partworn.'

'That's grotesque.'

'I know, but he's rather proud of it. Makes sure everyone gets it right: spells it out and all that.'

'I don't think I could ever marry anyone with a name like that. Percy's bad enough!'

'Funny thing with names. Most people think Percy's a pretty awful one and yet it isn't all that different from Peter. They each have five letters and three of them in common.'

'It's like if you say you have a bad foot, everyone immediately assumes you did it playing football or climbing a mountain, but if you say you have bad feet, they picture you with bunions and fallen arches.'

Machin laughed. 'I hadn't thought of that, but it's true.'

While they'd been talking, he'd been driving to the restaurant he'd selected for their evening out. Not that Arlebury offered a very wide choice of eating places. There were two hotels which had expensive restaurants with pretentious menus, indifferent service and food which tasted like dried peat through having been reheated so many times. At one of them, the speciality was to cook everything at the table with such an abundance of flame that all but the hardier guests recoiled from the scorching heat. However, a new Italian restaurant called Casa Nino had recently opened, and it was there that Machin had booked a table. It was actually run by Italians, served Italian food and was not too pricey.

'Have you been there?' he asked as he negotiated the

main square in the centre of town.

'No. But then I hardly ever eat out. Anyway, I wouldn't go to a place like that, I'd be nervous.'

'Nervous!'

'Well, isn't it terribly smart?'

'No. And even if it were, what's wrong with your own appearance?'

She blushed. 'What I really meant was that I wouldn't dare go to a place like that on my own. You're probably used to posh places.'

'That's one thing about the police, you see life from the highest to the lowest. One day you're in a ducal mansion, the next in a vermin-infested hovel. You're interviewing a lord in the morning and a criminal with a record as long as your arm in the afternoon.'

'You really do enjoy your work, don't you?'

'Yes. You have to. You couldn't keep on if you didn't. Nobody'd ever do it just for the money. It's the variety, the unexpectedness, the feeling that you're doing something useful which makes it a fascinating job. Mind you, like most jobs, it has its binds. There's far too much paper and form-filling and the discipline side can be irksome, especially when you're treated like a Guards' recruit and bawled out over something that's probably not your fault anyway, but just because somebody has got to be bawled out and you happen to show your face at that moment.'

'That doesn't sound fair.'

'It's not really as bad as I'm pretending,' he said, pulling up outside the restaurant. 'And, anyway, as I've said, I wouldn't swap my job for anyone's.' He got out and came round to open the passenger door, giving her a firm hand to help her to the pavement.

She was wearing a frilly white blouse and a woolly skirt which was the colour of burgundy with light shining through it. She had on black stockings and black shoes with plain silver buckles on them. Not for the first time that evening, Machin looked at her with approval. It was difficult at this moment to associate her with a twelve-year-old boy who had disappeared and who, in some unexplained way, was connected with a murder.

As soon as they were seated, he ordered a carafe of red wine. It took them some time to choose their meal and then in the end they accepted Nino's advice about what to have: 'I give you something delicious,' he said, having ascertained that both of them wanted veal. For first course, Susan opted for melon, but Machin ordered Spaghetti Bolognese. When it came, he set about it with the enthusiasm of a hungry schoolboy. Susan watched him and decided there was something rather engaging in the sight. From time to time he paused to mop sauce from his chin. It was a good firm chin, but at the same time without an aggressive appearance. He was one of those fair-haired men who needed to shave as often as someone much darker and she had noticed that he had obviously shaved just before coming out.

Susan had looked forward to the evening. There was something rather exciting about being taken out by a good-looking detective sergeant, certainly to someone who had led a relatively sheltered life by present-day standards. Though she had had a number of boy-friends, she had never been boy-mad as so many of her contemporaries were and had never regarded male company as an indispensable part of her life. Now, however, as they waited for their next course to arrive, she began to wonder what were Peter Machin's thoughts about her. Had he asked her out simply because she had floated across his line of vision when he had it in mind to date some girl anyway? Or had he been genuinely attracted by her? And if that was the case, what plans was he mentally hatching for that part of the evening which followed dinner? And what was her own reaction going to be? Somehow it had never occurred to her that policemen – detective sergeants in particular – were subject to the same human impulses as others. She'd always felt a similar thing about clergymen. She couldn't bring herself to believe that their children were conceived by the same rather ungainly process as other babies.

'A penny for your thoughts,' Machin said, bringing her to with a jolt.

'I'm sorry, my mind just drifted away. I wasn't thinking of anything in particular.'

He smiled. 'Not half from your expression, you weren't!'

She picked up her glass and took a sip of wine to try and cover her embarrassment. 'It really is very nice here,' she remarked, looking about her with exaggerated determination.

'I'm glad you like it,' he said drily. He wondered just what had been in her mind when he'd spoken. Of one thing he was certain, namely that her thoughts had involved himself. There was something pleasantly innocent about her.

Their main course arrived and was, indeed, as delicious as Nino had promised. Afterwards he insisted that they both have zabaglione which Susan had never tasted. She had not liked to admit that, in fact, she'd never even heard of it.

'I shall make it for you myself, Signorina,' he declared.

When he returned to their table with two tall, thin glasses filled with a delicate amber froth, he stood and watched them take their first mouthfuls.

'Delicious!' Susan said.

'Very good, Nino,' Machin chimed in, nodding his head. 'A bit like thin custard with sherry in it, if you ask me,' he added when Nino had moved away.

Susan giggled. 'And after he went to all that trouble!'

'All part of his act. And, anyway, we're going to pay for it. Nevertheless, I like old Nino, he's helped the police once or twice since he's been here, which is more than one can say for a good many of the locals. Some of them go out of their way to make things awkward all the time.'

Susan nodded gravely. The warm atmosphere, the food and, most of all, the wine had begun to make her feel sleepy and she was finding it increasingly difficult to make conversation. Her mind had, so to speak, kicked off its shoes and put its feet up and her responses had become reduced to smiles and nods and occasional monosyllables. If Peter Machin were to pick her up bodily and make a dash for his lair, she'd be unable to resist – at any rate, not at this stage.

However, nothing like that happened. He paid the bill and, with a hand on her elbow, guided her out to the car.

'Do you mind if I call in at the Station?' he said, as he got into the driving seat. 'I promised I'd look in about now. It won't take a second.'

'What'll you do if you have to go out somewhere?' she asked in a slightly unnatural tone.

He shot her a quick glance. 'I'll take you home first. But I'm not expecting to have to go out anywhere.'

Five minutes later he pulled up outside the police station.

'Shan't be a moment,' he said as he gave her hand a small squeeze before jumping out and clearing the three steps up to the entrance in one bound.

But, in fact, a full five minutes passed before he returned to the car. Susan saw immediately from his expression that something had happened, though the lapse of time had itself forewarned her.

'Kenny's been found,' he said, placing his hand over hers.

'Is he all right?' she broke in, with a catch in her voice.

'Yes, he's fine. He's at Shepherd's Bush Police Station. The news came through just a couple of minutes before we got here.' He paused and looked straight at her. 'I was wondering how you'd react to the suggestion that you and I drive up to London now and pick him up? Otherwise, someone'll have to go and fetch him in the morning.'

'Yes, let's go now,' she said eagerly.

'We'll be there just after midnight and back here between one and two.'

'He can spend the night at my flat.'

'That's what I thought.'

'Do my parents know?'

'I'll get a message to them now. I just wanted to find out

first how you felt about fetching him tonight.'

'Oh, I'm so relieved he's all right.'

'I told you he would be.'

'Perhaps now we'll find out why he ran away.'

'Let's hope so.' He drew her hand closer to him and enclosed it in both of his. 'If together we can't get him to talk,' he said, 'I'll run away myself.'

XVI

After leaving the Essex Arms, Brian Farmer took the Underground up to the West End – and went to a cinema, where he saw a film called 'Midnight Cowboy'. He sat through it engrossed. Though he laughed at the adventures of the eponymous hero, he did so with one hundred per cent identification. Like the hero, he lived in a world of unacknowledged fantasy: like him, he sought a change in his fortunes: and like him, too, he was only dimly aware that in the predatory corner in which he had chosen to dwell others were ever ready to outsmart him.

At all events, for Brian Farmer, two hours passed without so much as a reminder of the matter which had been uppermost in his mind when he had entered the cinema.

When he came out he went to a café near Leicester Square and ordered a plate of sausage, egg and chips and a cup of tea. It was as he began to embark on his meal that he began thinking again of the urgent need to get in touch with Kenny. It was out of the question to visit him at Long Gaisford. Perhaps the best thing would be to send him a letter couched in their own secret language asking him to come up to London. But there were dangers in that and, moreover, he didn't even know whether the Bostocks still lived in the village. They might have moved away, just as his own family had.

He finished his food and pushed his plate from him, at the same time reaching for his cup, which he cradled in both hands as he ruminated over his problem.

Of course, if the Bostocks *had* left the village, Kenny wouldn't know anything of what had happened. But if he was still around, then he was the only person who could provide the answer to the question which was burning his mind.

He put down his cup and lit a cigarette and gazed morosely out at the crowded pavement. He felt anxious and lonely. He wished he could see things more clearly. All he did realise was that Mick Edmunds was going to be pretty rough-tongued with him when he returned, but at this moment he felt worse things than that could happen to him.

Nevertheless he hung about the West End for several more hours before finally walking up to Oxford Circus and catching the Tube to Shepherd's Bush.

It was shortly after ten o'clock when he arrived at the house where his parents lived. He knocked on the door, which was opened by his nineteen-year-old brother, Roy.

For a few seconds Roy stood gaping at him, until Brian spoke.

'Are Mum or Dad in?'

'No. They won't be back till late.'

'Well, there's no need to look so bloody surprised. I haven't returned from the grave.'

'Do you want to come in?'

'I haven't come all this way just to chat to you on the doorstep. 'Course I want to come in.'

'Why've you come?'

Brian frowned. He'd never got on particularly well with his brother who represented most of the virtues which he himself lacked. He was studious, painfully law-abiding and quietly smug.

'What do you mean, why've I come? I've as much right to be here as you have.'

'It's not because of the police?'

Brian's head snapped back as he looked up sharply.

'Police! What's that about the police?'

'They came here looking for you.'

Brian who had taken a quick step inside the door now closed it firmly behind him.

'When was this?'

'Two days ago.'

'What did they say?'

'Just wanted to know where you were.'

'Why?'

'They didn't say.'

'Who spoke to them?'

'I did. No one else was at home.'

'What did you tell them?' His tone held a note of quiet menace and his brother gulped uncomfortably.

'Just that you didn't live here and I didn't know where you did live. I said you hadn't been here for about three months.'

'What did they say?'

'They just asked a lot more questions.'

'What sort of questions?'

'All about how they could get in touch with you. But I wasn't able to help them . . .' He retreated a rapid step as he observed the vicious look in his brother's eye.

'You weren't able to help them!' Brian ground out savagely.

'I didn't mean it like that. I meant that I didn't know anything about where you were or what you were doing.'

'How many policemen called?'

'Two. They were in plain clothes.'

'And they never said anything about why they wanted to see me?'

'No.'

'And you didn't ask them?'

'No. It wasn't any of my business. I mean they wouldn't have told me, anyway, would they?'

'Did you tell Mum and Dad they'd been?'

' 'Course I did.'

'What did they say?'

'They asked much the same questions as you have and I told them what I've told you.'

'Have they been back?'

'Not as far as I know.'

Brian glanced about him uneasily. The small hall seemed unbearably claustrophobic of a sudden. He gave a shiver.

'I wanted to see Mum,' he said, his voice that of a lost small boy.

'They won't be back till after one, but you can wait if you want.'

'I know I can bloody wait,' he said, his brother's tone causing his temper to flare again. 'But I'm not going to.'

'What's happened? Why've you come and what do the police want you for?' The questions came spilling out as Roy stared at him with blinking bewilderment. He hadn't shaved for several days and patches of whiskers sprouted sparsely on his face. There were three much longer hairs in the area of his adam's apple which had escaped the razor's attention for some time and which his brother had a vicious urge to seize and pull.

'Nothing's happened,' he said grimly, 'And how do I know what the police want to see me about?' The look which accompanied his words was potent enough for Roy Farmer to bottle his curiosity.

'Do you want me to tell Mum and Dad you came?'

'You can please yourself.' He turned and opened the front door. 'You will, anyway,' he added viciously as he stepped out into the night.

He had just reached the pavement and was fiddling with the latch of the gate when a voice spoke behind him.

'Excuse me – you, Brian Farmer?'

In the split second it took him to decide not to make a dash for it, a hand settled firmly on his shoulder. He shook it off and swung round to find a young police constable in uniform who didn't look a day older than himself.

'Yes,' he said with a faint note of truculence. 'I'm Brian Farmer. What do you want?'

'Would you mind coming along to the Station? One of our officers would like to have a word with you.'

'What about?'

'I think he'd like to tell you that himself.'

'I haven't done anything wrong.'

'Nobody's suggested you have.'

'Then why should I come to the police station?'

'To help Sergeant Cumnor with his enquiries.'

'You can't make me come.'

'Quite right.'

'Then piss off and leave me alone.'

The young police constable studied him mildly.

'It'll save everyone a lot of trouble if you do come along with me,' he said at length. 'And after all, if you've not done anything wrong, you've got nothing to worry about.'

There was something disturbingly calm and, at the same time, compelling about the officer. He was only an inch or two taller than Farmer and wasn't remotely tough-looking and yet he radiated a sort of unflappable confidence.

He seemed to realise that Brian was undecided whether to comply or to hurl a final word of defiance and he gave the impression of being perfectly ready for either.

In fact, if Brian had been able to see beyond the calmly assured exterior, he'd have known that P.C. Beresford's own mental processes were bubbling like a chemist's retort. He was a bright young officer (in fact, over a year younger than the person he was dealing with) who realised that bluff and native wit were about the only cards you had to play in a situation such as this. Everyone expected results; everyone, except a few who were wilfully obtuse, knew that you had to bend the rules to obtain them; but no one, least of all those in authority, wanted to know that this had occurred. You were out on your own like a spy in a foreign country. Supply the goods and quiet praise was heaped upon you.

Get caught and they couldn't act quickly enough to disown you. He had already committed a technical assault by laying a hand on Farmer and now he was standing in the shadow of an allegation of unlawful arrest, since, come what may, he hadn't the slightest intention of allowing Farmer just to walk away. By one means or another he was going to get him to the station. At the moment, there still seemed to be scope for a bit more persuasion.

He gave Brian a small smile.

'If you run off now,' he said, 'it'll look bad, won't it? It'll look as if you've got something to hide, that you're guilty of something or other. It'll just make it worse when you're found again. After all, if they want to question you about something, they'll go on looking for you, but with a bit more determination and then they'll want to know why you hopped it before. I mean, that stands to reason, doesn't it?'

'But why should I go with you, when I don't know what it's all about? Anything could happen.'

P.C. Beresford gave a good-natured chuckle. 'You sound like someone who has to go into hospital to have a wart removed and doesn't think he'll ever get out alive.'

'Wart removing can be a bloody painful business! I know!'

This time, the officer laughed outright. 'Trust me to pick the wrong example! Look, I don't know very much about it because I'm not in the C.I.D., but I think they want to see if you can help over a murder. Some old tramp was found dead near a quarry at Long Gaisford. You used to live there, didn't you?'

'Yes, but I don't know anything about a murder.'

P.C. Beresford noticed the look of strain which had increased on Farmer's face. The skin was white and taut, which added to the angry appearance of a pustule just below one corner of his mouth. He was constantly running his tongue across his lips.

'Nevertheless, you may be able to tell them something

which'll help. Police work consists almost entirely of collecting information, often from people who aren't aware that they've got any to give. Shall we make a move?'

Almost before he realised what was happening, Brian Farmer found himself walking along the pavement beside the officer, discussing England's chances in the World Cup. A somewhat one-sided discussion it may have been, since Brian contributed little more than the occasional monosyllable, but one which, by virtue of its hypnotic persistence, denied his mind time to dwell on what lay immediately ahead.

As they entered the station, P.C. Beresford called out to the desk sergeant:

'Someone to see Sergeant Cumnor, Sarge. I'll take him along to the C.I.D.'

The desk sergeant who was dealing with a volubly indignant old lady who was complaining that her neighbour had thrown a pail of water over her cat, merely grunted.

'This way,' P.C. Beresford said, leading a still bemused Brian through a glass-panelled door and down a passage. He paused before a door at the end and knocked on it. He could hear Sergeant Cumnor's voice inside.

'Come in.'

Beresford opened the door. He thought at first that Cumnor must have been on the telephone since he saw no one else in the room. Then looking in the same direction as the officer, he noticed a boy sitting on a chair in a corner of the room.

'Yes?' Sergeant Cumnor asked.

'I've found Brian Farmer, Sergeant,' he said in a stage whisper. 'He's here with me now.'

The effect on the boy was as though a current of electricity had been passed through him. His body jolted forward and he stared at the door with an expression of ferocious eagerness. But then he abruptly sat back and fixed an unwavering gaze on the wall behind Sergeant Cumnor's head. His whole movement had been as sudden and unexpected as the sharp flick of an ant-eater's tongue.

Cumnor got up quickly and came to the door.

'You stay here with the boy,' he said, as he went out.

P.C. Beresford closed the door and took off his helmet. Then running a hand through his flattened hair, he went and sat down in Sergeant Cumnor's chair and cast an interested look at the boy.

'The sarge didn't tell me your name. Mine's Beresford.'

'I'm Kenny Bostock.'

'Ah! I remember being told to look out for you when I went on duty. You've run away from home or something, haven't you?'

'No. I just came up to London yesterday and I didn't go home last night. That's not running away.'

'Where do you live?'

'Long Gaisford, if you've ever heard of it.'

'Where did you spend last night?' Beresford asked with interest. The odds were he oughtn't to be talking to the boy, certainly not questioning him, but he couldn't just sit there like a waxwork. And anyway, he had not been specifically told not to talk to him. It was obvious from his dramatic reaction that the boy knew Farmer, but it seemed that Farmer had been unaware of the boy's presence in the room.

'In the back of the lorry,' Kenny replied, with a touch of pride.

'That was a bit risky, wasn't it! You might have been driven off somewhere.'

'I'd have jumped out.'

'What did you come to London for?'

'No special reason.'

'Who found you?'

'Huh?'

'Did you come to the station on your own?'

'No, one of your blokes brought me here.'

'Are your parents coming to fetch you?'

Kenny shrugged. An hour ago, he'd been sunk in a mood

of dispirited apathy. But a good hot meal in the station canteen had gone a long way to restoring his morale and then a few minutes ago the unbelievable arrival of Brian had caused him to concentrate his mind as seldom before. He couldn't afford to relax his guard for a second. He'd already given himself dangerously away by his reaction just now, but he was as determined as ever that they wouldn't get anything further out of him. Brian could have been brought to the station for only one reason. If only he could find an opportunity of speaking to him. But he realised there was little chance of that and he felt suddenly ready to weep for the bitter frustration which welled up inside him.

'Feeling all right?' P.C. Beresford asked, observing his tight-lipped, puce-coloured look.

Kenny nodded curtly.

'Well, you'll be home soon, I expect.'

Beresford yawned. It had been quite an evening. He wished there were more like it. All too often, the hours passed in dreary routine. Or so he was apt to say when asked by friends not in the force. And yet when one came to think of it, most tours of duty produced an incident or two, certainly in an area populated by so many Irish, who never had to have an actual motive before embarking on a roistering fight. And if it wasn't the drunken Irish, it was the drunken English or the uninhibited West Indians who helped to keep busy the young police constable on his beat. But tonight had required the exercise of resource and ingenuity and he had enjoyed that. In a sense, all police work called for those two qualities, but some occasions more than others. Though he was not averse to a bit of strong-arm stuff (no more, of course, than was necessary in the execution of his duty), he preferred to deploy the more subtle arts in achieving his end. He smothered another yawn and glanced across at Kenny whose face had become set in an expression of concrete stubbornness.

The door opened and the desk sergeant looked in.

'Where's Sergeant Cumnor?'

'Don't know, Sarge. He went off to interview the chap I brought in.'

'There's an officer from Arlebury here. He's come to collect the lad. See if you can find Sergeant Cumnor.'

P.C. Beresford got up and made to leave the room. He became aware that Kenny's eyes were following him and looked across with a friendly smile, only to be met by a stare of implacable resentment.

XVII

On arriving at the station to pick up Kenny, Detective Sergeant Machin was taken wholly by surprise to learn that Brian Farmer was also there. His immediate reaction was that he must phone Detective Superintendent Page in order to obtain his instructions as to how to proceed. After all, Farmer was a suspect, though nothing more at the moment, and his interrogation could prove to be of crucial importance.

Page was in bed when the phone rang, having decided to have an early night for a change. He'd been asleep for about an hour and was surprised to see that it was only a quarter past twelve when he switched on the light and reached for the phone on the table at his bedside. He listened to Machin's news in silence, then said:

'You'd better have a talk with him and I'll join you as soon as I can. It may prove useful having him and the boy under the same roof. You might be able to do a bit of cross-checking – provided the boy is readier to talk. Do you think he will be?'

'I've not yet spoken to him myself, sir, but I gather he's still saying nothing. His sister may be able to get something out of him. I brought her with me.'

'Was that fortuitous or by design?'

'I don't follow you, sir.'

'How come you have Miss Bostock with you?'

'I happened to have dinner with her tonight.'

'Ah!'

'And I said I'd drive her up to town to collect Kenny.'

'Mmn, I see. Most convenient.'

After he had rung off, Page sat for a minute on the edge of his bed, staring morosely at a dirty mark on the opposite wall. Why couldn't Shem have waited a few more months before getting himself murdered! Then it would have been his successor's pleasure to be called out at all hours and to clamber through thickets and around dank caves, and to ask endless questions and receive an encyclopaedia of conflicting information. He telephoned the station for a car and began to dress. As he did so, his spirits rose. After all, the man he most wanted to see in connection with the case had been found. The end could be in sight.

Machin found Farmer sitting in a sparsely furnished room which was used for interviews. It contained a bare table and four hard chairs. Sergeant Cumnor who took him there made the introductions and said:

'I'll go and see if I can rustle up some tea.'

Machin sat down and pulled out a packet of cigarettes. He proffered it to Brian who took one.

'I gather you know why you've been brought here?'

'I haven't been brought here. I came on my own. Or rather I was asked to come and I came.'

'I'm sorry. I didn't mean to . . .'

'So I came here voluntary like, didn't I?'

'Sure. Now, I want to ask you a few questions. When were you last in Long Gaisford?'

Their eyes met before Brian flicked his gaze away.

'Three years ago,' he said in a curiously subdued tone.

'Not more recently?'

'Not that I remember.'

'Well, it's something you would remember, isn't it?'

'I expect so.'

'And do you?'

'I don't think so.'

'Where were you on Tuesday and Wednesday last week?'

'In London, I think.'

'You only think?'

'That's right.'

'Might you have been in Long Gaisford?'

'No.'

'Sure about that?'

'Yes.'

The answers came in the same unemphatic tone, as though he were living out a dream.

'Where've you been staying these past couple of weeks?'

'With a friend.'

'What address?'

'I don't want to say.'

'Why not?'

'Because I don't want him aggravated.'

'Why were you visiting your parents' home this evening?'

'Why shouldn't I?'

'You don't often go there, do you?'

Brian shrugged in reply.

'You know who Kenny Bostock is, don't you?'

'He's my cousin.'

'Seen him recently?'

'No.'

'Did you know he was here?'

Brian looked up sharply. 'What do you mean *here*?' His surprise appeared to be genuine.

'Here at this police station.'

'What for?' Brian asked, a puzzled frown on his face.

'He's been missing from home and was picked up wandering about London. If you ask me, I think he was trying to get in touch with you.'

For a full minute there was a silence, while Machin watched the transformation of Brian's expression from puzzled incomprehension to anxiety to blank wall. He quietly cursed himself. It looked as though mention of Kenny had been a tactical error.

'I said, I think he was trying to get in touch with you,' he repeated.

'I heard.'

'Well?'

'Well, what?'

'Do you think I'm right?'

'How should I know? I've not seen the kid since I left the village.'

Sergeant Cumnor came into the room carrying three mugs of tea. He raised a quizzical eyebrow at Machin who responded by turning down the corners of his mouth.

Machin looked across again at Brian who had seized the mug of tea with appreciation.

'Know who Shem is?'

'The old tramp?'

'Yes.'

'Yeah, I remember him. He's dead, isn't he?'

'How d'you know that?'

'Read it in the papers. And anyway, the young copper I came along here with mentioned it.'

'Oh!' Machin felt abashed and was not made more comfortable by the glance of sly amusement which Brian cast in his direction.

He rose and whispered to Sergeant Cumnor, 'I'm just going to have a word with the boy.'

The local officer nodded and Machin left the room. When he entered Sergeant Cumnor's office Susan gave him a look of relief. There was more than a touch of colour about her cheeks and she gave the impression of having reached her wits' end. Kenny was still sitting on the same chair and was glowering at anything which came within his vision.

Susan shook her head in answer to Machin's unspoken question. He turned to the boy with a sigh.

'Look, Kenny, it's time this nonsense stopped or you're going to find yourself in big trouble. Frustrating the police in a murder enquiry by withholding information is a very serious matter and the sooner that fact penetrates your stubborn little head, the better. I know why you came to London. It was to try and find your cousin Brian Farmer. He's at this station now, as you've discovered. What I propose to find out is why you wanted to see him?' He paused. 'Are you listening to me, Kenny?' he said fiercely.

Kenny's mouth trembled as though he was on the verge of tears.

'You can cry as much as you want,' Machin went on, 'but I'm going to get the truth out of you by one means or another. You've caused the hell of a lot of trouble and what you need is a bloody good thrashing, which is what you'll probably get if you don't decide to answer my questions.'

'Kenny, you must tell the police what you know,' Susan broke in urgently. 'You've got nothing to be afraid of. I promise that. Sergeant Machin just wants you to tell him what you know.' She walked across and stood beside him, putting an arm around his shoulders. 'Go on, love, do it for me and then we'll be able to go home – and you can come and stop at my place if you want.'

Kenny's head went forward and his whole body began to shake with uncontrollable sobbing. Susan gazed at him with heartfelt compassion and gently pulled his head against her side. Machin looked at them in mute despair.

'It's not my night,' he muttered helplessly. 'I shouldn't have torn into him like that. And yet . . .'

He rubbed a hand across his chin. It was still smooth and unbristled. For a second he was puzzled, then he remembered why he'd shaved that evening. That had turned out to be a waste of time, he reflected ruefully!

'He'll feel better after this,' Susan whispered.

For a couple of minutes the only sound in the room came

from Kenny. It was, moreover, a heartrending sound, which made Machin feel a wretch. But God knows they'd tried every other approach to get him to talk, so that a head-on verbal blast had seemed the only remaining expedient. He might yet begin to talk, but if he wouldn't, it didn't seem that any further means of persuasion were available. At the same time, Machin knew from experience that there was scarcely a living person – let alone a twelve-year-old boy – who couldn't be coaxed into talking. It was all a question of finding the right key. This was an almost universal truth which applied to the whole human race, including hardened criminals. It was the conscience's safety valve, provided by a Providence responsible for the original design.

Slowly, Kenny's sobs abated and came under control. Since he didn't have a handkerchief, Machin passed over his own – a minor act of atonement for having caused the breakdown in the first place.

'Feeling better?' he enquired, after Kenny had noisily blown his nose and wiped his face.

'Yes.' The tone, however, was not that of someone propitiated.

'Can we start talking again?' he asked in a cajoling voice.

Kenny shook his head.

'Do you mean you'd like a bit more time?'

'I don't want to talk. You can do what you like to me, but I won't talk.'

'Are you afraid of something? There has to be a reason for your refusing to say what's on your mind.'

But Kenny just stared ahead of him through puffy eyes and Machin realised he was as far away as ever from learning anything. It was a moment of enormous frustration. Here were he and Farmer in rooms within a few yards of one another, unable to communicate but each maintaining a wall of silence. The trouble was that the police were groping around in the dark. Without more precise information, it was impossible to apply pressure in the right place. There was something between the two of them, but what?

Shortly before half past one, Page arrived. By this time Kenny had fallen asleep, wrapped in a blanket, and Susan was dozing in the same room.

Machin gave him a quick résumé of his abortive interviews and said, 'If you agree, sir, I think we ought to send Susan and the boy back to Arlebury in your car and I can drive you back in mine when we've finished here, which mayn't be for a while.'

Page nodded. 'Go ahead and arrange that, will you. From what you say, we're not going to get anything out of the boy tonight and, therefore, the sooner he's out of the way, the better.'

Five minutes later, Machin escorted Susan and Kenny to the patrol car and instructed the driver to take them to Susan's flat.

'I'll call you tomorrow,' he whispered to her as he helped her into the back of the car. 'It hasn't been quite the evening I'd planned.'

She gave him a tired smile.

'Thanks for the dinner, Peter. It seems like a hundred years ago now.'

The driver had bent forward to search for something beneath his seat and Machin seized the opportunity to brush his lips against her cheek as she was getting in.

When he returned inside the station, he found Page and Sergeant Cumnor in the latter's office. Page was nibbling at a piece of loose skin at the side of his thumb and looking generally glum.

'I don't see how we can hold him,' he observed. 'It doesn't sound as though he's going to make any admissions and we certainly don't have enough evidence to charge him.'

'When are we going to get the lab findings on the stuff from the cave, sir?'

'Stevens only took it in today – yesterday – or wherever we are,' he said gloomily.

'Of course, if they do find anything which links Farmer

with the cave, then we're a big step forward, seeing that he denies being there.'

'We can't possibly hold him until we get a lab report. It'll be days, at least.'

'Incidentally, sir, I've got the butt of the cigarette he smoked while I was talking to him before you came. It may be useful as a control sample.'

Page nodded approvingly.

'You might have learnt something if you'd put him in with the boy and listened outside,' Sergeant Cumnor said in the silence which followed.

'A boy of twelve and at one o'clock in the morning,' Page remarked in a faintly scandalised tone.

Sergeant Cumnor shrugged. Some of these old country coppers still played it like a game of cricket, he thought. But it was their investigation, not his!

'Of course I'll have a talk to him myself, but I don't see that we're going to be able to do other than let him go in the end. Assuming he doesn't make a sudden confession, which seems unlikely.' Page's expression brightened. 'Unless, of course, we can find something else to pin on him. Has he been searched by any chance?'

'No, sir.'

'Well, we might test his co-operation a bit further,' Page went on, 'by inviting him to turn out his pockets. Who knows what mayn't be revealed! An offensive weapon, perhaps, or even a trace of cannabis!'

Sergeant Cumnor looked at the provincial superintendent with surprise and a gleam of respect.

Brian Farmer jumped to his feet as soon as the officers came into the room in which he had been left alone for the past fifteen minutes.

'I'm going,' he said in a truculent tone. 'You've got no right to keep me here.'

'I'm Detective Superintendent Page from Arlebury,' Page said, as though Brian had never spoken. 'I'm investigating the murder of an old tramp known as Shem ...'

'And I don't know nothing about it,' Brian broke in. 'I've already told him that.' He gestured at Machin.

'When were you last in Long Gaisford?'

'How many more times! I haven't been there for years, not since I left home.'

'Do you know a cave in Harrier's Wood just outside the village?' Page asked, his questions coming with the inexorability of waves breaking on the seashore.

An expression of the utmost wariness passed across Brian's face.

'Yeah, I believe there is a cave there,' he said.

'Have you ever been in it?'

'I may have been when I was a kid.'

'*May* have?'

'Yeah, *may* have.'

'You either have or you haven't!'

'I don't remember every place I've ever been.'

'Have you been in it since you were a kid?'

'Why do you want to know?'

'Because somebody has been in it quite recently and I wondered if it was you?'

'Why should you wonder if it were me?'

'Because I don't think many people knew of its existence, that's why.'

Brian made a scoffing sound.

'Lots of kids used to play there. Anyway, what's it matter!'

'You still haven't answered my question. Have you been there recently?'

'Not that I remember,' he said after a pause, looking up defiantly.

'You'd remember if you had been there, surely?'

'Possibly: possibly not.'

'You're not being very helpful, are you?'

'Why should I be! Anyway, I've had enough of this, I'm leaving.' He moved towards the door.

'Mind turning out your pockets?' Page enquired politely.

'Too right, I mind.'

'Sorry, boy,' Sergeant Cumnor broke in. 'According to information, you may have a weapon on you.'

'What bloody information!'

'Doesn't matter what information! Let's have your pockets out.'

'You've no right.'

'Let's have less talk and a bit more co-operation,' Sergeant Cumnor said, gently pushing him back towards the desk.

'Take your bloody hands off me!'

'Tch! That's no way to talk. Come on, now, empty those pockets.'

Slowly, and with extreme reluctance, Brian produced the contents of his pockets, placing the items on the desk. A packet of cigarettes, a cheap lighter, a ball-point pen, a wallet which was coming apart at its seams, four and eightpence in loose change. Page watched each movement as his hand went from pocket to desk and back again. Watched and waited...

'Is that the lot?' Sergeant Cumnor asked.

Brian passed a tongue across his lips and nodded.

'Sure?'

'Yes.'

'Mind if I have a look?'

Brian gave him a hard stare. 'Go ahead.'

Sergeant Cumnor stood in front of him and ran deft, practised hands over the outside of his clothing.

'Seems as though that is everything,' he remarked, turning to Page.

Brian gave them a triumphant smirk. 'And now perhaps you'll let me go. Nobody can say I haven't assisted the police in their enquiries.'

'Don't push it, boy,' Sergeant Cumnor growled.

Page let his glance go down Brian's jeans to the boots whose tops disappeared up inside them.

'Take off your boots,' he said.

The smirk abruptly left Brian's face and was replaced by an angry snarl.

'Why the bloody hell . . .'

'Go on, do as you're told,' Sergeant Cumnor said, moving closer towards him.

It was in the left boot that the discovery was made. A sheath knife neatly taped on the inner side. Sergeant Cumnor pulled it out and examined it.

'What do you carry this around for?' he asked.

'I use it in my work,' Brian replied sullenly.

Sergeant Cumnor grinned. 'What's that? Blowing up balloons? You're booked, my boy. A nastier bit of offensive weapon, I've not seen for a long while.' He winked at Page and Machin who had been observing the scene in silence. It was Sergeant Cumnor's manor and this part of the game was his.

Dawn broke while the two provincial officers were driving back to Arlebury. Page couldn't help reflecting that the poets who waxed with such romantic eloquence over this particular hour of the day must surely have become less enchanted if they had seen as many dawns as he had. He even wondered if some of them had ever seen one.

As it happened, Machin's feelings were much the same, though on a slightly more mundane level. If you had to see a dawn in, then there were better companions than your Detective Superintendent.

XVIII

Brian had appeared before a magistrate, charged with possession of an offensive weapon, and been remanded in custody for seven days, before Mick Edmunds heard what had happened.

When he did hear, he became angrier than anyone had seen him for a long time.

It was almost exactly twenty-four hours later that he and his two companions sat in the same room in which the four of them had conferred the day before.

'I only left him for a few minutes and he bloody 'as to wander off,' he said in a vicious tone.

'Where'd he go?'

'Christ knows! All we do know is that he got himself nicked and came up at court this morning and now 'e's at Brixton for the next seven days.'

'Don't know why he wanted to carry that boy-scout knife of his,' the shorter of the other two remarked. 'You couldn't sharpen a pencil with it.'

'Bloody police'll call a pencil an offensive weapon if it suits them,' Edmunds said.

'So what are we going to do?' the taller one asked, without looking up from the task of cleaning his nails.

'Stop poking at our nails for a start! What is that thing you're playing with, anyway?'

The nail-cleaner flicked the object on to the table. 'It's Brian's lucky tooth,' he said with a laugh. 'No wonder he got picked up. He didn't have it on him.'

Edmunds picked it up and glared. 'What flipping animal is it meant to come from?'

'A badger.'

'Well, sod all badgers!'

They laughed and the tension which had been building up was suddenly released. Edmunds went on:

'We've got seven days to find out exactly what's 'appened. Seven days to debrief Brian, as they say in the old spy circles, and seven days to rebrief him.'

'That shouldn't be too difficult. Not with him being on remand and at Brixton which is like a ruddy transit camp.'

'I suggest we see him as soon as possible, before anyone else gets at him.'

'Who?'

'I don't know. How do we know anything until we find out from him exactly what's happened.'

'The question is, who's going to visit him?' Edmunds said. 'Not me, for obvious reasons. And it'd be better if it weren't either of you. We've got to be careful about this.'

'What about Sandy? We can trust her.'

'Yes, I was thinking of Sandy. It's a good idea.' Edmunds glanced towards the taller man, who said:

'O.K., I'll fetch her along this evening.'

'Then she can go down to the prison tomorrow.'

'What's Brian likely to collect for this lot?' the shorter man asked.

'He ought to get away with a fine. He might even get probation. But you never know with some of these beaks. And it all depends on 'ow 'ard the police put the boot in. The whole thing could be a bloody fix. That's what we've got to find out – and quick.'

XIX

The next few days, though outwardly the scene of little activity, saw a good deal of coming and going behind the settled facade. Comings and goings which led to meetings; meetings which, in turn, gave birth to decisions; decisions, which, for their part, were to affect a number of people in a vital way. The fact that these decisions were destined to create further complications for others was also inevitable.

It was three days after Brian Farmer had been remanded in custody that Page and Machin drove one morning to the forensic science laboratory to learn at first-hand the results of the examination of all the carefully collected, packaged and labelled items which Detective Constable Stevens had handed over.

Their visit had been preceded by the usual fight to persuade the laboratory liaison officer that their case was more important and pressing than any of the dozens of others being currently considered by the overworked and understaffed team of scientific experts, upon whose single word a man's liberty could so often hang.

The liaison officer, part of whose job it was to protect the laboratory staff from unnecessary pressures, was used to being lobbied, cajoled and even misled – in fact, everything except actually bribed. However, when Page had explained how vital it was to know the results of the lab examination before Farmer's remand appearance, he had said he would do what he could. And three days later he had phoned to say that if they cared to call, he could give them the results, though it would be a while yet before a full written report could be expected. Since this was the usual routine, Page had thanked him, got hold of Machin and set off for the laboratory within thirty minutes.

The liaison officer greeted them with the slight reserve of one whose life is spent fending off the dissatisfied and the importunate. He had a sheaf of notes on loose pieces of paper before him.

'I suppose I'd better try and give you this in some sort of order,' he said, shuffling the notes with an air of resigned duty. 'Shall we start with blood?'

'Suits me,' Page remarked, while Machin got ready to make his own notes of the findings.

'The deceased's blood was group AB,' the liaison officer began in a dull monotone, his eye flicking over the pages of notes as he spoke, 'and, in fact, we've found no blood of any other group on any of the items. However, there were traces of blood on the collar of the deceased's coat, and on the sample of earth marked JS 12 – that's the sample from the scene of the crime.'

'Isn't it the sample from where the body was found?' Machin enquired, looking up.

'Aren't they the same place?'

'We think almost certainly not,' Page broke in. 'Everything indicates that the body was moved after death.'

'Ah!' The liaison officer grunted. 'Anyway. JS 12 is the sample from where the body was found and, as I say, it bore traces of blood of the deceased's group.' He glanced quickly over the notes again. 'There doesn't seem to be a weapon referred to.'

'We've never found one.'

'And that appears to be about all the traces of blood we've discovered,' he said slowly, his eye still moving up and down the sheets of paper he held in his hand. 'No, hang on a moment ... trouble is trying to decipher someone else's scrawl ... never yet met a scientist who could write, they're worse than doctors ... yes, there is a further reference to blood here. Some was found on the sample of earth taken from ... floor of cave, is it?' Page nodded and leant forward expectantly. 'But it wasn't sufficient to group,' the liaison officer added in a matter-of-fact tone, apparently unaware of the sense of anti-climax his news induced. 'And that really is the lot about blood. Now what else is there? A button! Yes, that's it, the button found in the cave had thread adhering to it which matched thread from the deceased's coat where a button was missing. That seems fairly conclusive,' he added, looking up.

'It definitely associates Shem with the cave,' Page observed, 'and, together with the blood trace, confirms my suspicion that he was killed there. The question is why did someone go to the trouble of taking his body and dumping it on the other side of the village.'

'If the murderer had left it in the cave,' Machin said, 'the odds are that it might never have been found. So it almost looks as if someone wanted it to be discovered.'

'There's certainly logic in that,' Page agreed. 'But people aren't always motivated by logic.'

'You can say that again,' the liaison officer remarked. 'I don't know why we spend so much time attributing logic to criminals. They're more irrational than most of us. Oh, I know all about patterns of behaviour,' he went on, 'but how often is a so-called pattern of behaviour one hundred per cent complete? Never! There's always one bit, at least, which doesn't fit. And it doesn't fit because the person concerned suddenly swerved off the great highway of logical behaviour. Most people don't know half the time why they act as they do ... not even police officers!'

Page, who had been listening with a polite expression, now said, 'One thing for sure, however, you don't hump dead bodies about the countryside without having some very good reason.'

The liaison officer, who appeared to have exhausted his interest in the subject, merely grunted and turned back to his notes.

'So much for the button! Four cigarette ends, items JS 13, 14, 15 and 20,' he read out. 'Saliva tests indicate that, of these numbers 13, 14 and 20 were all smoked by the same person.'

'Farmer,' Machine said excitedly to Page. 'Thirteen and fourteen were the two from the cave. Twenty is the one he smoked in my presence at the police station. That means he lied about not having recently been to the cave.'

'He said he didn't remember having been there,' Page corrected.

'Because he knew he had been and that we might be able to prove it. In so far as it wasn't an admission, it was a denial and now we can prove it to be a lie.'

'We need something else,' Page said, shaking his head.

'What, sir?'

'Just one further bit of evidence to connect him not so much with the cave but with Shem and the crime.'

Machin pulled a face. 'His clothing is not going to reveal anything after all this time.'

'Nevertheless, I think we should get hold of it.'

'We don't even know that what he's wearing in Brixton is what he had on when he was in the cave.'

Page pursed his lips in thought.

The liaison officer who had listened to this exchange with an expression of mild impatience now broke in. 'The fourth cigarette, JS 15, had been smoked by a different person, probably the deceased.'

'So we have a button and a cigarette end linking Shem with the cave and two cigarette ends which link Farmer with it. All we need is something to link Shem and Farmer together...' Page's voice drifted away as he fell into a frowning silence.

'It's possible we could help you there,' the liaison officer said.

'How?' Page said, looking up sharply.

'Quite a few hairs were found on the deceased's clothing. They're not his, but without any control samples we can't identify them.'

Page's expression was dubious. 'From the sort of places he was accustomed to sleeping in, I should think they're mostly animal hairs.'

'Some of them are, though one or two have the appearance of being human. If you can let us have a control sample of your suspect's head hair we'll make the further tests.'

'I noticed when I saw him at the station that he had loose hairs on his jacket collar,' Machin said excitedly, 'which means that he's one of those people who does shed hairs.'

The liaison officer glanced sourly at Machin's own well-groomed and strongly-rooted hair as he dusted his own shoulders with a hand.

'It's certainly well worth following up,' Page remarked. 'We'll go along to the prison right away and find out about his clothing at the same time.'

The liaison officer bade them a cursory farewell with the air of one who has tired of dispensing his favours, which came near to being the truth. He was efficient, but general disenchantment with life had removed any inclination to provide service with a smile.

However, neither Page nor Machin were in any mood to pass comment on this as they drove hopefully in the direction of Brixton prison.

XX

Kenny's return home had not been marked by any emotional atmosphere of forgiveness and reconciliation such as often accompanies such occasions.

Susan had failed completely to get him to talk and his parents had received him without either welcome or recrimination. His father had wanted to lay into him both verbally and physically, but had been dissuaded by his wife and daughter. His mother had wanted to talk to him about what had happened but hadn't known how. So Kenny had settled back, silent and withdrawn, in an atmosphere of greater estrangement than before.

Ray and Leo had called round on the day after his return and Kenny had gone with them to the quarries. Not the area where Shem had been found, but over on the farther side.

Ray had been eager to hear all about Kenny's escapade and had plugged him with questions. He had been dashed, and not a little hurt, however, when Kenny's reaction had, first, been snappish and then one of surly silence. He was bewildered by the change which had come over his friend. He could never have believed that Kenny would actually look at him with suspicion and hostility as though he were just another interfering grown-up.

On the next day when he had called round to see if Kenny would join him, he had received a direct rebuff. No, Kenny didn't want to come out, he preferred to remain on his own. After that, Ray didn't try again. If Kenny could manage without him, he could certainly get along without Kenny. Particularly as it was he who owned Leo. And Leo's mood, unlike Kenny's, was one of unvarying and buoyant friendliness.

It was on the day when Page and Machin visited the laboratory that Kenny set off in mid-morning on one of his now brooding meanders. He avoided the quarries where he knew that he would be bound to run into Ray and made his way to the field where he had met Shem that evening which now seemed a lifetime ago.

He was sitting against the same hedge not more than five yards from where Shem had been sitting when he suddenly felt that he was being watched. It was no more than a feeling since a quick look round failed to confirm anyone's presence. But it persisted, so that he got up and walked farther on until he reached a small copse. He entered the copse and sat down just inside from where he could look out. If anyone was trying to watch him, they wouldn't be able to continue without his knowledge.

For a couple of minutes nothing happened and then a man suddenly appeared through a gap in the hedge about fifty yards away. He was a large, strong-looking man whom Kenny had never seen before. He was dressed in fawn slacks, a dark blue shirt buttoned at the neck and a light beige jacket.

Kenny shrank back a little farther into the friendly cover of the wood, while the man looked about him and scratched his head. Then his gaze fastened on the copse and he began to walk slowly towards it. He was only ten yards away when he stopped and stared straight at where Kenny was crouching. Kenny held his breath. It seemed that the man must see him and yet, quite obviously, he didn't for, after a few seconds, his gaze roamed over the field which lay to the left of the copse.

Kenny bit his lip to try and stop the trembling which begun to seize his limbs. There was something quietly confident about the man, apart from his powerful build, which was intimidating. And there were just the two of them alone in the stillness of the autumn countryside. He had no doubt whatsoever that the man had been watching him before he moved his position and, a more chilling thought, that it was he, Kenny Bostock – and not anyone else – who was the definite object of interest.

What happened next took Kenny completely by surprise. Whatever he'd expected, it certainly wasn't to hear his name called out. Called out, moreover, in a quiet and friendly manner.

'Kenny! Can you 'ear me, Kenny? I want to talk to you, Kenny.'

The man looked hopefully about him, but Kenny remained where he was. How was he to know that this wasn't some trap! His instinct at this moment was that of an animal. Fear was still predominant, though admittedly not as strong as it had been before the man had called out.

While rational thought was beginning to filter into his mind, the man called out again.

'Kenny! If you can 'ear me, Kenny, come out. I'm not going to 'urt you. I'm a friend of Brian's.'

A friend of Brian's!

'It's Brian what sent me,' he added, as Kenny began to crawl out of his hiding-place.

The man's glance swung sharply to where the sound of crackling undergrowth indicated his presence.

As Kenny stood up and faced him, the man's face broke into a friendly smile.

'I'd never 'ave seen you in there,' he said admiringly. He held out his hand. 'My name's Mick Edmunds and I'm a friend of Brian's.'

They shook hands, Kenny keeping his eyes fixed all the time on the other's face, as though seeking some irrebuttable token of good faith.

Suddenly Edmunds thrust his free hand into his pocket and pulled out something. Holding it out for Kenny to see, he said:

'Brian said to show you this old tooth, Kenny. Then you'd know I was really 'is friend.'

For the first time since Shem's death, the tense, wary expression lifted from Kenny's face. He looked up at Edmunds with hope and eagerness shining in his eyes. An enemy had become an ally, a doubter had been converted and was now a disciple.

Edmunds noted the change of expression with relief and a certain amount of mild surprise. It had been a pushover. He wasn't used to such easy capitulations. He was a fighter who was accustomed to having to use his greater strength to get his way. More often than not he did get his way, the question merely being the degree of fight required to achieve it. But here was someone looking at him as though he were a modern saviour. Respect was something he exacted from his converts, simple faith had never before been voluntarily accorded him.

His smile broadened into a grin.

'Where can we talk?' he asked. He glanced at the dense undergrowth from which Kenny had just emerged. 'Do you think I could get in there, too?'

Kenny nodded. 'It's clearer once you're through that lot. Shall I go first?'

'You do just that, Kenny boy,' Edmunds said with a laugh.

After Kenny had crawled through, he turned to watch Edmunds make the last few yards, bent double and waving his arms ahead of him like a lobster's feelers. He arrived at Kenny's side and straightened up, brushing leaves and twigs from his clothing.

He gave Kenny a grin.

'You're better at that sort of thing than I am, Kenny boy. I likes feeling an 'ard pavement under my feet.' He glanced about him. 'What about propping ourselves against that old tree?'

He went and sat down and Kenny squatted beside him on his haunches, his attention riveted on this large man who exuded good humour and confidence. If Brian was in trouble, he seemed just the sort of friend he would need. And all Kenny was waiting to hear was what was required of himself.

Edmunds fixed Kenny with a clear, steady look. 'Brian's in trouble, Kenny boy, and you and I 'ave got to 'elp 'im. 'E's relying on us.' Kenny nodded. ' 'E's in the nick charged with possessing an offensive weapon, but that's only part of 'is trouble. The police are after 'im for something bigger than that. They want to 'ave 'im for murder.' Kenny licked his lips which felt suddenly dry. There was something hypnotic about the big man's manner. Though clearly unused to sitting propped against trees with his legs stuck out in front of him and consequently presenting a figure of restless squirms and wriggles, his gaze, which never wavered from Kenny's face, and his quiet, slightly gravelly, voice compelled attention. 'The thing is,' he went on, ' 'ow you and I can best 'elp 'im, Kenny boy.' He put out a hand and rested it firmly on Kenny's thigh. 'Let's start by you telling me everything you know about poor old Brian's trouble, O.K.?'

Kenny nodded.

'Fine. Off you go then, Kenny boy, I'm all ears. And mind you tell me everything. Everything, Kenny boy.'

XXI

Sergeant Machin sat in the poky room at Arlebury police station which he shared with another detective sergeant, trying to decide which of several matters merited the greater attention.

There had been a breaking at Yates Garage the previous night and £46 had been stolen. It didn't sound a particularly professional job and the indications were that it had been committed by an escapee from Borstal who had been briefly seen in the Arlebury area before disappearing from sight again. Then there was a complaint by an indignant mother that her daughter had been indecently assaulted by the art teacher at her school. He had already taken a statement from the girl who was clearly infatuated with the bearded giant who taught her art and had, Machin was sure, exaggerated whatever had happened, if indeed anything had. Her motive might be anything from a woman scorned to hopeful anticipation. And a psychiatrist would be able to conjure up a great many others. The teacher, whom Machin had interviewed the previous evening, had expressed himself forcibly about the allegation.

'It's the occupational hazard of my job if you're teaching girls of fourteen and fifteen,' he had said. 'You've only got to rest a hand on their shoulders and some of them hope you're going to commit rape – and are ready to say you have, anyway. As for Eileen Spragg, the sooner she gives up art and finds some boy to lay her, the better for everyone. But I can assure you it won't be me who provides the service.'

'She says you touched her thigh and then ran your hand up her leg and felt her private parts over the top of her panties,' Machin had said in a matter-of-fact tone.

'I wish she showed as much imagination in her art work.'

'Is that all you want to say about it?' he had enquired, pencil poised over notebook.

The art master had run a hand through his hair in a gesture of exasperation.

'No, it isn't. I must take it seriously. I've got a job and wife and kids to think of. But this sort of suggestion makes me bloody mad. I'm twenty-eight and happily married and I haven't stuck my hands up girls' skirts since I was at school myself.' He had sighed. 'What in fact happened was that I was standing beside her, bending over to show her how to make a cloud look like a cloud rather than a map of

Scotland when a pencil rolled off her desk on to the floor –
for all I know she did it deliberately. Anyway, when I bent
down to pick it up, she pulled her skirt back exposing a
great slab of thigh and shifted her position so that my hand
touched against her leg as I stood up again.'

'You say "her leg", do you mean "her thigh"?' Machin
had asked, remorselessly.

'Yes, very well, her thigh,' the art teacher had conceded
wearily.

'Do you want to make a written statement about it?
You're not obliged to, but . . .'

He had decided that he would make a statement and it
had been taken down there and then.

Machin now read it through twenty-four hours later. He
hadn't any doubt which version of events he believed, but
duty still required him to complete the enquiry. This would
entail interviewing other members of the class who might
have witnessed the incident and probing, to some extent
anyway, the background of the two participants.

He had just picked up a third docket relating to the sixth
case of attempted arson within four months at a toy factory
on the outskirts of town when the phone rang. For a moment, he didn't answer it while he reflected grimly on the
catastrophe which was inevitable unless they could detect
the person responsible before his attempts were translated
into reality. He must be an employee, certainly male and
equally certainly unhinged. But beyond that he might be
either someone with a grudge against his employers or
someone suffering from the curious aberration which links
arson with sexual satisfaction.

The phone rang again and Machin hauled his thoughts
away from the burrows down which they were darting like
an eager terrier.

'Detective Sergeant Machin,' he announced into the receiver.

'Is that you, Peter? This is Susan Bostock.'

'Hello, Susan,' he said in a cheerful tone. 'How are

things?'

'It's about Kenny. He's disappeared again.' She sounded both anxious and apprehensive.

'When did this happen?' he asked quickly.

'He went out this morning and nobody's seen him since.'

'When should he have been back?'

'Dinner-time . . . I mean lunch-time mid-day.'

'Any idea where he went?'

'No. He just wandered off on his own apparently, the way he does these days.'

'Somebody must have seen him!'

'Mum's asked everyone and they haven't.'

'Has she tried Mr Shelley? He seems to live in his window watching all the comings and goings. Meanwhile, I'll get on to the bus company and see if they remember having him as a passenger. He's probably run off to London again.'

'Do you really think so?'

'Don't you?'

'I don't know, Peter. I'm terribly worried about him. He's been acting so strangely . . . I even wondered whether he might have . . . well, killed himself.'

'I should think that's extremely unlikely,' Machin said robustly. 'Boys his age don't go in for suicide unless they're really round the bend. And there's been nothing to indicate that your brother's that way. No, my firm bet is that he's run off again. Anyway, I'll put out all the necessary messages and I'm sure we'll find him again soon. Only next time you'd better chain him to the kitchen stove.' He glanced at his watch. It showed a quarter past eight. 'Where are you speaking from?'

'The call-box opposite where I live.'

'Eaten yet?'

'Yes.'

'Pity.'

'Why?'

'I was going to suggest we went out and had a bite.'

'I could always drink a cup of coffee while you ate.'

'Great! Give me half an hour to get all this under way and I'll be round. I might even have news for you by then.'

But he hadn't; and all he could do was to reassure her of his certainty that Kenny would turn up again safe and sound.

'Can you bear to watch me eat a steak at Jock's?' he asked, as he started up the engine and engaged first gear in one swift movement. 'It's only an ordinary café, the chairs are hard and the tables usually need a wipe down, but the food's good, provided you stick to steak and chips, and Jock brews the best cup of tea in town. Though I wouldn't recommend his coffee if you're particular about having something that tastes of coffee.'

Susan gave a small laugh, but he could tell that it was more of a mindless reaction than an indication of rapport.

When they were seated in the café and Jock had bustled away to attend to their order, Machin leaned across the table and took her hand in his.

'You really are worried about that brother of yours, aren't you?' he said in a voice which reflected sympathy.

She nodded and gave him a fleeting smile. 'Yes, I am. It's so unlike him . . . it's . . .'

'It may be unlike the Kenny before Shem's death, but it's part of the only Kenny I know,' he broke in. 'I agree something's got into him. That stands out a mile. Something which has to do with Shem's death and also with Brian Farmer.' He paused. 'Is it going to upset you very much if your cousin is charged with murder?'

For several seconds she stared over his shoulder with unseeing eyes.

'Not because I have any particular feeling about Brian,' she said, at length, slowly, 'but the fact that he's a relation and once lived in the village is going to mean all sorts of gossip and publicity and I certainly don't look forward to that.'

'It mayn't be as bad as you fear.'

'Is he definitely going to be charged?'

'I can't say. It depends on evidence. It won't be my decision, anyway.' He spoke quickly, as though dismissing the subject. He must be more careful what he said. He had no right to discuss the propects of a charge, even with Susan in view of her links with the case. The trouble was that he felt he'd known her much longer than he had; that she was someone to whom he could open up without any thought of breach of confidence. Luckily she showed no inclination to follow up the subject – and, indeed, returned to the one which was uppermost in her own mind.

'But if Kenny has run away again like last time, where's he gone? You see, Peter, it can't be like last time, because then he was looking for Brian – or so we think – but now Brian's in prison. And if he's not trying to get in touch with Brian, what *is* he trying to do?' She gazed at him intently as though searching for an answer to her questions.

The trouble was that the same doubts were nagging Machin's mind and had been ever since she had telephoned him.

'In the first place,' he said, giving her hand a confident squeeze, 'we may have been wrong about the reason for his running away the first time. And even if we're not, it's quite on the cards that he's gone off to try and get in touch with him now. In fact, I'll ring the prison as soon as I get back to the station and find out if he's been there.'

Susan looked doubtful. 'Do you think that's possible?'

'Anything seems possible with your brother!'

'You don't think he could be in any danger?'

'What sort of danger?'

She shook her head helplessly. 'I don't know.'

'Nor do I! So forget about danger and watch me eat this steak. Like a bit?'

She smiled. 'No thanks.' Then: 'You're right about Jock's tea.'

Machin cut off a juicy piece of steak, covered it with mustard, added as many chips as the fork would hold and popped the lot quickly into his mouth.

'Best nosh there is!' he murmured with satisfaction as he prepared the next forkful.

It wasn't long before his plate was bare. At one moment while she had watched him eating, Susan had found herself wondering what it would be like to feed him as a permanent feature of life. She had, in fact, been indulging in such fantasies since their first meeting. To set eyes on him was sufficient to start up an itchy tingling in her veins. Even though he had done no more than hold her hand and brush her cheek in a butterfly kiss, her imagination had increasingly led her to wallow mentally in more sensual physical contact.

'A penny for your thoughts?' he said suddenly.

She blushed. She could hardly tell him that she had been picturing herself in bed with him: that she had (though this was something her mind didn't yet formally acknowledge) picked him as the man to whom she wished to give herself, never having done so to any man before.

'Come on,' he said with a grin, 'they looked interesting thoughts!'

She blushed further. 'I can't even remember them now,' she said.

'Liar!' His tone was good-humoured. 'Shall I tell you what I believe you were thinking about?'

'Yes.'

'And you'll tell me if I'm right?'

'No.'

'Then there's no point. It's not playing fair if you won't tell me.'

'All right,' she said slowly, experiencing a delicious small frisson somewhere in the lower lumbar region.

'You will tell me?'

'Yes.'

'Promise?'

'Yes, promise.'

'You were thinking about me. Right?'

'Ye-es.'

He laughed. 'Do you want me to go on?'

'Not if you don't want to.'

'Oh, so it's a challenge is it?'

'Who started it?'

He laughed again happily. Then taking her hand, he pulled it towards him, holding it palm upward. 'Shall I tell your fortune instead?'

'Seriously?'

'But of course. I'm Madame Vera in disguise, didn't you know!' He bent forward to study the hand more closely. 'I see that you were born in a village not far from here about twenty two years ago. You have a father and mother still alive. You also have three older brothers who are all married and a much younger brother of whom you are very fond. Correct so far?'

'Now tell me something which isn't in police records,' she said, looking gravely into his eyes.

He nodded and brought her hand closer under gaze.

'It says here that you're a very nice person, that you're kind and thoughtful and that you're a bit ... a bit old-fashioned.' He looked up with a quizzical smile. 'Right?'

'In what way am I meant to be old-fashioned?' she asked suspiciously.

'You don't do things just because others do. You have a sense of values. In fact, you're an individual and not just a mini-skirted sheep. How right am I?'

She pouted. 'You make me sound priggish.'

'You're certainly not that. I don't see any lines indicating priggishness here.'

'And goody-goody,' she added.

He gave her a wry look. 'I hope you're not goody-goody,' he said. 'Shall I give your hand another reading in a week's time?'

'No, tell me more now.'

'What do you particularly want to know?'

'Am I going ... going to get married?'

'Oh, certainly.'

'How soon?'

'I think it requires a more advanced reader than I to answer that.'

'And have children?' She felt suddenly light-headed and reckless. It was as if Jock's tea had contained properties which released her inhibitions.

'Yes, scads of them,' he said with a grin. 'You'll be worse than the old woman who lived in a shoe.'

'But she didn't have a husband.'

'There must have been a man in her life sometime! Anyway, not to worry, I'm pretty sure that this line here indicates you'll have a husband around the house to keep the children in order – and you, too.'

He quickly let go of her hand and glanced at his watch.

'Time I got back to the station. Maybe there'll be some news of Kenny. Then I'll drive you home afterwards.'

She was strangely silent as they drove through the near empty streets. Machin glanced at her once or twice and observed her expression of calm contentment. For the time being, at any rate, her anxiety about Kenny seemed to have abated. He hoped there'd be news of him when they reached the station.

'You'd better come in,' he said, as he parked in the small yard at the back. 'You can wait in my room. I'll pretend I've brought you in for grilling. After all, you are to do with the case.'

He led the way past the front desk, where he introduced Susan to the uniformed sergeant on duty, and up the narrow staircase at the back which provided a lesser used way to his office.

'Have a chair – the chair,' he said, as he stood aside for her to enter. His tone, while still friendly, was now brisker, almost as if the mantle of officialdom had fallen around his shoulders as soon as they passed inside the station.

He walked round to the front of his desk and riffled through the papers which had been put there while he'd been out. Susan watched him hopefully.

'Nothing here,' he said, half to himself. 'Let's make a few calls and see where we get.'

The first one was to the bus station where he learnt that no one answering Kenny's description had been seen by either of the two crews who had been plying the route between Arlebury and Long Gaisford that day.

A call to the railway station produced an equally negative response, though the man to whom he spoke was quick to point out that they couldn't be expected to remember every passenger who passed through in the course of a day; not even a twelve-year-old boy, since so many schoolchildren came in by train and poured out of the town again between four and five in the afternoon. Nevertheless, he had spoken to the booking clerks who'd been on duty and none of them recalled having sold a ticket to anyone who might have been Kenny. All the schoolchildren had season tickets, which added to the value of the clerks' recollection. Machin thanked him and rang off.

'He could have thumbed a lift, of course,' he said to Susan. 'Anyway, I'll now try the prison.'

But here again, he drew a nagative. It seemed that a twelve-year-old boy wouldn't have been allowed in as a visitor, anyway. Moreover, the officer to whom Machin spoke was sure he'd have heard if any such attempt had been made, even though he'd not been on duty in the earlier part of the day himself.

'Do we know how much money he had on him?' he asked Susan after he'd finished his round of telephone calls.

'It wouldn't have been very much. I didn't ask Mum when I spoke to her, but I doubt whether it would have been more than ten shillings at the very most.'

'That won't last him long. Indeed, it wouldn't even buy him a ticket to London. It seems as if he must have thumbed a lift. I'll get through to headquarters and we'll have a notice put out through the B.B.C. and the press. "Anyone who may have given a boy a lift . . ." something of that sort.' He looked at his watch. It was a quarter past ten.

'I reckon I'd better ring Mr Page and let him know the position.'

Page's relief was almost palpable once he gathered that Machin's call didn't require him to turn out himself that night. He had been sitting, slippers off, feet up, reading an article on the maturation of different sorts of honey when the telephone had rung. His sense of duty demanded that he answer it, but he had done so grudgingly and had found it impossible to keep a note of resentment out of his voice. He had listened to Machin in silence and at the end had spoken with the briskness of someone to whom a decision, for once, presented no problem.

'You'd better go out to Long Gaisford first thing in the morning, Sergeant, and see what you can find out about the boy's movements. That is, if he hasn't turned up by then.' Dryly, he added, 'You'll doubtless think it advisable to have a word with his sister.'

'Yes, sir,' Machin replied in a deadpan voice. 'Actually, it was she who reported the disappearance.'

'Ah! So you've possibly seen her already.'

'Yes, sir, I have.'

'I confess that when he has been found, my inclination will be to hold him upside down and shake him until there's nothing left inside. It's bad enough to be thwarted by someone his age, but when he's an active nuisance as well, something needs to be done.'

'I agree, sir.' He glanced across at Susan, but she didn't appear to be listening to the conversation with any measure of attention, which was just as well.

'With any luck, we'll soon have enough to charge Farmer and then, as far as I'm concerned, the boy can disappear for ever!'

Machin acknowledged this final simplification of the case with a neutral sort of grunt and Page rang off. He knew that the Detective Superintendent didn't really believe what he had said but that his eagerness to see the case disposed of lured him towards quick and easy solutions. He knew that when it came to the point, however, Page's natural caution and sense of duty would be in command as they always had been throughout his long police career.

He got up and came across to where Susan was sitting.

'Shall we go? Nothing more to be done here tonight. If we haven't heard anything by morning, I'm going out to Long Gaisford to make my own enquiries.'

She nodded. 'Was he very cross?'

'Who?'

'Mr Page. About Kenny.'

'No, he was just relieved that he hadn't got to turn out himself tonight. All he wants is a quiet life until he retires in a couple of months' time.'

'Do you like him?'

'Yes, I do. He's always been very fair to me and I've learnt a lot from him. He's a fine officer; it's just that since the amalgamation he's not been all that happy and what with his retirement coming up, anyway, he's lost a bit of his old steam. I'd be the same in his position.'

'He's not at all like I imagined a top detective to be.'

'He's not a TV character, if that's what you mean. Nor am I, I hope!'

She laughed. 'You could be for . . . for looks.'

'Watch it!'

When they had driven some distance from the station and away from the well-lit centre of town, Machin slowed down and, with his left arm, pulled her closer to him. A little farther on, he turned the car off the road and halted. As he leaned forward to switch off the lights, he felt her tremble slightly. A second later, his lips were on hers and he was kissing her with a fervour which transcended a mere physical lust. At first, her response was shy, but then she clung to him as if he was the last mortal on earth.

It was very late, indeed, when he dropped her outside her flat. As she held up her face for a last kiss, she didn't trust herself to speak – scarcely, even, to think.

As for Machin, he drove home feeling happier than he

had for a long time. It had been a wonderful, exhilarating evening, the more so for its unexpectedness. Never short of girl-friends, he realised that Susan had aroused in him feelings he had not previously experienced.

For the present, he was content to luxuriate in memories of the evening and had no desire to examine its implications.

XXII

Machin was aware of an overwhelming sense of euphoric well-being as soon as he woke up the next morning. Although he had had only four hours sleep, he felt alert and bright and full of confidence that the world was a very satisfactory place in which to live.

He ate an even larger breakfast than usual, looked in at the station soon after eight o'clock and ten minutes later was on his way to Long Gaisford.

He caught Mrs Bostock as she was about to leave the house on one of her numerous errands. It felt odd to be facing her so formally with last night's events brilliantly fresh in his memory: an air of unreality which was heightened when she addressed him as inspector and then apologised for not being able to remember his name. He had an urge to tell her that he wasn't just another policeman – an urge, however, which he quickly suppressed. It was as well to bear in mind the dangers of mixing business with pleasure, although that was, perhaps, already a little late in the day.

As it turned out, Mrs Bostock was able to add nothing to what he already knew. She had gone out the previous morning, leaving Kenny alone in the house, and hadn't returned until around five o'clock. The fact that he wasn't then in surprised, but didn't unduly worry, her. She had cooked a meal, expecting him back at any moment, but when he hadn't returned by seven she had gone to one or two neighbours' homes, only to discover that no one had seen him. It was shortly after this that she had phoned her daughter.

'I don't know what's got into him,' she remarked in a tone she might have used for commenting on an abrupt change in the weather. 'He's always been a perfectly normal boy until recently. All this running away. As if one didn't have enough things to worry about without him acting this way.'

Machin forebore to point out that she and her husband might care to consider their own responsibility for their son's recent conduct. He gathered that Mr Bostock was off again on one of his trips. It wasn't for him to sermonise, though he did wonder how they came to have a daughter of such apparently different outlook from themselves. She, alone, seemed to have any real affection for Kenny, and to care what happened to him for his own sake, as distinct from the sakes of those whose personal inconvenience was uppermost in their minds.

Mrs Bostock confirmed that her son was unlikely to have had more than a few shillings on him and she repeated again that she couldn't think what had got into him of late. Machin promised to keep her in touch with developments and they parted company on the pavement, she to go and clean up the vicarage, he to begin his round of enquiries. He shook his head resignedly as he walked away. It wasn't that she was an evil woman, or even, necessarily, a stupid one. She mightn't be a wholly selfish one, let alone a hardhearted one. It was just that so far as her youngest son was concerned she was an unminding one.

Machin turned into Mr Shelley's front gate, and saw the familiar figure sitting at the window. Mr Shelley smiled and gave a little wave as though he were awaiting an old friend. Machin responded with a formal nod and had to resist the urge to turn round and walk away. By the time he reached the door, Mr Shelley had opened it.

'Good morning, my friend, so the trail has brought you back to Long Gaisford. Come in and let me pour you a cup of tea. I have just made some fresh.'

He led the way into the small front parlour, which seemed more claustrophobic than before. Machin sat down on the edge of a chair and accepted the cup of tea which his host poured for him with elaborate fussiness.

'And how is your investigation going?' Mr Shelley enquired cheerfully as he gave himself a further cup.

'I've called to ask if you happened to see Kenny Bostock yesterday?'

'Ah yes, Kenny. He's disappeared again, I hear.'

'I wondered whether you'd seen him go past your house at any time yesterday?'

'No-o,' Mr Shelley said in a slowly thoughtful tone, 'I'm afraid I didn't see him at all yesterday, though I'm not surprised to hear he's gone off again.'

'Oh?'

Mr Shelley made a vague deprecating gesture with his hand. 'Please don't misunderstand me. It's not that I know anything; simply that if a boy runs away once, he's liable to run away again so long as the reason for his truancy remains.'

Machin pondered for a moment. 'It was you who first suggested that Brian Farmer had some part in all of this.'

Mr Shelley gave a small complacent nod. 'And I was right, wasn't I?'

'That still remains to be seen,' Machin replied, unwilling to crown the other's too obvious sense of self-satisfaction.

'I thought he was going to be charged with Shem's murder?'

'It's a question of evidence. No decision has been taken yet.'

'Well, evidence or no evidence, I think you'll agree that I put you on the right track?'

Machin pretended not to hear and said, 'Have you seen Kenny since he came back from running away the first time?'

'Yes.'

'To talk to?'

'Yes.'

Mr Shelley had an infuriating little smile on his face. It told Machin that if he wanted to know any more, he must sit up and beg for the information.

'Did he tell you anything which might be of interest to the police?' he asked stiffly.

Mr Shelley's voice bore a touch of malice as he said, 'I'm afraid he didn't seem to be very enamoured of the police.'

'We reciprocate the feeling.'

'I'm sure you must. It's understandable on both sides.'

'Why should he be anti-police?'

'Because you're after Brian Farmer, of course. He'll do anything he can to protect his cousin from trouble.'

'He told you that?'

'No, but it stands out further than ever.'

Machin decided that the interests of duty required him to swallow his pride and pander to Mr Shelley's smug omniscience.

'You've obviously thought quite a lot about the case and formed your own theories. I should be interested to hear what they are.'

Mr Shelley acknowledged the implied compliment with a nod.

'Yes, it's true that I have given the case considerable thought. Though my body may now be a trifle worn, I'm pleased to think that my mind is as keen as it ever was. And when one can't get out and about as much as one used to, inevitably it is the mind which receives the greater amount of exercise.' He seemed undeterred by Machin's glassy look as he went on, 'Of course, I've not only thought about the case but I've read all the newspaper reports – the *Arlebury Observer* has given it considerable coverage, as you probably know – and I've generally kept my ears open. My conclusion,' he continued in an oracular tone, 'is that Farmer murdered Shem and that Kenny Bostock witnessed it, if he didn't actually play a more active part – as an accessory.'

'Go on,' Machin said, when Mr Shelley cocked his head on one side and looked at him with a pleased expression.

'My dear Sergeant, what more! I've told you my theory. I'm not a detective, you know.'

'But *why* did Farmer murder Shem?'

'Ah! That's a very different question, isn't it? There could be any number of reasons.'

'Such as?'

'Shem was a witness to something between Farmer and the boy.'

'Are you suggesting Farmer's homosexual?'

A displeased frown passed across Mr Shelley's face. 'I'm not suggesting anything of the sort, though I suppose it's a possibility. Equally, Farmer may have killed him from motives of robbery. There were rumours that Shem was quite a wealthy man, that his pockets were stuffed with pound notes.'

'We've found no evidence to support that rumour,' Machin remarked.

'Anyway,' Mr Shelley said grandly, 'one can speculate endlessly about motives. The realm of the human mind is like the dark side of the moon, one can only guess at what lies there.'

Machin put down his cup and got up. Mr Shelley was no different from an ordinary busybody, apart from being rather more pompous. Nevertheless, it had to be remembered that busybodies were often the most fruitful source of information when it came to a police investigation. The present visit, however, could hardly be said to have justified the time or the uncomfortable pressure on his bladder occasioned by too much tea.

During the rest of the morning, he resisted invitations to step inside and remained steadfastly on the various doorsteps of the houses he visited. But at the end he was no further forward. No one was able to throw any light on Kenny's disappearance, though this didn't prevent his being subjected to a further spate of speculation. Almost everyone agreed that he was a nice boy; if something of a dark horse, as one or two people expressed it. In the course of his door-step interrogations, Machin also learnt that no mysterious strangers had been observed in the village. Kenny had vanished – apparently unaided.

The last person to whom Machin talked was Kenny's friend Ray, whom he caught on his way home from school.

'Do you mean he hasn't told you a thing?' Machin said, disbelievingly.

'Honest he hasn't,' Ray replied. Then: 'Do you think he murdered Shem?' His tone was eager, if not exactly hopeful. Machin shook his head. 'Perhaps someone's murdered *him*!'

'I doubt it.'

'I wonder what'll happen next,' he said, his eyes gleaming with excitement. 'Anyway, will I get a reward?'

'What for, finding the body?'

'Yes.'

'I'll see that Leo gets a bone.'

Ray laughed. 'I ought to get something, too.'

'You may yet. A boot up the backside!'

The next day a full-scale local search was made for Kenny, but without success. They didn't drag the quarry, nor did their resources stretch to searching every thicket and copse in the vicinity, but it was reasonably thorough.

The only thing was that though a couple of police dogs had been provided with Kenny's scent, they failed to find it anywhere beyond his own front door, which was frustrating as well as being patently absurd.

Moreover, no one came forward as a result of the appeal which was put out over the radio and which appeared in the press.

Kenny's disappearance was as complete as it was mysterious and the police viewed it with increasing concern.

XXIII

Three days later Brian Farmer appeared in court in London, on remand. On the previous day Page had learnt from the laboratory that two of the hairs found on Shem's clothing were identical with the control sample of Farmer's head hair which had been procured and sent along for examination. This was the link he had been hoping for and with this vital piece of evidence in his possession he decided that he had sufficient to justify charging Farmer with murder.

Accordingly, on the day of his appearance on the other charge, Page and Machin drove up to town early and met Detective Sergeant Cumnor at court. Apprised of their intentions, Cumnor had managed to dissuade Farmer from applying for legal aid and for an adjournment. He had pointed out that an adjournment would mean at least a further week in Brixton prison – since he, Sergeant Cumnor, would fight any application for bail – and that a quick plea of guilty now would be unlikely to result in more than a fine, especially since he, Sergeant Cumnor, was prepared to tell the magistrate that he accepted his, Brian Farmer's, assurance that he never had used the knife for an unlawful purpose, nor even had the intention of ever so using it.

It was, in fact, the sort of bargain which goes on all the time behind the court scenes, but which can never be openly admitted to by the police themselves, in view of the suggestions of improper pressure which would then be made – indeed, which frequently are made by a disgruntled defendant with afterthoughts and, with equal frequency, denied by an apparently shocked police officer.

What Sergeant Cumnor didn't fully perceive, however, was Farmer's readiness to be persuaded. He attributed this

151

entirely to his own subtle powers, in so far as he gave it any thought at all.

'Does he know we're going to charge him with the murder?' Page asked, as they stood in a corner of the jailer's office at court.

'No, I've not breathed a word to him. One thing for sure, however, he's a very worried boy. He's got something on his mind all right.'

'There are too many people connected with this case with things on their mind,' Page observed with a sigh. 'I wouldn't mind knowing what visitors he's had during his week in prison,' he added in a thoughtful voice. 'It's a pity we don't have better liaison all along the line with the prison people, instead of merely when a few high-powered prisoners are being transferred from one establishment to another. It's partly the old problem of manpower, of course, there just aren't enough officers for other than essential duties. And keeping eyes and ears on individual prisoners for our benefit can hardly be called an essential duty.'

'Not to mention the fact that every visitor to prison seems to walk in the shadow of his M.P. or some tame journalist,' Sergeant Cumnor remarked sourly. He glanced at his watch. 'I've arranged for it to be the first of the remands, and there aren't more than half a dozen overnight charges, so we should be through by about eleven.'

'Excellent. We'll take him straight back to Arlebury, charge him with the murder and get him before a justice this afternoon. I've already fixed that with the clerk. By this evening he'll be back in Brixton again.'

'Any leads on the young boy's whereabouts?' Sergeant Cumnor enquired, smothering a yawn.

Page shook his head. 'Not a thing. It's four days since he disappeared and we've not found so much as a trace.'

'Do you think he's dead? Fallen into a river or down some disused shaft?'

'It's a possibility which can't be excluded. I'm sure we'd have had news of him if he was merely wandering about like last time.'

'I'd certainly have thought so.'

The jailer's voice suddenly cut into their conversation.

'Quiet in here. Magistrate's on the bench.'

For the next few minutes, Page and Machin leaned against a wall and watched the familiar procession of defendants in and out of court. It was no different from their own local court, apart from the speed with which the cases were dealt with. Here, it seemed that the swing-door which separated the jailer's office from the court was in perpetual motion as defendants made their outward and, a very few seconds later, return journeys to pay their fines and sign the necessary documents connected with their release. Though an occasional offender was hurried past on his way to a cell beyond.

Just before Brian Farmer's case was called on, the two Arlebury officers stepped out into the hall of the court. They returned to the jailer's office, however, as soon as Farmer had passed through from the cell in which he had been fretfully waiting since his arrival from the prison.

It was several minutes before the door swung open again and the uniformed officer who was the court's master of ceremonies called out to a colleague who was at the receipt of custom:

'Fined ten pounds, seven days to pay or one month.'

'Got ten pounds?' the desk officer asked breezily. Brian Farmer shook his head. 'Can you pay in seven days?'

'Yes.'

'Well, it's either that or a month inside.'

Sergeant Cumnor now came through the door and up to where Farmer was standing.

'There's someone here wants to see you,' he said.

'Who?' Farmer looked quickly around, his expression freezing into one of fear and hostility as he caught sight of Page and Machin.

The two officers moved forward and Sergeant Cumnor led the way to a small room off the corridor which led to the cells.

'I have to tell you,' Page intoned, as they stood like a badly rehearsed group of stage conversationists, 'that you are going to be taken back to Arlebury where you will be charged with the murder of Joshua Clapp. You are not obliged to say anything, but anything you do say will be taken down in writing and may be given in evidence.'

What Farmer did say was short, explicit and of no evidential value. If it assisted his own feelings, it didn't disturb those of the officers who were used to such explosive misuse of language.

As Machin passed through the jailer's office on his way to fetch the car round to a side door, the uniformed officer on duty said:

'There was a girl enquiring after your chap just now. Wanted to know where he was. I told her I'd ask if she could see him before you took him away, but the next moment she'd disappeared.'

'Wonder if she's still hanging around outside?'

'Hang on a tick and I'll come and have a look.'

Leaving another officer in charge, he accompanied Machin into the hall. 'Don't see her here.' He went to the entrance and glanced up and down the street. 'That's her there, talking to that bloke.'

Machin looked where the uniformed officer was indicating and saw a girl with blonde, cropped hair talking animatedly to a man who appeared to be around the mid-twenties and who was listening to her with a grim expression, his hands thrust deep into the pockets of the short camel-hair motoring coat he was wearing.

'Thanks,' Machin said, returning inside. 'I think I'll be able to recognise them again if necessary.'

When, ten minutes later, the car containing him, Page and Farmer turned into the street, there was no longer any sign of the couple.

'What happens after I've been charged?' Farmer asked suddenly, breaking his silence as the car weaved its way through the midday suburban traffic.

Page gave a small inward sigh of satisfaction. He'd wanted to converse, but hadn't wished to take the initiative as this might have had the effect of driving Farmer into deeper silence.

'You'll make a brief appearance in court and be remanded for seven days.'

'Back in Brixton?'

'Yes. The court'll probably grant you legal aid. I imagine you want that?'

'I suppose so.'

'Anyone you want me to tell about your arrest?'

Farmer appeared to ponder the question for several seconds before replying. 'No.'

'What about your parents?'

'Can if you want!'

'Only if you want.'

'They'll see it in the papers, so why bother?'

'Did they visit you this last week?'

'Mum came once.'

'Have any other visitors?'

'A few.'

'A girl-friend, perhaps?'

'Perhaps.'

'Like me to let her know what's happened?'

'No.'

There was a further silence, then Page said, 'As far as I'm concerned, this is all off the record. You know your cousin Kenny Bostock has disappeared?'

'Yeah, I read it in the paper.'

'Any ideas what can have happened to him?'

'Why should I have any ideas? I haven't seen the kid for years.' His tone was edgy and he turned his head abruptly away and stared out of the window.

'He's very fond of you from all accounts.'

'How do you mean?'

'Several people have told us how he used to idolise you

and how he's never got over your leaving the village.' Page had decided to pitch it high.

'Balls! All kids have somebody they look up to like an older brother – or an older boy at school. Kenny happened to look up to me when I was around. Then I left and I don't expect he's given me any thought since.'

'That's certainly not true. Moreover, you know it isn't.'

'How do I know?'

'Because the first time he ran away it was to look for you.'

'That's a load of cock!'

'I don't think it is and I don't believe that you think it is.'

'What did he want to find me for, anyway?'

'Ah! Wouldn't you like to answer the question as well as ask it?'

Farmer shook his head angrily. 'This whole conversation's bloody stupid. As I've told you, I haven't seen Kenny for over three years and I've no idea what's happened to him or why he's left home again. I just know it's nothing to do with me.'

'I wish I could believe that.'

'It's none of my business what you believe or don't believe.'

'Why are you so tetchy on the subject of Kenny?' Page said mildly.

'Who's tetchy?'

'There you go again.'

'I'm tired of your nagging questions, that's all.'

'Don't you agree, Sergeant, that he's tetchy whenever his cousin's name is mentioned?' Page enquired, turning his head in Machin's direction.

'I do indeed, sir. He's probably worried about him.'

'Are you?'

'What've I got to be worried about him for?'

Page let out an exaggerated sigh. 'Because he's disappeared and you know something about it.'

'And because he may be in danger,' Machin added.

'What sort of danger? How do you know he's in danger?'

'The sergeant merely said "may be". Look, Farmer, it stands out a mile you know something about him. If it's anything which'll help us to find him, it's your duty to tell us. Just think about that quietly for a few minutes. If you have any feelings at all for a young boy who once regarded you as his hero, you'll come clean.'

But Farmer's expression already foreshadowed the answer he would give, doubt and fear merging into a look of stubborn refusal.

'Well?' Page said after several minutes. 'Thought about it?'

'I don't know nothing about him and that's final.'

The rest of the journey was completed in silence.

On arrival at the station Farmer was formally charged with Shem's murder and locked in a cell where he was brought a meal. When the uniformed sergeant went to collect the plate, he found the food untouched.

'Not hungry?' he asked in surprise, eyeing a congealed mess of steak pie and cabbage. 'Don't want no plums and custard?'

Farmer shook his head.

Three-quarters of an hour later, Machin fetched him from the cell.

'We're going across to court now.'

When they arrived there, Farmer was placed in yet another cell, but this time for only ten minutes. The uniformed officer who came for him led him into a virtually empty court-room and announced his name.

Apart from the magistrate, the clerk, Page and Machin, the only other occupants were two local newspaper reporters.

Unlike the court in which he had appeared in London that morning, this was a new building with leather tip-up seats which wheezed like deflating bagpipes every time anyone sat down. The decor was a smart dark blue and gold where the other had been institutional cream and brown. In fact, as someone had once remarked, Arlebury Court lacked nothing save an organ to come up through the floor.

Page stepped into the witness-box which was of such eminence that an archbishop would have been proud to have preached from it. In tones suitable to the occasion, he gave evidence of arrest and charging and asked for a week's remand in custody.

The clerk asked Farmer if he wished to put any questions to the Superintendent (he shook his head) or say anything against the remand (another shake of the head).

The clerk then turned and spoke to the magistrate sitting above and behind him. This was achieved by his standing on tip-toe and by the magistrate leaning forward until their heads were in suitable proximity for the transmission of whispered advice.

'You'll be remanded in custody for seven days,' the magistrate said in the tone of one making a surprise announcement with determined boldness.

'Do you apply for legal aid?' the clerk enquired. Farmer nodded. 'Then you will be informed the name of the solicitor allocated to your defence.'

And that concluded the proceedings.

The next morning, however, the clerk phoned Page to say he thought he would be interested to hear that Farmer had withdrawn his application for legal aid and that he was now going to be defended by Mr Jason Butters of London. Mr Butters had himself informed the court of the change in representation.

Page was not only interested but extremely curious, for Mr Butters had the reputation of being one of the flyest solicitors in criminal practice. It was to him that the big boys invariably turned when the law closed about them.

If his arrival on the scene did nothing else, it certainly emphasised to Page that there was a good deal more to the case than he'd discovered.

XXIV

Mick Edmunds and the two men he was fond of referring to as his colleagues sat round the same first-floor room of the house in a South London side street in which they'd held all their meetings. On this occasion, the girl named Sandy was also present. She sat on the arm of the chair occupied by the taller of the two men.

'The whole thing's one bloody aggravation,' Edmunds said in disgust. 'I'd like to screw Brian's 'ead off, getting 'imself charged with murder like that.'

'The question is what's he going to say when he comes up in court,' the shorter man remarked.

'I don't think we need worry about that, I've discussed the position fully with Butters and he'll be visiting 'im in Brixton today or tomorrow, and we'll soon 'ave that bit sorted out. It's the bloody delay what makes me wild. And all because of 'im!'

'Why do we have to wait?' the tall man asked.

'Because Brian's acting up like a prima donna and it seems we've no alternative but to pacify 'im.'

'I know how I'd pacify him!'

'Well, you can't, so it's no good talking that way.'

'O.K., Mick, no need to get stroppy with me. It was you who was saying just now that you'd like to screw his head off.'

'So I would too!'

'What's the difference between that and pacifying him?' the short one enquired mildly. 'Let's be practical about this. Brian's tucked away and there's a bit of a stalemate, but as soon as the case is over, we're out on top again. It's just a question of a bit of patience.'

''Ow do you fancy being patient for the next twenty years?' Edmunds demanded in a scathing tone. 'You 'adn't thought of that, 'ad you! Because that's what it'll be if Brian's convicted.'

The short man frowned. 'What the hell is Jason Butters for, 'cept to see that he isn't convicted?' he said at length.

'He's a lawyer, not a miracle-man. We don't yet know what evidence they've got against Brian.'

'Enough to charge him.'

'Exactly.'

'That doesn't mean to say he'll be convicted.'

'Too true it don't and we've got to 'ope 'e won't be.'

'And if he is?'

'We'll jump that 'urdle when we comes to it,' Edmunds said grimly.

Mr Jason Butters was a man of about forty five and had a generally square appearance. He was broad-shouldered and had a large squarish head, with black hair brushed straight back without a parting, a full but well-trimmed moustache and a pair of heavy horn-rimmed spectacles. The eyes which peered at the world through these were sharp and wary, but at the same time capable of twinkling in a most disarming way. He was well-dressed without being flashy and his only sartorial extravagance was the pearl pin which he always wore below the knot of his tie. He certainly didn't resemble many people's idea of a solicitor, least of all one whose conduct in almost every case he undertook would at some point cause him to be struck off if it ever came to light. But it never did; or rather never in such a way as to be capable of proof against him. It followed that he was the most sought after solicitor by those criminals who had the money to buy his services. He wasn't cheap, nor could be having regard to the risks he was prepared to run in meeting the requirements of his clients' defences.

On the day of Brian Farmer's remand appearance at Arlebury magistrates court, Mr Butters drove down from

London in his this year's Ford Zodiac. He parked in front of the court and strolled in a relaxed manner over to the police station. He'd arrived early as he wanted to have a word with Page beforehand and then speak to his client before the court sat.

On being informed that Page wasn't at the station, he politely asked if there was any other officer he could talk to about the case. It was thus that Machin came, for the first time, face to face with the solicitor whose reputation was as formidable as it was dubious. Nobody had ever described Mr Butters' physical appearance to him and he was quite unprepared for the genial approach of a rather heavy-featured man. Neither fitted his pre-conceived picture of the solicitor.

'Good morning,' Mr Butters said, holding out his hand, 'I'm Jason Butters. I'm defending this fellow Farmer. What's our position today?'

'We'll be asking for a further remand, sir.'

'I guessed you would. Not had much time to get your tackle in order yet, I suppose?'

'No, sir.'

'Is the D.P.P.'s representative attending today?'

'No. Superintendent Page will be asking for the remand.'

Mr Butters pulled at his lower lip.

'Off the record, what sort of a case have you got against my chap?'

Machin blinked. 'We think it's a good one or we wouldn't have charged him.'

'What's your main evidence?' Mr Butters enquired with an indulgent smile.

'We've got a bit of everything,' Machin replied blandly.

Mr Butters laughed, though without amusement. 'Well, as far as I'm concerned, the sooner the case can be dealt with the better. The defence certainly don't want any de-lays. We'll be ready for trial at the forthcoming Assizes.'

'But they're less than three weeks off.'

'What of it! Let's have a bit of speed on this one. I'm

ready for a committal today.'

'You'll accept a section one committal?'

'Certainly.'

'Oh, I thought you might want some of the witnesses to give oral evidence before the magistrates.'

'No, no,' Mr Butters said, sweeping away the suggestion with a broad gesture of his right arm. 'We're ready for a paper committal. Shan't even want the statements read. Get the whole thing over at this stage in a couple of minutes. If you can let me have a copy of the statements now, we can have the committal this morning.'

'It's the D.P.P. who'll be serving the statements on you, not the police.'

'D.P.P., police, what's it matter? I'm just trying to save everyone some time.'

Machin stared at the solicitor impassively. As soon as he had heard that Jason Butters was defending, he'd envisaged that the case would become bitterly contested at every turn, that nothing would be accepted by the defence which made the prosecution's task simpler. And yet here was Farmer's lawyer agreeing to a formal committal for trial without consideration of any of the evidence by the committing magistrates, and not only that, but also urging that the trial should be held at the Assizes which opened in about three weeks time.

Either Mr Butters had undergone a conversion as dramatic as Saul's on the road to Damascus or something was up. Machin had little doubt which was the more probable alternative. On the other hand he didn't see why he shouldn't play Mr Butters at his own game.

'It sounds as if your client is proposing to plead guilty,' he remarked.

'Who are you trying to fool?' Mr Butters replied briskly. 'That'll be the day when one of my clients pleads guilty!'

'I just thought from all this desire for speed and getting to trial without any delay that you might have a plea of guilty in mind.'

'Neither in mind, nor anywhere else!' Mr Butters retorted. 'We've got a good defence to this charge and one which, when the time comes, will see my man free. That's the reason I don't want any delay, since every day of waiting means an unnecessary day in prison for my client.'

'You sound very confident.'

'I certainly am confident.'

'It must be a good defence you have up your sleeve.'

'It is, and that's where it's staying until the right moment, so you needn't waste any more time trailing your coat under my nose.'

'Of course, if it's an alibi you have to give us notice,' Machin went on unabashed.

'Nor do I particularly want to receive a lecture on the law,' Mr Butters said energetically. 'Anyway, it's time I went over to court and saw any client.' His eyes glinted behind his spectacles as he gave Machin a final appraising glance before walking away.

Machin went up to Page's office to see if he had come in and to report on his conversation with the solicitor. Page was there, reading a newspaper. He laid it on one side in such a way as to reproach Machin for his interruption.

When Machin had finished, he said, 'I've never yet known a defending solicitor say his client's not got a hope in hell and that his defence won't hold up any better than a sandcastle against the incoming tide.' He paused in reflection. 'Well, not very often anyway.'

'Oh, I don't know, sir, people plead guilty often enough, sometimes even to murder.'

'Not in my cases, they don't,' Page observed gloomily.

A quarter of an hour later, the two officers made their way over to court. Mr Butters was already sitting in the row reserved for lawyers and Machin took Page across to introduce him. But on this occasion the defending solicitor remained uncommunicative.

However, as soon as Farmer's name had been called and

he had been brought up into the dock, and Page had asked for a further week's remand in custody, Mr Butters rose and conveyed to the bench the same views he had expressed to Machin. His language, though more forensic, was no less pungent in its effect and the three magistrates looked nonplussed as the unexpected barrage hit them.

The upshot was that the remand was made, but the prosecution were urged to be ready for a formal committal for trial the following week.

When it was all over and they were outside, the solicitor came over to where Page and Machin were talking.

'Tell the D.P.P. to send me over the statements as soon as possible. He needn't trouble to tie them with pretty ribbon. As long as I can read them, that'll be fine.'

'It's going to be a bit of a rush to have this case ready for trial at the next Assizes,' Page remarked. 'The Prison Medical Officer has to make a report and a hundred other things have to be done.'

'I'll hand you one thing on a plate, Superintendent,' Mr Butters said with a wolfish grin. 'I'm not concerned with a medical defence. No question of pleading diminished responsibility in this case. So you can stuff the P.M.O.'s report for all I care.' He turned to go. 'See you next week.'

'He's like a stiff breeze,' Machin remarked as they watched his retreating back.

'More like a bucket of acid, if you ask me,' Page replied sourly. 'Why can't he stick to London? What's he want to get involved in one of our cases for?'

'If we knew that, sir, we'd know a lot.'

But Page merely grunted. Mr Butters' intrusion in the case had unsettled him considerably. Why couldn't he be allowed to retire quietly!

It was three days later that a letter arrived at the Bostocks' home. It was addressed to Mr and Mrs Bostock and bore a Liverpool postmark, indicating that it had been posted in that city two days previously. In the envelope was

a single sheet of ruled paper which appeared to have been
torn from a notebook and on this was written:

'Dear Mum and Dad,
   'Sorry I haven't written before but I am all right so
don't worry. Don't try and find me as I'm moving about.
I'll explain everything when I get home.
                                    'Yours faithfully,
                                      'Kenny Bostock.'

The police learnt of the arrival of the letter later the
same day, when Susan phoned Machin. He at once got into
a car and drove over to Long Gaisford to see Mrs Bostock.
   She greeted him with the slight reserve which charac-
terised her meetings with the police. It wasn't that she was
ever actually hostile, but there was always a noticeable
wariness, even a sort of estrangement, about her manner.
She invited him into the kitchen and handed him the letter.
   'Is it Kenny's writing?' he asked, after he had read it.
   'Yes.'
   'No doubt about that?'
   She shook her head. 'No, it's his writing all right.'
   'Is there anything about it which strikes you as curious?'
   'I don't think so,' she replied, in a faintly puzzled tone.
   'Would you expect him to sign his full name when writ-
ing to you?'
   'He's never written to us before, I don't think. Oh, I
suppose we must have had cards when he's been away with
the school, but I've never noticed how he writes his name at
the end.'
   'And "yours faithfully" seems a funny way to finish off a
letter to your mother and father,' Machin remarked, giving
her a questioning glance.
   'A lot of letters end that way, don't they?'
   'Not personal letters usually. I'd have expected him to
have put "love from" or something of that sort.' But Mrs
Bostock merely looked at him blankly. 'What I had in

mind,' he went on, 'was whether you felt this was a spontaneous letter or whether you thought it might have been written at someone's dictation?' She gave a helpless shrug. 'Do you have any family or friends up in the Liverpool area?'

'No.'

'Has Kenny ever talked about the place?'

She shook her head. 'No.'

'Well, all we can do is notify the police up there and get something into the newspapers.'

She made a face. 'I suppose all those reporters will come round again asking their questions.'

'I doubt whether they'll bother you to the same extent this time, if at all.'

'Lot of nosey parkers! What's it got to do with them how we live! And hinting that Kenny wasn't happy at home or that he knew something about the murder and had run away because he was afraid! I told them to go and stick their noses into someone else's affairs; all I knew was that Kenny had disappeared and it was someone's job to find him.'

For the first time since he had known her, she had exhibited a degree of vehemence about something, but then, Machin reflected sardonically, the press were able to achieve this reaction in the mildest-mannered people with their relentless probing of the personal details of those lives which circumstances had shoved under their microscope. He was still, however, unable to decide what precisely were Mrs Bostock's reactions to her son's disappearance. If she were worried, it didn't seem to spring from any true concern about what might have happened to him.

'Well, at least, this letter proves that Kenny's alive,' he said. From her expression he realised it had never occurred to her that he might not be.

'I don't know what we're going to do with him when he comes back,' she remarked. 'Perhaps he could join up.'

'Join up?'

'Go into the army. They do have boy soldiers, don't they?'

'Oh, I see what you mean. Yes, I think they do.'

Shortly afterwards he left, taking the letter with him.

That evening when he and Susan were sitting in front of the fire at her flat, he asked:

'Is your mother worried about Kenny?'

'Of course. Wouldn't you be if your son vanished?'

'Yes, but ... well, I just wondered. She doesn't show it, that's all.' He paused. 'Does she know about us?'

Susan lifted her head from his lap and gazed up at him. 'She knows I've seen you a bit, but I've not told her any more. She doesn't know ... that we've slept together.'

'I should hope not!' Machin exclaimed in a tone of shock which sent Susan into giggles.

She raised a hand and pulled his head down towards her own. 'Please kiss me, Peter.'

Machin grinned. 'You sound like a polite little girl asking if she may have a plum,' he replied, before complying with her request.

Not for the first time since their relationship had developed, he wondered vaguely at the back of his mind whether there was anything in the police code to cover their situation. Almost certainly there was! But not for the first time either, he now firmly pushed this worm of a thought back into the furthermost part of his mind.

He had reached a point where he was happy to have his heart rule his head ...

When Farmer appeared a week later in the magistrates' court, he was committed for trial with as little fuss and bother as Mr Butters had foreshadowed. The whole proceedings lasted no more than ten minutes and the defending solicitor, himself, uttered not a single word throughout.

It was, as Page remarked afterwards, extremely ominous.

XXV

Brian Farmer's trial opened at Arlebury Assizes seventeen days later. During that time, nothing further happened. The prosecution's case neither grew nor diminished in strength, and no word came as to what line the defence might be taking, which at least indicated that they weren't proposing to adduce alibi evidence since advance notice of this was now a legal requirement. There'd been no further word from Kenny and his disappearance remained a mystery which showed no signs of solution.

Page's sense of uneasiness about various aspects of the whole case was tempered only by the knowledge that each day brought him nearer to retirement and that this would go on whatever disagreeable surprises might be in store for him. He derived mordant comfort in the knowledge that nothing could actually halt the clock. Time would continue to pass however much buffeting awaited him.

Machin, for his part, had continued to see more and more of Susan and though neither spoke of it, there was a tacit understanding that theirs was now the sort of relationship which could end quite naturally in marriage.

And so the seventeen days passed without any outward sign of dramatic activity, but with a great deal of busy preparation being undertaken behind the scenes in the camps of all concerned.

The trial came on before Mr Justice Sarrow, an enormously distinguished lawyer who had not set foot in a criminal court since he was a pupil at the Bar until his appointment as a Judge of the Queen's Bench Division. He found trying criminal cases utterly distasteful and to an even greater extent did he dislike the travelling involved as an itinerant judge of Assize. He was a man of mild manner whose method of summing up a case was to read out the law from a textbook and the evidence of all the witnesses from his notebook in which he had recorded it in detail, and with great speed in his own brand of shorthand. Though this frequently left the jury careening like a rudderless ship, it ensured that he could never be upset on appeal. Where his more determined and colourful brethren on the Bench would give clear and pithy indications of their own view of various aspects of a case, Mr Justice Sarrow would play it straight down the middle. When he did make some comment on the evidence, he would follow it almost immediately by another to cancel the effect of the first comment.

To say that Mr Jason Butters rubbed his hands in delight at the propsect of his client's case being tried by this particular judge would be to understate his reaction. Indeed, it was the very prospect which had determined him to get the case to trial at Arlebury Assizes. The leading counsel he had briefed was no less satisfied. This was Mr Vincent Paynter, Q.C., who received a lot of work from Mr Butters and who viewed his instructing solicitor with a certain detached respect and without any of the righteous indignation affected by others of his profession. His junior counsel in the case was a Mr Crooke.

Leading for the Crown was Mr Aubrey Wotell, Q.C. (pronounced Wo-tell; though more often, to his annoyance, either deliberately or unwittingly, made to rhyme with bottle). Mr Wotell was someone of mediocre attainment and no sense of humour. He hid both, though none too successfully, under a pompous and hectoring manner which had become so much part of him that he carried it everywhere he went, including into his own home where his wife and two unmarried grown-up daughters and an old retainer had learnt to live with it, so that it no longer bothered them any more than cold weather bothers the inhabitants of the arctic.

Mr Wotell's junior counsel was Mr Strang.

The court into which these various men of law and others squeezed themselves was very different from the magistrates court which lay in another part of town. Arlebury Assize Court was three hundred years old and an historic monument. It was, in addition, quite the least suitable building for its purpose that anyone could have devised. Hexagonal in shape, with walls of darkest oak and seating accommodation of primitive discomfort, it constituted one vast frustration to those who were obliged to work in it. In its centre sat the dock surrounded by a double iron rail. Ranged round the dock was divided off banks of narrow seats with even narrower ledges in front of them from which papers were frequently slithering to the floor. But perhaps the designer's most original touch had been to ensure that the only way of getting from one part of the court to another was to leave through the door nearest to you, scoot briskly round the corridor which formed the outside perimeter of the court-room, guess which was the appropriate door to bring you where you wished to be, and re-enter.

It was no very great exaggeration to say that anyone could almost touch anyone else from where he sat. And it was this atmosphere of chaotic propinquity which caused Brian Farmer, tense though he was, to blink with surprise as he came up into the dock on the first morning of his trial.

The judge appeared to blink back at him from a few feet away while just below and to his right was a huddle of bewigged barristers. Behind them sat Mr Butters and other solicitors as though squashed together in the dickey of an ancient coupé. To his left were the jury sitting in what looked like an open crate. Farmer gripped the iron rail which ran along the front edge of the dock and sucked at his lower lip. He felt anything but calm and this congested scene did nothing to reassure him. It was like being thrown into the arena to find the lions waiting there in a small tight circle. When the clerk of Assize asked him whether he pleaded guilty or not guilty to murdering one Joshua

Clapp, he could at first only stare at him. Then he managed to say 'not guilty' in a low whisper and was allowed to sit down while the jury was sworn. He paid no attention to this, but just stared at the floor between his feet. He felt lonely and frightened, but knew that he had no choice other than to go through with what had been arranged. He just wished that he didn't feel so alone. He wasn't a solitary person by nature and the burden he was now being required to carry all on his own made his head throb. He was out of his depth, but he knew that he couldn't afford to give in. He had to fight all the way. He glanced across at Mr Butters who was staring at him warily. The solicitor gave him a small nod of encouragement before being eclipsed from view by Mr Aubrey Wotell rising to open the case to the jury.

Everyone's gaze turned towards the tall, ample-girthed, but still imposing figure of prosecuting counsel as he stood like a famous actor waiting for the last rustle of movement to die away before he began to speak.

'May it please your lordship,' he said in a tone which managed to give the impression that he was addressing a lesser actor. 'Members of the jury, in this case I appear on behalf of the crown with my learned friend, Mr Strang and the prisoner' – to Mr Wotell, persons in the dock were always prisoners, never accused or defendants – 'has the advantage of being represented by my learned friends Mr Paynter and Mr er-er . . .' Mr Wotell reached imperiously for a piece of paper in front of him and read it. 'Mr er Crooke.'

Junior defence counsel shot a look at Mr Wotell's back which expressed clearly his own view of this aberration. It was as well that Mr Wotell was unable to see it.

'Members of the jury, the prisoner stands indicted with the murder of Joshua Clapp. For some reason with which we are not concerned, the dead man was apparently known as Shem. He was, not to place too fine an edge on it, a tramp. But the fact that he *was* a tramp,' Mr Wotell went on, 'doesn't mean that he didn't have as much right to live as you or I, members of the jury.' His tone, however, clearly belied this belief. 'In this country, everyone is entitled to enjoy the Queen's peace, whatever his place in society.'

When Mr Wotell came on to the evidence which he would be calling, he dealt with its every facet in ponderous, and not infrequently inaccurate, detail. It fell to his hapless junior to hiss whispered corrections of the more outrageous errors of fact and to come under pitiless fire for his help.

'It was the Tuesday, not the Thursday,' he whispered, giving a small tug at Mr Wotell's gown.

'What's that? I wish you wouldn't interrupt me ... Tuesday, you say. Isn't that what I said? ... Members of the jury, whether it was the Tuesday or the Thursday, you'll probably consider quite unimportant...'

'It was the Tuesday,' Mr Justice Sarrow said in his quiet, desiccated tone.

'I am much obliged to your lordship,' Mr Wotell said, glaring at the small red-robed figure on the bench. 'As I was saying, members of the jury ...'

An hour and three quarters later, Mr Wotell was approaching the end of his opening speech.

'Let me just summarise the case for the crown against the prisoner. First, you have his denials that he was anywhere near the scene of the crime at the relevant time, albeit denials of a somewhat ambiguous character. But, members of the jury,' he went on in a heartily scornful tone, 'you will probably come to the conclusion that he was merely being evasive. Evasive because he felt himself being driven into the corner from which there could be no escape from guilt. And as against his denials, you have this most important scientific evidence which not only links the prisoner with the dead man, but also links each of them with the cave in Harrier's Wood where the murder was so clearly committed.' He threw the jury a triumphant look, as though himself was personally responsible for all these feats of scientific detection. 'And now, members of the jury, with the assistance of my learned friend, I will call the evidence before you.'

Mr Wotell sat down and in so doing managed to sweep most of his junior's papers to the ground.

'Like working in a pig-sty,' he muttered graciously as Mr Strang groped to retrieve his scattered brief.

The first two witnesses were the plan-drawer and the photographer, of neither of whom Mr Paynter asked any questions in cross-examination.

'I don't know why these witnesses were required to attend,' the judge remarked. 'Their statements could quite well have been read in the circumstances.' But since this observation didn't appear to be directed at anyone in particular, and since Mr Justice Sarrow himself didn't seem to be greatly interested in any reply, none was forthcoming.

Ray was the next witness and described the finding of Shem's body. Mr Wotell treated him with heavy avuncularity, but again Mr Paynter had no questions to put in cross-examination. Ray, who had expected to be asked all about Kenny, left the witness-box with a feeling of let-down. Kenny's name hadn't even been mentioned. And to make matters worse, the judge directed that he might be released from further attendance, so that he wasn't even going to be able to sit and listen to the rest of the case. His thoughts, as he departed from the court-room, were anything but complimentary about those conducting the trial.

There followed Dr Leary, the pathologist, spruce and mint-fresh as always. He and Mr Wotell eyed one another across the small court-room without visible pleasure. The trouble was that when Mr Wotell was questioning a witness, he liked to make it very plain that he was in charge, whereas Dr Leary, who regarded a good many of the questions he was asked in court as inept, preferred to give the evidence which he knew to be relevant with the minimum of interruption. As far as he was concerned, his was the star performance and counsel was merely the feed man. It was therefore fortunate that his evidence in the case was short.

With a final glare at the witness, Mr Wotell resumed his seat. 'Conceited little ass!' he muttered to his junior.

Attention was quickly diverted to Mr Paynter who rose for the first time in the course of the trial. He regarded Dr Leary with a faintly quizzical smile.

'You say that the deceased died of a sub-dural haemorrhage as a result of a fractured skull, following a blow to the back of the head?'

'That is so.'

'As you're doubtless aware, no weapon has ever been found . . .'

'So I understand.'

'But was this injury of which you speak consistent with having been caused by a stone?'

Dr Leary smiled indulgently. 'What sort of stone do you have in mind?'

'Oh, the sort of stone you'd find on a beach?' Mr Paynter said almost casually.

'Yes, it could have been. A stone or a hammer.'

'How much force would have been required to cause the injuries you've described with such a stone?'

'A moderately hard blow.'

'Moderate or moderately hard?'

The witness smiled again as he was enjoying this civilised battle of wits with defence counsel after brawling with Mr Wotell.

'Moderately hard,' he replied after a second's pause. 'Though the deceased's skull was, as I've already said in my evidence, a fraction thinner than average.'

'And he was an old man?'

'He was sixty-eight, I understand,' the pathologist said, casting the judge a sly glance.

'And had lived a hard life?'

'Yes, his body certainly indicated that.'

'Thank you,' Mr Paynter said and sat down.

Mr Wotell heaved himself up, stared balefully at the witness for a couple of seconds and then said, 'I have no questions I wish to put in re-examination, my lord.'

Dr Leary gave the judge a small bow and hurried out of court as though he had already accorded everyone there more of his time than they deserved.

It was at this point that the judge indicated that the court would adjourn for lunch – and exited, a small, spare, remote figure, through the pair of heavy dark brown curtains which covered the door behind his seat.

Brian Farmer had just been given his own lunch – a plate of stew dominated by an enormous dumpling and a mound of chopped cabbage stalk – when Mr Butters arrived in the bleak cell below the court in which he was having his meal.

'How are you feeling?' he enquired, rather in the manner of a fight promoter eyeing a novice to the ring.

'All right, I suppose.'

'You won't be giving evidence today, anyway,' Mr Butters remarked as if to reassure his client. 'You haven't forgotten all I've told you, have you?' Farmer shook his head. 'Good. A lot depends on it.'

'You're telling me!'

'I mean on the impression you make.'

He gave his client a final appraising glance and departed. His own lunch consisted of a quick double Scotch in the pub opposite the court and he was back in his place with several minutes in hand.

'I had a word with Farmer during the adjournment,' he said to Mr Paynter who came in just after him. 'I think he's suitably anxious.'

Mr Paynter smiled faintly. 'It's not exactly an *anxious* look that's needed.'

'Oh, I think he's got the other all right, too. What one doesn't want from him is any display of cockiness.'

'I agree.'

'I think we've got the other side puzzled.'

Mr Paynter chuckled. 'It's always a pleasure to puzzle old Wotell.'

At this point, the judge made his entrance and after the usual exchange of bows, everyone sat down again, save for Mr Wotell who announced:

'I now call Charles Henry Adey.'

'Freeston,' whispered Mr Strang.

'What? Who?'

'His name's Charles Henry Adey Freeston.'

'That's what I said! It's the witness from the laboratory, my lord – a Mr Freeston.'

The judge nodded without looking up from what he was reading.

Mr Freeston who spent as much time in court as he did in the laboratory was equally at home in both. The evidence he had to give was long and detailed and further complicated by the number of exhibits to which he had to refer in the course of it. It was no thanks to Mr Wotell that he reached its conclusion without the jury having arrived at a state of utter confusion. There was one point, however, when it had seemed that disentanglement would prove beyond human endeavour. This had come when Mr Freeston was speaking of the accused's clothing and Mr Wotell thought he was referring to that of the dead man.

'I also examined the trousers, exhibit 18,' said the witness.

'Exhibit 12,' Mr Wotell corrected.

'Exhibit 12 is a sample of hair.'

'I mean exhibit 10.'

'Exhibit 10 are the deceased's trousers.'

'According to my list, they're exhibit 23.'

'What are?'

'A pair of trousers.'

'Exhibit 23 is a pair of pants.'

'Does that mean under-pants?'

'Yes.'

'It'd be better if it said so. Then what's exhibit 17?'

'Scrapings taken from the turn-ups of the deceased's trousers.'

'And that's what you're about to tell us about?'

'No. I was about to deal with exhibit 18, which are the accused's trousers.'

'Very well.' Prosecuting counsel glanced across at the judge. 'I hope your lordship has been able to follow this.'

'I haven't tried, Mr Wotell,' Mr Justice Sarrow said in a voice devoid of all expression.

When, eventually, Mr Fresston had completed his evidence in chief and Mr Wotell had slumped back into his seat, attention was once more turned on Mr Paynter. He rose, gave the witness a small, almost apologetic smile, and said:

'I have no questions to ask this witness, my lord.'

A short-lived buzz of conversation broke out and even the judge reacted with a look of mild surprise, since the whole purport of the witness's evidence had been to link Farmer indisputably with the dead man. And now apparently there was going to be no attempt to dispute the link.

The only witnesses who remained to be called to complete the prosecution's case were police officers – and they were quickly disposed of, since Mr Paynter equally failed to cross-examine any of them. The last witness of all was Page who dealt patiently with Mr Wotell's clumsy handling of his evidence. It was five o'clock by the time it was completed and the judge, without bothering to find out whether or not Mr Paynter was proposing to cross-examine the witness, adjourned the trial until the next morning.

'What do you think the defence are up to?' Machin asked in a baffled tone, as he and Page made their way back to the station.

Page made a face. 'We'll know soon enough tomorrow.'

'I mean, so far they've cross-examined only one witness. And yet they've pleaded not guilty. I suppose they have got a defence?'

'You bet they have! Jason Butters doesn't waste his time unnecessarily.'

177

'I'd like to know who's paying for it.'

'So would I!'

There was a silence, then shaking his head with a puzzled air, Machin said, 'Know how the whole trial strikes me, sir? It's just not like real. It's more like a sort of charade.'

Page nodded. 'I know what you mean.'

'The fact that there's no mention of Kenny when we're darned certain that his disappearance is closely tied up with the case. That's unreal for a start.'

'There's no mention of *him*,' Page replied, 'because it's not evidence of anything. I suppose the defence might try and introduce it, but his disappearance is no part of the prosecution's case. It's not even admissible evidence.'

'It ought to be,' Machin said in a tone of frustration.

'To prove what?'

'I don't know, sir, but . . .'

'There's your answer. It's not material to anything. Or rather we can't prove that it is.'

'I sometimes wonder, sir, if the rules of evidence aren't too narrow, too much like the sort of rules for playing a game.'

'But British justice is a game! It isn't a search for truth so much as a lottery. Even some lawyers agree that,' Page added sardonically. He turned towards Machin and went on, 'I've been in the police thirty years and I've given evidence in a good many thousand cases in that time and I can tell you that the rules of evidence in a criminal trial ensure not only that a large number of villains go free, but that the lawyers are kept in business.'

Machin was taken aback. It was rare for the Detective Superintendent to speak with such vehemence and he hadn't known that this particular subject was one on which he held strong views. At one time or another, most police officers felt – and usually with sound reason – that the balance was tilted unfairly in favour of the criminal, but once their pique over a particular case had passed, they were usually to be found on the side of those who vaunted British justice as the envy of the rest of the world. What such people really meant was that British sense of fair play was an admirable facet of character and that the world would be a better place if other nations were similarly endowed. In which they were probably right. Machin himself was certainly an adherent to this view.

'Well, sir,' he said after a pause, 'it's still better that nine guilty men should go free than that one innocent one should be convicted.'

'Balls to that!' Page observed crisply as they turned into the entrance to the station.

Later that evening, Machin found himself assailed by a not dissimilar, if less articulately advanced, argument when he took Susan out to dinner. She had been reading an account of the trial in the local evening paper and found it incomprehensible that her brother's disappearance had not figured prominently.

'How can you say it's not relevant?' she demanded hotly.

'It's not I who says it's not: it's the rules of evidence,' Machin replied defensively.

'Well, I think it's disgraceful.'

'Well, there's no need to take it out on me,' he said, engaging his leg with hers beneath the table.

She smiled at him fondly. 'I don't know what I'd have done without you, Peter,' she whispered. 'You've been so wonderful to me, I sometimes feel I want to cry.'

He glanced at her anxiously. 'You'll make your chips all soggy.'

'Why do you have to be facetious?'

'Masculine embarrassment in the face of feminine emotion in public. It's our natural reaction.'

'Only British men are like that!'

'British men and British justice are having a thin time this evening,' he said, glancing at her hopefully.

For several seconds she stared at her plate of half-eaten food. Then she looked up at him and said, 'I'm not really interested in British justice and I'm only interested in *one* British man.'

'Say no more! I'll get the bill.'

XXVI

When Mr Justice Sarrow took his place on the bench at half past ten the next morning, the scene was at once re-set as it had been left the previous evening. Page stepped back into the witness-box and the judge looked towards Mr Paynter, who rose.

'I have only one question I want to ask you, Superintendent,' he said, obviously relishing the ripple of interest occasioned by this statement. Page half turned in his direction. He had been expecting some strenuous cross-examination concerning his interviews with Farmer. The normal line of defence of Mr Butter's clients was to make a vicious attack on police, alleging duress, physical assault and 'verbals'. But this could hardly all be wrapped up in one single question. Page waited, with that tingle of apprehension known to most witnesses as they stand on the threshold of cross-examination.

'Tell me,' Mr Paynter went on, after a deliberate pause to heighten the effect of his question, 'did the deceased have any previous convictions?'

Page blinked. 'Nothing recent, sir.'

'Any at all?'

'Might I look at my file, sir? I think there may ...'

'Might he look at his papers, my lord?'

Mr Justice Sarrow nodded.

Page thumbed through his working file till he came to the sheet he was looking for.

'Yes, sir, he had one conviction. It was over thirty years

ago. At Bow Street Magistrates Court, he was fined £5.'

'For what?'

'For importuning as a male person.'

'Thank you. That's all I want to ask the witness, my lord.'

'That, then, is the case for the Crown, my lord,' Mr Wotell announced, with a meaning look at the jury.

'I call my client,' Mr Paynter said briskly.

There was the sound of an ancient bolt being pulled back and a door in the rear of the dock was opened to allow Brian Farmer access to the witness-box. He took the oath in a gulped, nervous tone and then stood facing Mr Paynter like a small boy summoned by the headmaster, while Mr Wotell glared at him as though he'd gate-crashed a Palace garden party. He was wearing a pair of dark brown slacks, a sober sports jacket of grey-green cloth, a neat striped shirt and an undemonstrative tie. His hair was cut to a length to please an older generation and it was immediately noticeable that the two women on the jury cast him looks of maternal interest.

'Is your full name Brian Richard Farmer?' Mr Paynter asked in a tone which had a friendly, and almost welcoming, ring to it.

'Yes.'

'And how old are you?'

'Twenty-one.'

'Is it a fact that about eight months ago you were released from Borstal?'

'Yes.'

'For what offence were you sent for Borstal training?' Mr Paynter made it sound like an army course for the specially chosen.

'Burglary.' Farmer's tone was little above a whisper.

'Is that your only conviction?'

'Yes.'

'Just for the benefit of the jury, perhaps I should ask you this further question: was it an offence which involved any violence towards anyone?'

'No.'

'Now,' Mr Paynter went on, casting the jury a significant look, 'let there be no beating about the bush, were you the cause of Shem's death?'

Farmer hung his head. 'Yes, but I never meant to kill him. I didn't even want to hurt him.'

'Silence,' bellowed an usher as excited murmurs erupted all over the court-room.

'Now that we have got that out of the way, let me take you back in time and move forward to the date of Shem's death. Until you were about seventeen, did you live in the village of Long Gaisford?'

'Yes.'

'Your parents lived there at that time?'

'Yes.'

'And after you left, did you ever return?'

'No ... well, that is, not until ... not until the day of Shem's death.'

'I now want you to tell my lord and the jury, how you came to return to Long Gaisford that particular day?'

'I didn't actually go to the village, it was to this cave in Harrier's Wood.'

'Why did you go there? Just keep your voice up and tell the court why you went to the cave.'

'When I was a kid living in the village, I used to go and play there. It was a sort of secret place. No one else knew about it, see.'

'Yes?'

'Well, I suddenly wanted to go back and look at it again. I had this feeling like when you want to see your old home, except with me it was this cave. I'd been thinking about it and wondering if anyone else had been using it and ... well, I decided to go and see. It was one of them on the spur of the moment things. I'd been feeling a bit low for a few days, thinking about when I used to live in the country and then suddenly I decided I'd go that day.' He paused and added in a wistful tone, 'I wish now I never had.'

'So what did you do?'

'I drove down there in the afternoon.'

'With anybody?'

'No, alone.'

'Whose car?'

'A mate's. He'd lent it to me for a few days while he was away. It was having the use of a car what really decided me to go.'

'Yes, go on.'

'I got down there around four o'clock and parked the car on the track which leads into the wood.'

'Stop there a moment,' Mr Paynter broke in. 'How far up the track did you take the car?'

'Right up to the edge of the wood as far as you can go.'

'What did you do then?'

'I walked to the cave.'

'Yes.'

'At first it didn't look as if anyone'd been there. It's all hidden by creepers and stuff, and I pushed my way through. But as soon as I got inside, I knew someone had been there, I could smell cigarettes.'

'What did you do?'

'I sat down and had a smoke myself.'

'How many cigarettes did you smoke altogether while you were in the cave?'

'A couple, I think.'

'We've heard that two cigarette ends were found on the floor of the cave which bear saliva traces showing they were smoked by you, so that's right?'

'Yes.'

'You made no attempt to conceal the fact you smoked in the cave?'

'No, why should I?'

'Anyway, you say you sat down and had a smoke, what happened next?'

'I heard sounds outside the cave and someone came in. It

was the old tramp.'

'Shem?'

'Yes.'

'Did you know who he was?'

'Not then. But I realised later he was the same old tramp who used to come around when we lived in the village.'

'What happened next?'

'He was surprised to find me there and he got kind of funny.'

'In what way?'

'Well, he came over and sat down close beside me and started making ... well, sexy remarks.'

'What did you do?'

'I didn't take any notice at first, but then he suddenly made a grab at my privates.'

'Yes?'

'I knocked his hand away, but he did it again and more or less rolled on top of my body. I tried to push him off, but he was bigger than me ...'

'When you say bigger, do you mean taller?'

'Yes.'

'How tall are you?'

'Five feet six inches.'

'And we've heard from Dr Leary that the deceased was five feet ten.'

'He seemed to weigh quite a bit, too.'

'What happened next?'

'I was telling him all the time to get off and not be a fool. I kept telling him I wasn't interested in that sort of thing.'

'By which you meant homosexual conduct?'

'Yes.'

'Did he take any notice?'

'No, he just tried all the harder to get his hand inside my trousers. And then I got into a sort of panic because I couldn't get free from him and I suddenly felt a stone under my hand and I clutched it and I hit him on the head with it.'

'How many times, did you hit him?'

'I don't remember. Several times.'

'How hard?'

'Not very hard, because he was on top of me and I couldn't use my arm properly.'

'And then?'

'Well, suddenly he sort of stopped struggling and he half rolled off me and I was able to get free and stand up.'

'And what about him?'

'He just lay on the floor.' Farmer's lower lip began to quiver and he bit at it. 'I bent down and shook him by the shoulder and it was then I realised he was dead. He just slumped over and I could see the blood on his head.'

'Tell me, how much light was there in the cave at this time?'

'It was sort of dark, but you could see a bit when your eyes got used to it.'

'But you say that you saw blood on his head?'

'Well, I did and I also felt it.'

'What did you do next?'

'I was in a proper panic. I didn't know what to do. In the end, I decided I'd have to shift his body.'

'Why?'

'Because I thought, if somebody knows he's living in the cave, they'll find him, but if I leave his body somewhere else, it'll make it more difficult for them.'

'For who?'

'The police.'

'You were frightened that the police would be able to trace you more easily if they found the body in the cave?'

'Yes, that was it,' Farmer said, with a grateful nod.

'So you carried the body to your car, is that what happened?'

Mr Wotell rose to his feet. 'I really must ask my learned friend not to lead on such an important matter,' he said in a huffy voice.

'I'm sorry to have upset my friend,' Mr Paynter remarked in a faintly patronising tone, 'but it didn't occur to me that there could be any dispute.' He turned back to Farmer. 'How did you get the body from the cave to your car?'

'I dragged it.'

'There you go again,' Mr Wotell broke in crossly. 'He's never said anything about removing the body in his car. You're putting words into his mouth.'

'How did you transport the body?' Mr Paynter asked with exaggerated weariness.

'In the car.'

'And where did you take it?'

'To the quarries.'

'Why there?'

'I intended . . .' He broke off and appeared to be about to cry.

'Yes, go on. What was it you intended?'

'I'm afraid I intended to put his body in the water. I hoped it'd sink.'

'And why didn't you do that?'

'I hadn't the strength to drag him that far. It was going to take too long and I wanted to get away.'

'What was your state of mind at this time?'

'I was in a terrible panic.'

'I should have asked you this before, what time was it when you took the body to the area of the quarries?'

'Around midnight.'

'And what time had the struggle in the cave taken place?'

'About four or five o'clock, I suppose.'

'And what were you doing between then and midnight?'

'Just waiting.'

'Waiting for what?'

'For there to be nobody about.'

Mr Paynter turned the pages of his brief in a thoughtful manner and then leant over to have a word with his junior. He gave a nod and straightened up again.

'What happened to the stone with which you hit the deceased over the head?'

'I threw it into one of the quarries.'

'Into the water there?'

'Yes.'

Mr Paynter sat slowly down and Mr Wotell rose with the air of a self-appointed avenger.

'So you didn't mean to kill this unfortunate man, is that what you're telling the jury?'

'Yes.'

'And yet you tried to dispose of his body afterwards, didn't you?'

'I moved it, yes.'

'Intending to commit it to the deep waters of an anonymous quarry?'

'As far as I'm aware, we don't have any evidence as to the depth of the water,' Mr Paynter murmured audibly from his seat.

'If my learned friend has something to say, perhaps he'll have the courtesy to stand up and address the court properly,' Mr Wotell observed with an angry glance in his opponent's direction.

The judge looked from one to the other, but kept his thoughts to himself.

'Well, Farmer, you intended casting this unfortunate man's body into the water, hoping it would sink and never be found, that's right, isn't it?'

'Yes, because I was in a panic.'

'So you say! Do you . . .'

'Really!' Mr Paynter broke in, this time jumping to his feet. 'That is a gross comment and far removed from the realm of proper cross-examination.'

'I'm sure we'd get on much better if counsel would avoid bickering,' Mr Justice Sarrow remarked, though without much hope in his tone that his admonition would go heeded.

'Do you call that the conduct of an innocent man?' Mr

Wotell asked, while Mr Paynter shook his head in weary resignation.

'I tell you I was scared.'

'I suggest you were coldly calculating.'

'No . . .'

'And that your evidence is one long cock and bull story from beginning to end.'

'It's the truth.'

'We'll see. Now . . .'

And so prosecuting counsel pursued his cross-examination for a further forty minutes, at the end of which time he sat down red in the face, but with a sweepingly triumphant look at the jury.

Farmer for his part looked pale and drawn. He hadn't understood half of it, all he'd been conscious of was a barrage of loud and angry words. But he'd clung steadfastly to the account he'd given under examination-in-chief. It had been like clinging to a spar of wood in a stormy sea. All he could think of was that he mustn't let go. And now the storm had suddenly abated and his own counsel was facing him with a reassuring look.

'My lord, I have no questions I wish to put in re-examination,' Mr Paynter said.

Mr Justice Sarrow turned his head to look straight at Farmer for a few seconds. Then he made a small gesture indicating that he should return to the dock and turned his attention back to his notebook in which he had effortlessly recorded the evidence with an old-fashioned fountain pen.

'Then, my lord,' Mr Paynter went on, 'that is the case for the defence.'

The judge glanced up and nodded and looked towards Mr Wotell, who rose with the air of one with an unquenchable sense of self-imposed duty.

'May it please your lordship, members of the jury, it now falls to me to address you for the last time on behalf of the Crown and to direct your mind to those unassailable pieces of evidence which show quite clearly, in my submission, that the crown has amply discharged the onus placed upon it by law of proving that the prisoner is guilty of the murder of Joshua Clapp.' Mr Wotell once more went through the evidence in support of the crown's case and then turned to Farmer's own testimony. 'And what is the prisoner's story?' he asked in a tone of scorn. 'It is that he was subjected to a homosexual assault by the deceased. Can you believe it, members of the jury? Can you really believe *that*? Or is it just the invention – the despicable invention – of a vile mind? The invention of someone who is ready to stoop as low as the ground itself in order to try and save his shameless skin.'

'My God!' Mr Paynter muttered to his junior. 'He's just like a ham actor in a Victorian melodrama. Shameless skin, indeed! I suppose he didn't say foreskin by any chance?'

The junior sniggered, but Mr Wotell, who was now in full spate, didn't hear. It was some time later that he reached his peroration.

'Members of the jury, soon this case will pass finally and irrevocably into your hands and I know that you will not shrink from performing your duty in accordance with the solemn oaths you have taken. Let nothing sway you from that path of duty which, as citizens called to carry out the highest duty to which Her Majesty's subjects can be called upon to perform, namely to act as jurors at the trial of a fellow citizen, you ... it ... Let nothing deflect you from returning a true verdict, which, the Crown say, must be a verdict of guilty.'

'Members of the jury,' Mr Paynter said in a brisk, conversational tone, as he stood up to make his final speech. 'I am asking you for nothing less than my client's acquittal. My lord will direct you as to the law, but my submission to you is this. If you accept Farmer's account of what took place in the cave and you find that he used no more force than was reasonable to repel this loathsome attack on him, then it is your duty to find him not guilty.

'Of course, I know you only have one side of what took

place. The only other person who could have helped you is now dead. But I am going to suggest to you why you should accept what you've heard from Farmer's own lips. You will recall that one of my few questions in cross-examination of the crown's witness elicited the fact that the dead man had once been convicted of importuning.' Mr Paynter paused and gave the jury a significant look. 'Admittedly it was some time ago, but it still indicates, does it not, that the deceased was a man with these unfortunate proclivities? They're a streak in a man's character which remain there for the whole of his life. They don't disappear like a pimple on the face or a cut on the finger. They are part of the person, a facet of his personality. So when Farmer tells you that the deceased made this sudden assault on him, do you really have very much difficulty in accepting it as the truth, in the light of that previous conviction?'

Mr Paynter went on to compare the difference in height of the two men and to liken the struggle in the darkened cave to one between a larger man with the advantage of surprise on his side and a smaller man who, but for suddenly finding a stone under his hand, might himself have become the victim of murder. 'And a particularly revolting murder at that,' he had added.

And as to Farmer's conduct afterwards, well, said Mr Paynter, was there anything in it not consistent with panic? And who would not have fallen into panic in the circumstances described? His client had, moreover, frankly told them that he was not a person of unblemished character – he hadn't been obliged to tell them, but he had chosen to do so – he'd been in Borstal, but that didn't make him a murderer. *His* offence had not involved any personal violence. Unlike the deceased's conviction, it had no evidential bearing on the facts of the case they were considering.

In all, Mr Paynter addressed the jury for rather less time than Mr Wotell, but he did so with far greater persuasive force.

But juries are enigmatic entities and it's a rash person

who thinks he can divine their verdict from their corporate appearance. All that could be said was that they seemed to listen to defending counsel with more interest than they'd shown his opponent. But Mr Paynter was too experienced a hand to allow this to lull him into a false sense of security. When the fate of his clients rested in the hands of a jury, he left nothing to chance.

For some moments after he had sat down, nothing happened and Mr Justice Sarrow, upon whom everyone's eyes had turned, merely went on writing in his notebook. Finally he laid down his pen, blinked around the court a few times and faced the jury who were watching him expectantly. His interventions in the course of the trial had been so minimal, it came almost as a surprise to discover that he could utter a complete sentence.

His voice was in keeping with his appearance, dry, remote and unemotional, and he proceeded to instruct the jury on the principles of law involved in a criminal trial and, in particular, in a case of murder. Having given them a scholarly lecture which left several of them looking like members of an audience who were expecting to witness a Brian Rix farce but find they've strayed in error into a performance of *King Lear*, his lordship began to recapitulate the facts. With scrupulous thoroughness, he regurgitated the evidence they had heard from every witness. It all took a very long time and when he had finished, he glanced up at the clock which faced him just below the public gallery.

'Having regard to the hour, we will now adjourn and I will complete my summing-up tomorrow morning.' He paused. 'Unless you would sooner retire this evening,' he added, looking at the foreman.

The foreman, a large, red-faced man whose wheezy breathing had been audible throughout the trial, heaved himself round and murmured to his colleagues, who broke into urgent whispers among themselves. Then he stood up.

'We'd like to get it done with tonight,' he announced.

'Very well.'

'If that's O.K. for your lordship?' he added as a polite afterthought.

'The choice is yours.'

A couple of minutes later, they had filed out of court to consider their verdict, the judge had departed to a cup of tea in his room, Farmer had returned to his cell beneath the dock and everyone else had spilled out into the narrow corridor which ran round the hexagonal perimeter of the court-room.

'They'll acquit him all right,' Mr Butters remarked to his two counsel, as they stood together near to the porticoed entrance. 'There's more than enough to raise a reasonable doubt as to his guilt.'

' 'Fraid they didn't get much help from the judge,' Mr Paynter observed.

'Somebody ought to put him back in the British Museum,' Mr Butters retorted. 'And put Mr Wotell in the Chamber of Horrors!'

Mr Paynter smiled thinly. 'You, at any rate, sound confident of the result.'

'I am.'

A little way off, Mr Wotell had at last managed to light his pipe and was puffing out clouds of smoke to his own obvious satisfaction.

'Never know what a jury'll do,' he observed to his junior, 'but they ought to convict. Thought Farmer looked a nasty bit of work. Typical young layabout. Sort of worthless creature makes you want to bring back hanging.'

The junior nodded, since it seemed the easiest thing to do.

Farther on round one of the kinks in the corridor, Page and Machin stood together.

'What do you think they'll do, sir?' Machin asked.

'Disagree.'

'Do you really think that?'

'Why not! After that summing-up, they won't know what to make of the case, so each'll chase after his own pet theory and they'll end up in utter confusion.'

'That'll mean a retrial.'

'Yes,' Page said gloomily, 'and probably the postponement of my retirement.'

But the jury didn't disagree.

After thirty-five minutes, they returned to court and announced that they had reached an unanimous verdict, which was 'not guilty'.

Fifteen minutes later, when the court-room was empty, Farmer came up the stairs into the dock on his way to freedom. Before anyone had a chance to speak to him, however, Mr Butters had closed in and was steering him firmly and rapidly towards his parked car.

The last that Page and Machin saw of him was sitting in the passenger seat, looking pale and tense, as the car accelerated away towards the London road with a burst of exhaust fumes.

'Wonder what the hurry is!' Page remarked thoughtfully.

'Almost as if his solicitor was kidnapping him,' Machin added, as the car disappeared from view.

XXVII

Farmer's acquittal received little attention in the national press. It needed much more than a mere suggestion of a homosexual assault to interest the public at large in a murder trial these days. Though, of course, the local papers gave it full coverage and the residents of Long Gaisford had every reason to go on talking about it. Not only had the accused been a local boy, but there was the added mystery of Kenny Bostock's disappearance. No one had any doubt that he was in some way connected with the murder, but thereafter speculation branched out in a dozen divergent directions.

Page didn't really know what he had expected to happen after the trial, but he *did* know that he felt most uneasy. He could only regard the situation as a lull. But a lull before what, he had no idea.

It hadn't occurred to him that Farmer was going to be snatched away from under his nose and the more he thought about it, the more ominous it appeared. It had been his intention to have a long talk with him in the hope of finding out some of the unexplained background of the case and, in particular, to question him about Kenny. With his acquittal, the normal inhibitions about interviewing an accused had been removed. There was no reason why Farmer shouldn't have been co-operative in an off-the-record session. But it was now very clear that Mr Butters had been intent on seeing that no such opportunity was afforded the police. Farmer had been swept up and spirited away before anyone could speak to him. It was almost, as Machin had remarked, as if his solicitor was kidnapping him.

However, there seemed to be nothing Page could now do, save hope that the weeks up to his retirement would pass off without event. It was with considerable fretfulness that he doubted this. A lull was a lull – and only a lull.

Two days after his trial, Farmer was again sitting in the first-floor room which was the regular meeting-place of himself, Edmunds and the other two.

''Ow's it feel to be free again, Brian?' Edmunds asked cheerfully.

'Fine.'

''E doesn't exactly look as if 'e's full of the joys of spring, does 'e?' he enquired of the other two.

The short one curled his lip and the tall one said, 'What's wrong with you, Brian? You ought to be thanking us.

We've been put to a lot of trouble all on account of you and all you do is look like a bloody Scottish funeral.'

'I'm all right —'

'Too bloody true you're all right,' Edmunds said. 'It cost a tidy bit of money, too. You want to show a bit of gratitude like 'e says.'

'What have I got to be grateful for?'

For a moment, there was a stunned silence, not so much for what was said as for the tone in which he'd spoken, for the words had come out in a bitter spew.

'You want to watch the way you talk,' Edmunds said, with a dangerous edge to his tone. 'You've got a lot to be grateful for. If it 'adn't been for me, you'd still be in the nick, and be there for a long time as well. The jury would 'ave 'ad you for murder, if I 'adn't got old Jason Butters to take on the case.' He glanced at the other two who nodded in agreement. 'That's what you got to be grateful for!' He got up and walked across to where Farmer was slouched in a chair. 'Come on, Brian, let's see a bit of enthusiasm. This isn't the moment for sulks. We've got work to do.'

'P'raps he's missing old Shem's warm embraces,' the tall one said with a grin.

'Cut that out!' Edmunds said sharply. 'We don't want no bitchy talk here.'

'Well, from the way he's carrying on, I wondered if Brian wasn't one of them...'

'Enough, I said!' Two strides brought Edmunds to where the other was sitting. 'Another word and I'll stuff your rotten teeth down your stinking throat.'

The tall man shrugged, but said nothing more and Edmunds went back to his own chair.

'Now,' he said, 'let's just run through things, shall we, because it's my view we can go ahead next week.'

'What about the boy?' Farmer broke in.

Edmunds frowned. 'What about 'im, Brian?' he enquired in a tone which carried more than a hint of menace.

'When are you going to let him go?'

195

Edmund's frown grew. 'We'll talk about that later,' he said.

Farmer shook his head. 'No we won't, Mick, we'll talk about it now.'

For a second it looked as though Edmunds was going to fly across the room at Farmer, then with an obvious effort at self-control, he sat back in his chair.

'O.K., Brian, go ahead.' A silence followed and he added in a heckling tone, 'Well, go ahead and talk about 'im, if that's what you want. I'm listening, but don't take all bloody night about it, that's all.'

'I've kept my side of the bargain,' Farmer said in a tense voice, 'and I think you ought to keep yours.'

'Oh, so we're on to bargains now, are we!'

'Yes. You said you'd release him as soon as the case was finished. I've kept my side . . .'

'I've kept my side,' Edmunds mimicked angrily. 'Who do you think you are? The bloody United Nations?'

'I want you to release him,' Farmer said quietly, but in a tone as menacing in its way as Edmunds' had been. 'In fact, I'm telling you to.'

The atmosphere in the room had become suddenly so charged that a struck match might have caused an explosion. Then as suddenly, the tension slackened.

'I don't know what you're so worried about him for. 'E's a nice kid and 'e's all right. Anyone'd think 'e was in some danger to 'ear you talk. 'E's not, 'e's fine. Nobody's going to 'urt 'im, so what's all the worry about?'

'The worry,' Farmer said, 'is whether Mick Edmunds can be trusted to keep his word. It seems . . .'

Before he had time to finish the sentence, Edmunds was standing over him and had delivered two stinging slaps across his face.

'I've 'ad enough of your talk, Brian. I'm the boss around 'ere and it's time you remembered it. And also remembered that you're only a small number in this outfit. The boy'll be released when I say and not before. He mightn't be released at all unless his big cousin learns to behave sensible and to do as 'e's told.' He paused and stared dispassionately at Farmer whose left cheek was now an angry red. 'Got that message, Brian? You'll behave sensible-like or else . . .' He turned towards the other two. 'Anyone got any comments before we get down to business?' They shook their heads with the same degree of indifference that had marked their attitude towards the whole episode. They'd been like two cats quietly observing a veteran tom suddenly turn on a much younger cat. 'Good, then let's not waste any more time on silly talk about bargains. We're in this together for our own benefit and we don't want no more setbacks. The old bugger's death 'as been enough.' He threw Farmer an amused smile. 'But Brian's managed to get off that 'ook and we certainly don't want to see 'im on another, do we? So let bygones be bygones, I say. O.K., Brian?'

Farmer seemed about to say something, but thought better of it. He gave a brief nod and leant forward as Edmunds went on speaking.

'That's fine, then. And our old plan's fine, too. All we got to do is make one change and that's what we got to talk about now . . .'

XXVIII

For the first week or so, Kenny's sense of excitement had been sustained. It was all a big adventure; an adventure to help Brian. Moreover, everyone had been friendly – not that he'd seen more than a couple of people – and had treated him as a sort of V.I.P. He'd been given almost everything he asked for and the tall man and the blonde girl with him had been at pains to keep him amused. The only snag had been that he hadn't been allowed out. They'd said he might be recognised and had stressed how important it was that he shouldn't be seen so long as Brian remained in trouble. They had hinted that Brian's release would largely depend on Kenny himself and that he must therefore stay under cover until the right moment came. Without questioning what this moment might be, Kenny accepted their suggestion that an inability to go out was a small sacrifice to pay if it was going to help Brian. It was at the tall man's dictation he had later written the note to his parents.

Mick Edmunds had driven Kenny to London on the day of their meeting and that in itself had been an adventure, since Edmunds had driven very fast and had made him duck down out of sight whenever they passed a policeman. He had brought him straight to the house where he had been ever since. Kenny had no idea where it was, save that it was somewhere in London and once later when he had asked the tall man, he'd been told it was better he shouldn't know in Brian's interests. It was a modern semi-detached with a garden, though he was never allowed there. The windows were hung with lace curtains, and the road outside looked like one out of a television commercial showing housewives discussing detergents on their doorsteps.

He had never seen Edmunds again, though when they had parted, he'd been led to believe that Edmunds would be dropping by almost every day to give him details of the plans to help Brian. In the beginning the tall man had made excuses for his failure to appear, saying that he'd been held up on important business but that he'd probably look in the next day. But after a time, he ceased to bother to make excuses and Edmunds' absence became a fact of life.

It was only after the sense of adventure had become dulled and excitement had given way to boredom that Edmunds' failure to reappear began to cause Kenny uneasiness. He was like someone who had eagerly answered a call to the colours and then found himself confined to base camp when he'd expected to be in the front line.

With the onset of frustration had also come a change in

the attitude of his jailers, not that he yet thought of them as such. They became more offhand and less inclined to spend time talking to him and indulging his wishes. The girl, in particular, would manifest impatience and once or twice snapped at him. One evening he had heard her complaining to the tall young man, saying that she was fed up with having Kenny in the house and how much longer was it going on.

He hadn't heard the reply, but shortly afterwards the man had come up to Kenny's room and been friendlier than he had for several days. They'd played a game of draughts which Kenny had won and the man had said how pleased Brian was that Kenny was helping him and how Brian had great confidence in him, Kenny, which, now they'd come to know him, the others all shared. He enjoined patience and said he hoped it wouldn't be long before things began to happen, by which, he quickly added, he meant that Kenny would be told how he was going to help Brian get out of trouble.

But still the days went by and nothing happened and Kenny's boredom began to yield to fear. Unimaginative boy though he was, he was suddenly assailed by doubts and anxiety as to the future. He wondered whether his current existence would ever reach an end. By now the house had become a prison and his only desire was to get out of it.

After one particularly bad day when he and the girl had had a sullen confrontation, the tall young man had once again acted as peacemaker. He said he knew how Kenny must be feeling, but that it was now more important than ever he should remain under cover. Nevertheless, he suggested that he should take him for a drive round the lighted shopping streets to give him a change of scene, provided he would promise not to attract attention in any way.

Kenny promised and the drive took place and when they got back to the house, the man said they'd have another run around later in the week, as he'd enjoyed it as much as Kenny had.

However, the next night Kenny had a shattering nightmare. He dreamt that he was shut in a room and couldn't get out and nobody answered his screams. He awoke from it soaked by his own sweat and in a state of terror. He leapt from his bed and dashed to the door to find it locked. In a panic, he rattled it furiously and shouted and beat on the panels with his fist.

Suddenly, the key was turned and he fell back as the door was thrust open. A light was switched on and the tall young man stood there, tousle-headed and naked.

'What the hell's up?' he demanded, angrily.

'I had a bad dream,' Kenny said, looking at him urgently in search of comfort.

For several seconds, the man just gazed back at him as though uncertain what to do, while Kenny continued staring at him, mesmerised by his nakedness.

'Well, get back into bed and don't have any more bad dreams. Making all that noise in the middle of the night'll get us in wrong with the neighbours.'

Slowly Kenny backed towards the bed and got in, pulling the blanket up to his chin.

'Feeling O.K. now?'

He nodded. 'You won't lock the door again, will you?'

The man frowned. 'Not if you promise to behave yourself. Promise?'

'Yes.'

'Well, go to sleep, then.' He switched off the light and closed the door. Kenny strained his ears to hear if the key was turned but was satisfied that it was not. Later he cried himself to sleep.

But from then on, his fear grew. And with it, grew a frightening sense of complete captivity.

XXIX

In the ten days which followed the end of Brian Farmer's trial, Machin found himself fully occupied, so that his only reminder of the case was Susan, whom he continued to meet several times a week. Kenny's name was hardly ever mentioned, if only because there was nothing new for either of them to say, but he, nevertheless, still loomed large in both their minds. To Susan his disappearance was a dull ache in her heart: to Machin a reminder of baffled impotence.

The day after the trial finished, Machin was put on a delicate enquiry involving a number of allegations of bribery against an official in the local housing department. Just as he had got going on this, he had to drop it to deal with the attempted murder of a woman by her postman husband, who had attacked her with a pair of scissors on discovering that she was having an affair with a good-looking young man who was the butcher's assistant.

He had nearly completed the preliminary investigation of the attempted murder and was preparing to pick up the threads of the bribery case when yet another violent crime intervened.

It was a Thursday morning and eleven o'clock. He was on the point of setting out to interview further witnesses, who'd alleged that they'd been told they'd have a better chance of obtaining a house quickly if they slid the particular official a small present, when the phone rang. He immediately recognised the voice of the officer on duty in the information room below.

'There's been a robbery over at Flatchet at Keenan's Electrics,' the officer said. 'Information's still coming in.

Four men wearing stocking masks held up the two clerks who were making up the pay packets. One of the men was armed and fired at one of the clerks who got a bullet through his shoulder.'

'Did they get away?'

'It seems so, but with only a few hundred pounds. It appears there was a fair amount of confusion and they fled without getting very much.'

'Who's gone to the scene?'

'A couple of patrol cars are on their way and so is Detective Constable Porter. He's the only C.I.D. officer available at Flatchet at the moment.'

'Have you informed Superintendent Page?'

'No, I thought you would. Anyway, he's out.'

'How the hell am I to tell him then?'

'Thought you might know where he was.'

'Well, I don't! O.K., pass a message and say that I'm leaving straight away. And then try and find Mr Page and let him know what's happened.'

'Will do.'

It took Machin twenty-five minutes to reach Flatchet and a further five to navigate his way through the congested high street and out the other side to where Keenan's Electrics was situated. As he swung his car through the main gate of the factory, the scene which met his eyes was reminiscent of a TV crime serial. Three police patrol cars were pulled up at odd angles to one another, an ambulance was parked over against a low prefabricated building and various officers were standing about in attitudes of intense purposefulness. It was the standard tableau.

One of the patrol car officers who recognised Machin came across.

'They've taken the injured man off to hospital and Detective Constable Porter's talking to the other clerk in the office. He's pretty shaken by his experience.'

'What exactly happened?'

'The clerks had just finished making up the wages when

the lock was shot off the door and four masked men charged in. One of them was carrying a canvas holdall and he began to shovel the money into that while the other three covered the clerks.'

'Were they all armed?'

'One had a gun and the other two were carrying coshes. Anyway, the injured clerk made a dive for an alarm bell and that was when he got shot. There then seems to have been a certain amount of panic. The chap who was filling the bag dropped it and most of the money fell out and they fled just grabbing what they could in their hands.'

'I gather they got only a few hundred?'

'Nobody's made a proper check yet, there hasn't been time. But they can't have taken much.'

'How much was there altogether?'

'Around ten thousand pounds.'

Machin glanced about him. 'Where was their car?'

'They drove right up to the office door.'

'What about the chap on the gate, how'd he come to let them through?'

'They cracked him over the nut and bundled him inside his cubby-hole. He was still unconscious when it was all over.'

'Didn't the shooting attract attention?'

'Apparently, there are quite often noises like rifle shots around the factory, so nobody took particular notice. But I think that may be where their plan started to go wrong. It's only recently that the clerks have taken to locking themselves in when making up the wage packets, and it looks as if these villains hadn't expected to find the door locked.'

'Have road blocks been set up?'

'Yes. But this whole area is a maze of lanes. They could easily slip through.'

'How much start did they get?'

'A good quarter of an hour before anything effective could be done.'

'Well, I'd better go and find Detective Constable Porter,'

Machin remarked, moving off in the direction of the nearest building. It was a spaciously laid out factory with lawns and flower beds between the various buildings, which were all one storey. A high wire fence surrounded the area and the only entrance was that through which Machin had driven. He had just reached the administration block when one of the officers who'd been sitting in his car receiving and transmitting messages hailed him.

'Hey, Sarge! Here a moment!'

Machin went over to the car.

'What is it?'

The officer held up a delaying hand, as he went on listening intently.

'I'll tell Sergeant Machin right away. He's here beside me now.' He turned to Machin. 'That was Arlebury on the line. They've just received a message that a man is lying in a ditch about four miles from here. I've got the reference. A farmer found him. He's dead and he's got a stocking over his head.'

Machin pulled open the rear door, jumped in and shouted to the driver who had been talking to another officer. He came running up and a few seconds later, they were swirling along the narrow road away from Flatchet.

They had no difficulty in finding the spot, since the farmer who'd made the discovery was standing guard as though he had taken a prisoner and was waiting to hand him over.

He stepped back as the officers spilled out of the car and watched them as they stared at the sprawled form lying face downwards in the ditch.

Machin knelt beside the body and gingerly lifted the stockinged head. There was no sign of any blood but it lolled grotesquely as soon as he removed his hand.

Slipping his other hand into the dead man's jacket pocket he felt around for some clue as to identification. His fingers closed on something faintly familiar and he pulled it out.

'What the hell's that?' the radio operator asked, gazing

mystified at the small object which Machin was holding in the palm of his hand.

Machin looked up. 'A badger's tooth,' he said.

XXX

Kenny had spent the morning playing bagatelle by himself. The tall man had brought him the board the previous evening and he had found himself hypnotised by the small steel ball as it pinged off the pins. There was also something satisfactory in releasing the spring which set the ball in motion. At first he had done it too vigorously so that the ball frequently jumped right off the board and he had to go crawling under the furniture to retrieve it. Subsequently he settled down to try and break a new record with each turn.

The blonde woman had looked in once or twice, but gone away again as soon as she'd seen that he was peaceably engaged.

Lying on his tummy on the floor had given him an appetite and he was glad when he smelt cooking down below. He and the blonde normally ate together in the kitchen, where they were occasionally joined by the tall young man. But more often than not he didn't come home until the evening.

Kenny got up off the floor and went across to the window. It was a dull grey day with more than a hint of fog hanging around.

In his absorption in the bagatelle board, he had temporarily forgotten his plight, but now as he gazed out on the empty street, he was again filled with anxious bewilderment. Life had reached a state beyond his comprehension and his mind was quite unable to cope with the situation.

As he stood looking out of the window, a car came racing

down the road. He recognised it as the tall man's Vauxhall and it was clear that the driver was in a tearing hurry. It pulled up outside the house as though doing a braking test and the tall man leapt out of the driver's seat and rushed into the house, slamming doors behind him.

Kenny went across to his bedroom door and opened it.

'We've got to leave at once,' the tall man was saying urgently. 'At once! Now! Grab anything you want from upstairs, but for Chrissake don't start trying to pack. There's no time for that.'

'What about the kid?'

'Forget him. Forget what you're cooking, too. Now, for God's sake, get your skates on! I'll give you just two minutes.'

The blonde came scampering up the stairs and disappeared into their bedroom. A minute later, she reappeared wearing a coat and carrying a small case which she was trying to fasten as she went. The man was waiting in the hall.

'Do you mean we just leave him up there?' she asked, glancing back up at Kenny's door.

'Yes.'

'I suppose you know best?'

'We haven't time to do anything about him and that's all there is to it. We don't want another murder on our hands. One's enough for today!' The blonde gasped. 'Let the catch on the door down,' the man shouted as he dashed ahead to the car.

Kenny hurried over to the window and watched them drive away with the same vicious speed that had marked the car's arrival a few minutes before.

For some time after it had disappeared, he continued staring out. Then he recrossed to the door and went downstairs. He found that the burners on the kitchen stove were still alight. He peered in one of the saucepans and found that it contained a bubbling stew. Fetching a plate, he helped himself and sat down at the table to eat it.

He felt strangely safe now that he knew they wouldn't be coming back. On the other hand he wanted a bit of time to decide what he was going to do himself. He was by no means sure that he meant to go home. That would involve facing another barrage of questions from the police. It had been bad enough before. Next time it would be even worse; though he'd still hold out.

He wondered what had happened to make the couple leave the house in such haste. The man had mentioned a murder. Kenny pondered the implications of this, but his mind failed to come up with any sort of answer. But so much had happened to him in the past month which he hadn't understood, that the words made no great impact. His mind had become water-logged.

He finished his meal and then searched the house to see if they had left any money behind. But all he found was a new 20-pence piece on top of the TV set.

Ten minutes later, he let himself out and set off down the road. His sense of liberation was complete, even if he was still quite undecided what to do.

XXXI

For half an hour, Machin, the two uniformed officers and the farmer maintained their curious vigil round the body.

'Well, aren't you going to do something?' the farmer had asked in an affronted tone. 'Aren't you going to see who he is? You can't just leave him lying there like a dead beast.'

'We'll have to leave him just as he is until the doctor and the photographer have come,' Machin said. 'Anyway, there's nothing we can do for him.'

'No, but it doesn't seem natural just to let him lie in a ditch.'

'It won't be for long.'

The farmer had stepped closer and peered at the body again with a puzzled expression. 'Can't see any blood. How do you think he died?'

'No idea. Have to wait for the doctor,' Machin replied, his mind elsewhere.

'Know who he is?'

'Perhaps.'

'You a countryman yourself?'

'Cornish. Why?'

'I wondered how you came to recognise a badger's tooth?'

'Oh! I happen to have seen others recently.'

The farmer pushed his cap back and scratched the front of his head. 'Poor sod!' he observed in a troubled voice. 'What a way to end up! In a ditch with a stocking over your head. A woman's stocking! It's kind of undignified.'

'Death often is.'

'It oughtn't to be. The Good Lord never intended folk to die like that.'

Machin shrugged. 'Why don't you go and sit in our car?'

'I'll stay. I found him, didn't I? I'll stay till he's taken away.'

Soon after this, a car pulled up and a small man with a bald head got out. He was carrying his badge of office, a black bag.

'I'm Dr Fenwick. I received a message to come out here. Some accident, I was told . . .' His glance fell on the body. 'Is that the chap?'

'I'm expecting the photographer any minute,' Machin said, 'so I'd be grateful if you didn't disturb the scene more than necessary.'

The doctor grunted and bent down over the copse. When he stood up, he said, 'He's dead and that's all I can tell you. I can't see any sign of injury. Want me to hang on until the photographer's been and we can remove the stocking?'

'If you would.'

'Half an hour won't make much difference. I've only got

a couple more visits before lunch and neither of them urgent.' He glanced at the body again. 'I suppose he was involved in this hold-up at Keenan's Electrics?'

Machin nodded. 'For sure.'

During the half hour he'd been at the scene, Machin had been doing some hard thinking. He wasn't yet ready to voice his conclusions aloud, but he felt he now had a reasonably complete picture of recent happenings. Part of it was still based on guesswork. But this time it was intelligent guesswork, as distinct from floundering speculation.

Accordingly, it was no surprise to him, when the moment at last came to peel off the stocking mask, to find himself looking down on the pale, terror-fixed features of Brian Farmer.

XXXII

Whereas Shem's death had aroused very little newspaper interest, Farmer's made, within a few hours of its occurrence, national headlines, as well as receiving radio and television coverage from on the spot reporters.

The wages snatch was in itself a newsworthy event, but when it could be linked with a dead body in a ditch only a few miles away and the dead person turned out to be someone who had himself recently stood trial for murder, it took news precedence over every other event of the day. Nothing could compete with it for eye-catching readability.

Police headquarters at Arlebury were besieged by reporters who invested every coming and going with overblown significance.

Page and Machin on their way back from the mortuary had had to run the gauntlet of cameras, microphones and jabbing ball-point pens.

As they reached the steps of the station, Page turned and faced the throng. Immediately a dozen questions came at him, but he held up his hand for silence.

'I've just come from the mortuary where Dr Leary has conducted a post-mortem on Farmer,' he announced, as though about to declare the result of an election. 'The cause of death was asphyxia...'

'Does that mean he was strangled?' a louder voice than most called out.

'No, he wasn't strangled.'

'What was the cause of the asphyxia then? Dr Leary must have given an opinion.'

'I was about to tell you when you interrupted me...'

'Come on, Professor,' someone else called out, 'we want news, not a lecture.'

But Page continued staring stolidly at his vociferous audience. 'The asphyxia,' he went on with slow deliberation, 'was consistent with having been caused by a sharp blow to the side of the neck.'

'A karate chop, something of that sort do you mean?'

'Yes, something of that sort.'

'Any clues as to who did it?'

'No comment.'

'You mean you have?'

'I mean, no comment.'

'Where does Kenny Bostock fit into this?'

'We have to find him to discover that.'

'Do you think he's still alive?'

'There's no evidence to the contrary.'

'But you're certain he does fit into the picture.'

'I never said that.'

'It was an inference.'

'Inferences are your business, not mine.'

He turned on his heel and walked into the station.

'Don't let any of that lot inside,' he said firmly to the desk sergeant, 'and while you're at it, pray for a heavy shower of rain.'

Accompanied by Machin, he went up to his office.

'Now let's sort out our thoughts,' he said as he slumped into the chair behind his desk, 'or, rather, assemble our facts and see what shape they come out.'

'Can we work backwards, sir?' Machin said in an eager tone. 'I think it'll be easier.'

'Go ahead.'

'Four masked men took part in a well-planned wages snatch at Keenan's Electrics this morning . . .'

'If it had been better planned, they'd have known the door of the wages office would be locked. But go on.'

'It came unstuck for the reason you mention. One of the men was Brian Farmer. During the escape one of the others struck him a blow on the neck which killed him and his body was dumped.'

'Why did someone strike him at all?'

'I don't know, sir.'

'Can't you guess?'

'He was responsible for the botch-up.'

'Possibly. More likely he was showing himself to be a weak link. He was proving to be a threat to the others. Things must have been pretty hectic for them at that moment. It was no time for cool argument and leisurely decision. They must all have had raw-ended nerves. Violence would have been very much in the air. Anyway, go on.'

'Do you remember, sir, where Farmer worked for a short time before he left Long Gaisford?' Page shook his head. 'Keenan's Electrics.'

'Ah!' Page gave a satisfied nod. 'So it was probably he who suggested doing the job.'

'That's my bet, sir.'

'What's the link between today's effort and Shem's death?'

'I'm sure the robbers' use of the cave in Harriers Wood comes into it somehow. Shem was murdered because he crossed their path and threatened them in some way.'

'And the boy, what about him?'

'He witnessed something.'

'His cousin murdering Shem?'

'It fits.'

Page let out a sigh. 'With any luck, we'll soon be able to put out descriptions of the men we're looking for. When a job goes as seriously wrong as this one, clues are always dropped. Anyway, Keenan's are offering a reward, which should bring somebody out of his hole with information. Meanwhile, we can check on Farmer's Borstal associates. That's where this little lot was originally conceived, you mark my word.'

The phone rang and Page put out a lazy hand for the receiver. For several seconds he listened in silence, though his eyes began to shine with unusual excitement.

'Hold him and I'll come straight there,' he announced briskly. He replaced the receiver and gave Machin a triumphant look. 'Kenny Bostock's at the Yard. Walked in and gave himself up, so to speak. More important, he's ready to talk!'

XXXIII

Machin had never driven a car faster than he did to London that evening.

At one point, Page had said, 'Watch it, I'm keen to retire in one piece,' but otherwise the journey passed in virtual silence.

They found Kenny playing draughts with an extremely attractive policewoman. He stared at them phlegmatically as they entered the room. He might be ready to talk, but there was no evidence of an urgent need on his part.

'Hello, Kenny,' Page said in a faintly reproachful tone.

' 'llo.'

There was an awkward silence.

'What's been happening?'

'They killed Brian,' he said baldly. 'I read it in the paper.'

'Who killed him?'

'Mick Edmunds and his lot.'

Page took a deep breath. 'I think it'd be best, Kenny, if you began at the beginning and told us everything you know.'

'Do you mean starting with Shem?'

'Yes, that's a good point to start.'

'Shem hadn't got anywhere to sleep, so I told him about the cave,' Kenny said. In short bursts of speech he went on, 'I hadn't been there since Brian went away. It was our secret place. You could only go if you had the secret pass. A badger's tooth. I gave Shem one. When I saw him the next day, he said someone else had been there. I knew it must be Brian, because nobody else knew about the cave. I went to look for him but he wasn't there. I went two or three times. The last time I went, I saw Brian, but he never saw me. He and another man were carrying Shem out of the cave. Shem's head was rolling all funny, like he was dead and I ran away. I was frightened.'

'Did you see who the other man was?'

'No. I didn't see him properly. It was Brian I was looking at.'

'And when Shem's body was found, you naturally thought Brian had killed him?'

'Yes.'

'And you decided to cover up for him?'

The boy nodded. 'I'd do anything for Brian.'

'Which is why you're here now?'

He nodded again. Page was silent for a while. The boy's sense of loyalty to his cousin had clearly transcended every other motive. In retrospect it could be seen as something admirable, obstructive though it had proved to police enquiries.

Later, Kenny went on to describe how he had encountered Edmunds, who had taken him to London on the pretext that he was going to help Brian get out of trouble. How he had been living in a house (it turned out to have been in the Dartford area) with the blonde and the tall young man. How he had subsequently seen Edmunds once only, but was always being told that he was helping Brian by staying there out of sight.

'Did you ever see Brian?' Page asked.

'No.' It came out as a reproach against the whole world.

Finally, he described what had happened that morning when the tall young man came bursting back to the house, only to leave again accompanied by the blonde.

He, Kenny, had been undecided what to do until he read of Brian's death in the evening paper. Thereafter all doubt had been removed from his mind.

As a result of this information, Edmunds' description was circulated, together with those of the tall young man and the blonde woman, all of whom, it was believed, could assist the police with their enquiries into the wages snatch at Keenan's Electrics.

By a quirk, however, it was none of these three, but the short man who fell first into the police net.

His name was Dennis Bowers and he had been in Borstal with Brian Farmer. He was arrested as he was leaving a pub, where he had spent the evening getting completely tight, in the course of which he had dropped a few incautious hints as to the day's events within the hearing of the licensee who happened also to be a police informer.

This final shock, coming on top of all else, persuaded him to cough; and cough he did to the beguiled ears of Page and Machin.

He told of how he had introduced Brian Farmer to Edmunds with a view to setting up the robbery – and of how the tall young man, whose name was Etley, was recruited as the fourth member of the gang. He said that when Edmunds had mentioned that the most dangerous part of such an operation was breaking through the cordon which the police could set up very quickly, Farmer had drawn attention to the existence of the cave in Harrier's Wood. This was less then five miles from Flatchet and, after Farmer and Edmunds had made a reconnaissance, it was decided to use it as a staging post. They'd hole up there for twenty four hours until the immediate heat was off and then set off quietly for London once it was safe to do so.

But Shem had fouled up that plan by his sudden truculent appearance and Edmunds had killed him.

Later, as they all knew, the enquiry had concentrated on the search for Farmer and after he had been found and charged with possessing an offensive weapon, and subsequently with murder, he had been persuaded to go through with the trial without letting out the truth.

Edmunds got Jason Butters to suggest a defence which would fit the facts and he then ensured Farmer's compliance by 'kidnapping' Kenny. He told Farmer that if he didn't play it as directed Kenny would suffer. Farmer had responded by saying that if any harm did come to the boy he'd blow everyone, himself included, sky-high. Thus a stalemate situation had been produced and had lasted until after Farmer's acquittal. But then Edmunds had refused to consider Kenny's release as he had promised.

The raid on Keenan's Electrics had been replanned, use of the cave being now out of the question. But whereas before Shem's death, they had been eager and united, there was now dissension and squabbling. Moreover, Brian Farmer showed a number of signs of having lost his nerve.

The raid itself was a disaster, as everyone now knew, and their only concern afterwards was to save their skins.

Bowers said none of them knew that Edmunds was carrying a firearm and they were badly shaken when he shot at one of the clerks. Farmer, however, was more than shaken.

He ranted and raged at him in the car until Edmunds suddenly turned and struck him viciously across the side of the neck. When they realised he was dead, they just heaved him out into a ditch – on Edmunds' instructions, he was quick to add.

And so the pieces of the puzzle fell into place.

Etley and his girl-friend were arrested two days later on the South Coast, but Edmunds wasn't caught for a further week. By that time he'd grown a beard and changed his hair style, but he was recognised by an old associate who decided that the reward was sufficient to overcome any qualms about retaliation. Also, Edmunds was a relative small-timer in the hierarchy. He didn't have strong-arm minions at his command. There was no reason not to grass, decided this person, particularly as the object of his treachery was going to be put out of circulation for a great number of years. Anyway, treachery? He was performing a public service.

With Kenny restored home and strangely unmoved by everything that had happened, including the vital part he was due to play in the court proceedings ahead, life for Page and Machin settled down into a busy routine of preparation. It was rather like cleaning up after an earthquake. Much to be done, but little excitement in doing it.

Machin had now made up his mind to propose to Susan as soon as the case was over. He wasn't quite sure why he felt it necessary to wait until then, but somehow it seemed the proper thing to do.

When he mentioned to Page that he was contemplating marriage, his Detective Superintendent said, 'I know of a nice freehold cave if you're looking for somewhere to live.'

'I'd sooner have a suite of cells here, sir ...' Then: 'Reckon the trial's going to hold up your retirement?' he asked.

Page shook his head and looked at him with an amiable expression.

'I've just been through all the statements and I find that there isn't one single item of evidence in my own statement which can't be equally well given by another witness.'

He turned to the calendar which hung on the wall at his side and with a happy smile drew a thick red ring round a certain Friday three weeks ahead.

>>> If you've enjoyed this book and would like to discover more great vintage crime and thriller titles, as well as the most exciting crime and thriller authors writing today, visit: >>>

The Murder Room
Where Criminal Minds Meet

themurderroom.com

www.ingramcontent.com/pod-product-compliance
Ingram Content Group UK Ltd.
Pitfield, Milton Keynes, MK11 3LW, UK
UKHW022315280225
455674UK00004B/313